Praise for the novels of

BELLA ANDRE

"Sensual, empowered stories
enveloped in heady romance."
—*Publishers Weekly*

"The perfect combination of sexy heat and tender heart."
—Barbara Freethy,#1 *New York Times* bestselling author

"Bella Andre writes warm, sexy contemporary romance
that always gives me a much needed pick me up.
Reading one of her books is truly a pleasure."
— Maya Banks, *New York Times* bestselling author

"I can't wait for more Sullivans!"
— Carly Phillips, *New York Times* bestselling author

"Loveable characters, sizzling chemistry,
and poignant emotion."
—Christie Ridgway, *USA TODAY* bestselling author

"I'm hooked on the Sullivans!"
—Marie Force, bestselling author
of *Falling For Love*

"No one does sexy like Bella Andre."
—Sarah MacLean,
New York Times bestselling author

"The chemistry is explosive!"
—*Reading, Eating and Dreaming* blog
on *Can't Help Falling in Love*

BELLA ANDRE

Come a Little Bit Closer

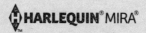

Recycling programs
for this product may
not exist in your area.

ISBN-13: 978-0-7783-1608-4

COME A LITTLE BIT CLOSER

Harlequin MIRA/March 2014

First published by Bella Andre

Printed in U.S.A.

Dear Reader,

From the start of my Sullivan series, I have been waiting for the chance to write about Smith Sullivan. As a movie star, he's larger-than-life, but he's also an incredibly loving brother and son. What, I wondered as he appeared in each book and promptly stole every scene he was in, was going to happen to him when he finally fell in love? And how could he possibly have a "normal" relationship with anyone with cameras and journalists following his every move?

I absolutely adored every minute I spent with Smith and Valentina while writing *Come a Little Bit Closer*. A man as strong as Smith needs a woman with just as much strength...and I can't wait for you to read their super sexy—and emotional—love story.

I'd also like to take a moment to say thank you to every single one of you for reading my books! I can't tell you how much it means to me to know that you've fallen in love with my Sullivans just as much as I have, and that you've been taking the time to spread the word to your friends and family. Your emails, tweets, Facebook and Goodreads posts make my busy days working on the next Sullivan book even better!

I can't wait to hear from you after you finish reading Smith's book. Especially the scene where he... Well, I should probably let you read it for yourself, shouldn't I?

Happy reading,

Bella

Come a Little Bit Closer

One

Smith Sullivan loved his fans. They'd supported him from the start of his career and had helped his movies gross nearly two billion dollars worldwide. Without them, he wouldn't be in San Francisco today, about to begin filming the most important movie of his career.

So, even though he had at least a dozen other important things to take care of before filming could begin, Smith headed straight toward the large group of women gathered outside the barriers his crew had erected around Union Square where they'd be filming today. Some of the women had brought their young children with them, but most of them were alone, and quite clearly available.

As he approached, he said, "Good morning," with a smile that held even as the crowd pushed in closer to him.

One smile and two simple words was all it took for a woman to reach out to shake his hand. She pressed a piece of paper with her name and phone number into his palm. She was dressed in a tight V-neck top and short skirt despite the cool fog hanging over the square.

"I'm so excited about your new movie, Smith," she purred. She ran her hand up his arm as if they'd met before, and knew each other well enough that he'd want her to touch him.

"Thank you…" He paused waiting for her to say her name, since he'd never set eyes on her before this morning.

"Brittany."

He smiled down at her. "I'm looking forward to you watching it, Brittany."

"Oh, I can't wait," she said in a husky voice. "And I want you to know that I'm free anytime while you're filming, if you want to talk about it. Or—" she licked her lips "—for anything else you want to do while you're in San Francisco."

Following her lead, one after the other, the women shook his hand and passed him their phone numbers while telling him that he was their favorite actor and that they'd seen all of his movies. This same scene had played out hundreds of times over the past fifteen years, and the truth was that if he'd still been in his twenties, Smith would have been more than happy to take his pick of the beauties back to his place for a night, a week or even longer if the woman was easy enough to be with.

But thirty-six was a long way from those early, wild years…and he was tired of waking up next to naked women whose names he didn't remember, who had never made him laugh, whose families he'd never meet. What a contrast that was to the way so many of his siblings had recently found love. They all seemed to be getting married and having children. Every week he updated the screensaver on his phone with a new picture of his little niece, Emma. Soon, his sister Sophie would have her twins, and he couldn't wait to upload a picture of all three Sullivan babies.

Still, even after witnessing just how powerful real love could be, and just what amazing things could come from that love, it was hard to break the cycle. Because without those strangers in his bed, he was alone.

Alone in another hotel. Alone in another city. Alone in another country. Away from his family and friends. Surrounded by people who either wanted something from him, or treated him like a god rather than a man.

Yes, he could have his pick of these women, but he knew what they wanted: to date *Smith Sullivan*. And as the past couple of years had ticked by, part of him had begun to wonder if he would ever find a woman who not only meant something beyond a few hot hours between the sheets, but who also wanted him for more than his fame.

Of course, Smith was still a man. A very sensual man who adored women of all shapes and sizes. He knew that a few nights of hot sex didn't add up to much in the long run, but he would never be immune to beautiful women.

More specifically, he thought as Valentina Landon walked past in a thick, long wool coat to fight the early-morning chill, her eyebrows raised as she took in the women gathered and giggling around him, he was drawn to one woman in particular.

"Valentina," he said with the intention of making her stop in her tracks.

She turned to look at him without the slightest bit of the flirtatiousness that the two dozen women he'd just been speaking to had been pouring all over him. "Yes?"

"Do you and Tatiana have everything you need this morning?"

"Everything's perfectly in order, thank you," she said in a crisp voice. "Do you need anything from us before filming begins in—" she looked at the slim watch on her wrist "—an hour?"

"Just let me know if you or Tatiana have any problems, or need anything from me at all."

She nodded, her pretty mouth softening slightly as she said, "Thanks. We will." Unfortunately, just then her gaze caught the pile of telephone numbers that had been pressed into his hands, and her eyes narrowed in disgust.

And yet, as she walked away with her lips pressed together in clear disapproval, she was beautiful.

Smith turned back to his fans and thanked them all for their support one more time before heading back to the trailer that was doubling as his office during filming. Dumping the women's numbers on his desk without giving them a second thought, he grabbed his script and laptop and walked back out. He was just sitting down in the makeup trailer when his phone buzzed; the key electric was alerting him to a lighting issue that needed to be worked out before filming could begin.

It was just the beginning of what would be an incredibly busy day, on a set that was all his this time. And as Smith dealt with the first problem of what would surely be many before the day was through, he knew he wouldn't want to trade his career for any other. Not for the beauty of his brother Marcus's winery in Napa Valley, not for the thrill of Ryan's World Series wins pitching for the Hawks, not for the speed of Zach's race cars.

Smith couldn't wait to begin filming *Gravity*.

The young woman in the middle of the sidewalk was utterly beautiful, and yet, the way she moved, dressed, wore her hair with pink streaks, her makeup artfully smudged and dark around her eyes, gave her away in an instant as an overwhelmed early-twentysomething on her own in a big city for the first time. With wide eyes she took in San Francisco—the buildings, the traffic, the people rushing all around, the fog rolling in from the bay. For a moment, her mouth almost curved into a smile, but a flash of something that looked too much like fear held that smile back from her full lips.

A stray dog skittered over her cheap red plastic boots and the longing on the girl's face was almost painful as she knelt down to reach out to the mangy animal. Instead of coming toward her open hand, the dirty little dog turned and ran as fast as it could in the other direction.

Her big green eyes suddenly filled with the slightest sheen of tears, which were blinked away just as quickly. It was impossible not to wish that she'd find happiness, and love, and everything else she'd come to San Francisco for.

Down the street, a businessman dressed in a dark suit, impeccably tailored and very, very expensive, was talking on a phone and moving fast, faster than anyone else on the sidewalk. His conversation held his complete attention, his expression forbidding as he issued directives one after another in a hard voice. Everything about him spoke of his power...and to just how closed off his heart was.

Fury crossed the man's face a beat before he spoke loudly into his phone, his entire attention turned to the conversation so that he didn't take notice of anyone on the street around him. There wasn't even the slightest pause in his gait as he kicked the girl who was still kneeling on the pavement staring after the dog who hadn't dared to trust her.

Thousand-dollar Italian shoes jabbed hard into her stomach, and as she cried out in pain, he finally stopped cursing into his phone, looked down at the dirty sidewalk and noticed her.

It was the ultimate picture of how far the girl had fallen. And yet, in that moment when she should have been cringing, her fear and sadness finally receded.

This time, she was the angry one, and even though the man had kicked her hard enough to shove the air from her lungs, she was young and agile enough to be back up on her feet and in the man's face fewer than thirty seconds later.

It didn't matter that she was so much smaller than he. It didn't matter that his clothes were worth more than what she'd managed to save over the past year working double shifts in the ice-cream shop in her hometown.

It didn't even matter to her that people had stopped on the sidewalk to watch the scene.

"Do you think you're the only person who matters?" she yelled at him. "Talking on your phone, ignoring everyone, kicking anyone who gets in your way?"

Before he could answer, she got closer and poked him in the chest.

"I matter, too!" Her mouth trembled now, just barely, but somehow she managed to get it under control as she repeated, "I matter, too."

Throughout her tirade, the man stared down at her, the phone still held to his ear, his dark eyes utterly unreadable. He was clearly surprised by what had happened. Not just that he'd stumbled over her, but by the way she had sprung up to scream at him. And yet, there was more than surprise in his eyes.

There was awareness that had nothing to do with anger...and everything to do with her incredible beauty, made even more potent by the flush on her cheeks and the fire in her eyes.

Everything that surrounded the two of them fell away as she searched the businessman's face for a reaction, but he was impossible to read—and on a sound of disgust, she pushed away from him and started to move back down the sidewalk.

But before she could get lost in the crowd, a large, strong hand wrapped around her upper arm and stopped her from getting away. She whipped around to shake him off. "Get the he—"

"I'm sorry."

His voice resonated with genuine regret—deeper, truer, than anyone who worked with him might have thought he was capable of feeling. Even, perhaps, the man himself.

Bravado had been all that held the young woman together. She did not know that this was a man who had never apologized to anyone for anything in his life. Hearing his words, she lost hold of the strength she'd been clinging to by her fingernails.

Her first tear had barely begun to fall when she finally pulled herself free and started running through the crowds, intent on getting away from the man whose apology had touched her despite her anger.

The man's deep voice called out to the girl as she pushed through the crowd. She was small and fast and he lost her at the busy Union Square intersection. The pink streaks in her hair were the last thing he glimpsed.

As the rest of the world rushed around him, most people either talking or texting on their phones, their attention on anything but the people around them, the man stood perfectly still.

And utterly alone.

* * *

Valentina Landon held her breath until "Cut!" rang out. Moments later, applause and cheering came from the crew who had been held spellbound by the scene.

Somehow she got her hands to move, to come together in a basic approximation of clapping, but she was too moved by what she'd seen to put anything behind it. That had been the first scene on the first day of photography for *Gravity*. The story had immediately grabbed her gut and twisted it hard. Smith Sullivan had not only written the screenplay, but he was also directing, producing and starring in the film.

Tatiana Landon, Valentina's younger sister, was an incredibly talented actress with ten years of experience behind her. She'd been hired for dozens of TV episodes, had shot a couple of sitcom pilots over the years and, most recently, had played important supporting roles in two feature films. But *Gravity* was her first lead in a major motion picture.

Valentina had always been proud of her sister, but what they'd all just witnessed from Tatiana had been so stunningly good that Valentina was still having trouble catching her breath. And she knew why.

Smith Sullivan had brought out every last ounce of magic her sister possessed.

Just then, Tatiana moved back down the sidewalk toward Smith. Valentina could read her sister like an open book, and though she was smiling at the applause from the rest of the cast and crew, it was clear that the person she really wanted a comment from was Smith.

So much like the character he was playing, for a moment it was hard to read his face until he reached out to put his hands on either side of Tatiana's shoulders and said loudly enough for everyone to hear, "You. Are. Perfect." He was grinning widely as he planted a kiss on her forehead.

Tatiana blinked up at Smith, pleasure and pride mixing with the stars in her eyes a moment before her lovely face broke into a blinding smile.

In the span of one terrible heartbeat, the ground fell away from Valentina's feet as she watched the interaction between her sister and the movie star…and every one of her fears for her sister's welfare pushed to the forefront.

She couldn't forget the way he'd flirted and charmed the legion of female fans who had waited to catch a glimpse of him just outside the set earlier that morning. He was the cliché of a movie star. The women had fawned all over him and she had no doubt that he'd loved every second of the attention, not to mention the dozen phone numbers he'd held in his hand. Valentina had no trouble imagining just how giddy with anticipation the women were over whom he would pick to warm his bed tonight.

Like hell if it was going to be her own sister.

So when Smith went to watch playback, Valentina didn't think, didn't stop to assess whether her actions were wise as she pushed through the crew to get to him.

"We need to talk. In private. Now."

She kept her voice pitched low and even, though

she knew everyone would likely be gossiping about her nervy move within seconds of their leaving the set. They would all be wondering what possible beef she could have with the great Smith Sullivan.

Valentina headed toward Smith's trailer, which had been moved to the Union Square site for the first day of filming, and even though she hadn't waited for his reply, she could feel his larger-than-life presence behind her every step of the way.

Two

Gravity was the story Smith had been waiting to tell his entire career. It wasn't a big-budget, smash-'em-up blockbuster. Nor was it a period film with impeccably researched costumes and sets. Instead, it was a pure, honest story about love and family and what really mattered.

And he was staking his entire reputation on the deceptively simple story.

If ever there was a time for focus, for pure and total concentration, it was now and through the next eight weeks of filming. He couldn't afford to let anything—or anyone—distract him from making the best movie he had in him.

However, as he followed Valentina to his trailer, her waist, hips and legs gorgeous in her formfitting pencil skirt, he already knew holding that intense focus wasn't going to be easy.

Valentina Landon had attracted him from the start with her exotic looks that she downplayed into cool, businesslike reserve. He couldn't miss the slightly seductive tone to her voice, or the fact that her scent was pure, rich sensuality. If she thought she was putting anyone off with her suits, her soft golden hair pulled back into a simple ponytail and her thick-framed glasses she slid on when she was poring over contracts, she was way off base.

Didn't she know that all those carefully constructed conservative elements made a guy like him want to find out just how deep her passions ran? Especially when she was so intent on hiding them. Not, of course, that she'd even come close to letting him find out the answer to that question.

During rehearsals, she was always either with her sister or making her way out of a room the second he walked into it. He'd been impressed with her business acumen during the past weeks. She took very good care of Tatiana's career. She also took care of her sister on a personal level. Valentina didn't hover but, at the same time, she was there whenever Tatiana needed her.

As the second-oldest brother in a family of eight siblings, Smith knew just how hard it was to watch over his brothers and sisters while letting them spread their wings and live their lives without his constant interference. Family meant the world to him, but he craved his independence, and his work, too. It was a constant balancing act, but one he wouldn't have given up for all the peace and quiet and spare time in the world.

From the beginning of his career, just after college,

he'd started with whatever scraps he could get and built on things from there. He knew people thought he'd been handed his acting career on a silver platter, that his looks had paved the road with gold bricks and Hollywood stars. In truth, his looks had made being taken seriously extremely difficult in the first couple of years of countless auditions. He'd almost resorted to taking one of the dozens of underwear commercials he'd been offered. Until, finally, an older actor had given him his chance to prove that he was more than just a pretty face. Smith had grabbed that chance with both hands, and when the movie was a box-office hit, other doors finally began to open.

It was one of the reasons he'd been so interested in casting Tatiana Landon. Yes, Valentina's younger sister was beautiful. No question, she was going to be a star, one way or another. But when she worked, he saw several qualities in her that he recognized and admired. Determination. Concentration. And joy.

Yes, he thought as Valentina threw open his trailer door without waiting for him to let her inside, there was much to admire about the Landon women. Particularly the older sister he hadn't been able to get out of his head since he'd met her in that initial casting meeting two months ago.

Talk about determination and concentration. Valentina had clearly taught her sister everything she knew. But when Valentina was with Tatiana, when they were laughing together the way sisters did when they were very close, her own joy rang out loud and clear.

Smith had just stepped inside and closed the door behind him when Valentina turned and faced him down.

"My sister is not going to become one of your little playthings."

Momentarily taken aback, Smith simply echoed, "Playthings?"

Valentina didn't have the obvious, more conventional beauty of her younger sister, but to Smith that made her face even more alluring. A man had to look beneath the surface with Valentina, but once he did, he was paid back richly with the contours of high cheekbones, incredibly long, unpainted lashes, eyes that tilted up slightly at the corners and a Cupid's bow on full lips that couldn't help but whisper of sex and heat no matter how tightly they were pursed.

Just the way they were right this second, in fact.

"Tatiana and I have been in this business for ten years," she said in a frosty voice. "I know exactly how this world works, Mr. Sullivan."

He had to cut her off then, if only because he hated the way she used the *Mr.* as yet another way to keep distance between them. Not another damn person on his set called him Mr. Sullivan. He wouldn't let her do it, either, whatever her reasons for wanting to keep her distance.

"Call me Smith. Please."

Her mouth tightened even further, her eyes flashing yet again even as she nodded and said, in a very soft voice, "Smith." Her long, slender fingers twisted in her grip as she stared back at him. "You're older. You're successful. You're extremely good-look—"

She stopped just short of the full word and it was all but impossible to keep himself from smirking just a little bit. And from saying, "Thank you, Valentina. I'm glad to know you think so."

Her eyes widened at the way he spoke her name; his tone held more than a little heat. Any woman would have noticed she'd captured his attention weeks ago. But she hadn't been looking for his attention— she had just stopped short of running from it, in fact.

Valentina was the opposite of every woman he knew in Hollywood. Instead of trying to draw attention to herself, she worked to deflect it. As an actor, Smith had transformed himself into many different characters over the course of his career. He knew all it would take were a few simple changes to her hair, clothes, makeup and body language to shift her message from *back off* to *come closer*.

She was an incredibly intelligent woman. Despite that, he didn't think she realized just how much her reserve and aloofness was drawing him in, making him want to discover who she really was. And why she was so intent on dismissing the male attention she deserved. Especially his.

Nor did she realize just how refreshing it was for him to finally meet a woman who wasn't overeager and ready to throw herself at *Smith Sullivan*'s feet. Especially just when he'd been convinced there wasn't a woman alive who could see beyond his fame and all the shiny things that came with it.

Now, as he watched Valentina work to suppress her anger, it occurred to him what an excellent actress she would have been. Emotion simmered just beneath the surface of her eyes, her mouth, her skin, all covered in an outward calm that could fool even the closest observer. A shared family trait, one Valentina had perfected in real life, while her sister merely played it out for the camera.

One sister so contained, the other so open.

Smith couldn't help but wonder—had Valentina sacrificed her own openness so that her sister could have such freedom?

She gestured to the pile of phone numbers that littered his desk, her upper lip curling slightly. "You have plenty of women falling for you. More than enough for any man to enjoy making his way through."

If he hadn't been in a hurry earlier that morning, he would have thrown the numbers away instead of just dumping them on his desk. With anyone else, he likely would have explained just that. But he found he didn't like having to defend himself to Valentina, especially when he hadn't done anything wrong.

"I meant it when I told you I wanted you to come to me if anything was wrong," he said in an even voice. "I'm glad you felt comfortable enough to pull me aside this morning, but I'm afraid I don't understand what's bothering you."

"I'll tell you exactly what's bothering me. You and I both know the power you hold. We also both know that my sister is perfect in this film."

He nodded in agreement. "You just heard me tell her that."

"And it meant the world to her." But instead of looking happy about it, a flash of deep-seated worry crossed Valentina's face. "Tatiana looks up to you. She has never been so committed to a production. All she wants is to do her best for you, and I know she's going to give a thousand percent to do just that." Her gaze was direct, unblinking, as she said, "And in return, I want you to give me your word that you will not cross any professional lines with her."

Damn it, he hadn't signed Tatiana to star in his film with nefarious plans of seduction. He'd signed her because she was a great actress who was going to get better and better.

Were it not for two unfounded accusations in the span of minutes, he would have taken the time to answer Valentina more carefully. But as it stood, she'd been questioning his honor since the first second he'd met her sister. Silently, perhaps, but it had been there nonetheless.

His honor was everything to him, and now he felt like a bear poked one too many times by a long stick, coming out of his lair grumpy, with teeth bared in warning. Which was why he gave her an answer he knew was bound to aggravate more than soothe.

"Your sister has already signed the contracts."

Instead of backing off at what many people would have construed as a warning, Valentina came closer to him, so close that he could smell the lavender in her shampoo.

"I asked around about you before we signed on for this movie. Everyone told me you were different." Her eyes slid again to the phone numbers on his desk, then back to him. "But you're just the same as everybody else, aren't you?" Fire leaped to new heights in her eyes as she told him, "I don't give a damn what she's signed. If you do one single thing to hurt my sister, if you dare toy with her emotions or her body, I'll—"

"Damn it, Valentina," he said in a voice loud enough to break through to her, "I'm not going to seduce your sister!" He had to work to gentle his voice as he said, "Tatiana is young and beautiful and I'm going to work like hell to make sure she wins an Oscar for her performance in my movie. But I don't *want* her."

And yet, even as he reassured her about his intentions toward her sister, there was no way for him to keep the silent words *I want you* from hanging in the air between them.

He was sure that was what had her taking a step away from him as she said, "I saw the way you grabbed her and kissed her after the scene. And I saw the way she looked at you—like you hold the key to the secrets of the universe."

It was because he had two sisters and a mother he loved that he realized just how badly he'd misplayed this situation with Valentina. Instead of going on the defensive and throwing the signed contracts in her face like the big bad movie star who only had to snap his fingers for the world to fall at his feet, he should have done whatever he could to reassure her that Tatiana was in safe hands.

"Your sister did such a great job with the first scene that I got excited, and I wanted her to know how thrilled I am to be working with her. But I honestly don't think she took my enthusiasm for her performance in the way you thought she did."

He could see that Valentina was still wary, but she took a deep breath and finally backed down enough to say, "I sure hope not."

He'd thought her eyes were a dimmer green than her sister's, but now he could see that they were a beautiful hazel, a clear green on the inside, deep brown on the outside. Smith had never been much interested in perfect, even less so after so many years in Hollywood where people hired doctors to rip them open and put them back together until they looked like the dolls his sisters had played with as kids.

He was also finally close enough to see the slightly dark smudges beneath the delicate skin under her eyes.

"It's got to be exhausting being your sister's watchdog all the time."

"I'm not her watchdog. I'm her sister and I love her. I—" She sighed, letting her exhaustion come through for a moment. "I just need to make sure she's safe. Always."

"Your sister is lucky to have you to protect her, Valentina. But who's protecting you?"

Her eyes met his again, wide with surprise…and an answering desire that she could no longer effectively mask as her hazel eyes dilated until the green near her pupil pushed out all of the brown along the rim.

Hot damn if he didn't want to kiss her beautiful mouth as she lifted her chin and her eyes flashed at him one more time.

"I don't need anybody to protect me."

She walked out of his trailer without a backward glance.

"Val, there you are!"

Valentina could see that Tatiana was still glowing from both her excellent performance and Smith's praise, but she was also clearly concerned about why her business-manager sister had yanked the executive producer and directing star of her new movie into his trailer after the first big take.

"You were fabulous," Valentina said as she put her arms around her younger sister.

Where she was lean, her sister was curvy. While she was tall, her sister was small. She'd never been the beauty that Tatiana was, but Valentina had never wanted that. Not when she knew just how much responsibility came with great beauty—and how much pressure shone down through every spotlight.

"Do you need anything before you do close-ups?"

"No, I feel great," Tatiana said, before adding, "Is everything okay?"

"Yes." Valentina smiled. "Better than okay."

And it was, at least where Smith's designs on her sister were concerned. The last thing she wanted for her sister was to end up in a Hollywood relationship. Miraculously so far, it hadn't been a problem with any of the men Tatiana had worked with, but Smith was at least a thousand times more charismatic than any of her previous costars.

Still, for all his charm and good looks and power, Valentina had believed him when he'd said he wasn't going to seduce her sister. Yes, he was an amazing actor, but every instinct she had told her he hadn't been acting when he'd said that.

Unfortunately, those instincts also told her other things.

Like how merely standing in the same room with him made her heart leap around in her chest as if she was a crushed-out teenager.

And how just the sound of her full name on his lips— everyone else called her Val, why did he have to be the one person on earth who always said *Valentina?*— made her long to hear him whisper it against the curve of her neck right before he kissed the sensitive skin there.

Valentina wasn't angry with him for those things. How could she be? But she was angry with herself for being so much weaker than she'd ever thought she was. Because when she'd moved close to him in his trailer and made the mistake of looking into his eyes, she'd been hit with such a hard rush of desire it actually stole her breath away.

Smith Sullivan looked great on-screen, but in person, he was even more arresting. She could have been blindfolded and known that he was in the room. He had that much presence.

There was inherent sensuality in every look, every movement. Smith didn't try to attract people. He just did. Everything from the masculine shape of his jawline to the way the cords in his neck moved as he turned his head made him, hands down, a shockingly beautiful man.

At the same time, she wasn't foolish enough to just write him off as a pretty face who'd been lucky. No question, he was a natural actor. And yet, she'd seen again and again throughout rehearsals just how hard he worked to get every nuance of every scene just right.

Clearly relieved by her response that everything was fine, Tatiana looped an arm through hers as they walked back over to the set. Smith was already there, discussing something with the director of photography.

"Did you know that before we started shooting this morning, he told me again how excited he is to work with me?" Tatiana asked. "And that if there's ever anything I'm uncomfortable with, I should tell him right away."

"That's great." And far more considerate than any other actor or director her sister had worked with before now.

More than once over the years, Valentina had asked her sister to explain why she wanted to be an actress. Each time, the reasons Tatiana gave—she loved to entertain and make people happy and forget about their lives for a while—made intellectual sense, and yet Valentina still couldn't understand why anyone would choose to live their life under a microscope. Because when Tatiana became a really big star like Smith, that's exactly how her life would be: every move would be made in the spotlight, captured by thousands of cameras, and detailed in newspapers, magazines and blogs.

Just the thought of living a life like that made Valentina shiver in horror.

Tatiana gave a sigh that bordered on worship. "He's amazing, isn't he? I still can't believe I get to work with him."

Valentina tried to read whether there was anything more than professional appreciation beneath her sister's simple statement. Because, really, how could there not be? Smith was gorgeous, talented, kind—

She cut herself off at *kind.* It was one thing to acknowledge his looks and acting skills. It was another entirely to start rhapsodizing about what a fantastic person he was when she barely knew him.

Fortunately, her sister didn't have time to wait for her reply regarding how amazing Smith was or wasn't, because she was called back in front of the cameras.

For the next few hours, Valentina watched her sister do her job with a deep sense of pride. Valentina had not only never let an actor emotionally hurt her sister, she had also made it a point never to let people treat Tatiana like a pretty airhead. It was a large part of the reason they chose her roles so carefully, rather than always just taking the highest financial offer.

Perception, Valentina knew, was everything in Hollywood. And no one would ever have a chance to whisper that the Landon women were easy or bubbleheaded.

At least, not the current generation, she thought as her cell phone buzzed in her pocket and she looked down at the screen to see that her mother was calling. She'd been wondering when Ava Landon was going to request a visit to the set.

Or, more to the point, to meet Smith Sullivan.

Valentina sighed as she pushed the phone back into her fitted jacket pocket. Her mother wasn't a bad person, she just had a weakness for good-looking, famous men who made their living in front of cameras.

Valentina may have shared her mother's love of chocolate ice cream, sunsets on the beach and fifties singers…but she absolutely refused to let genetics pull her down the same path as far as men were concerned.

One day, when Tatiana's career was a bit more on autopilot, Valentina planned to meet a nice man and fall in love. He would be good-looking, intelligent, with strong hands and a ready smile.

And he'd have absolutely, positively nothing to do with the entertainment business. Popcorn and Red Vines on a Saturday night would be as close to the film industry as her future husband would ever come.

Three

One week later, Valentina paused on the front step of Smith's house and took a deep breath that was perfumed with the scent of flowers. Beautiful, and not always easy to grow, lily of the valley was sprinkled all along his wide front drive. They were an unexpectedly soft touch for such a powerfully masculine man.

She'd spent the past ten years attending meetings similar to this one—stars often liked to show off their homes—so there was no reason to feel so off-kilter. Besides, her sister would be here shortly, so it wasn't as if Valentina was going to be all alone with Tatiana's costar for very long.

She'd decided over the past few days of filming that the best way to think of Smith was as *Tatiana's costar.* It depersonified him, made him almost a prop.

God forbid she forget herself and let herself think of him as a man, just as she'd caught herself doing a couple of times during the past week. If only she could have remembered that two days ago when they'd filmed the scene where he was working out without a shirt on. Had she realized, she would have made certain to steer clear of the set on that day. Her mouth had dropped wide open when she caught sight of his tanned, muscular shoulders, his well-defined biceps, triceps and washboard abs. Boy, had it been difficult to turn away from all that incredible male beauty. So difficult, in fact, that she hadn't actually managed it.

Unfortunately, she was pretty sure Smith had caught her drooling over him, judging by the knowing look in his eyes when he'd moved from the weights to the monitors to watch playback.

Clutching her leather bag tightly, Valentina finally rang the doorbell. She was surprised when a pretty woman with a radiant smile opened the door.

"Hi, come in. I'm Nicola. You must be Valentina. Smith said you would be here any second now." Valentina automatically shook the woman's hand as she said, "The boys are in the kitchen whipping up a batch of celebration margaritas."

It took Valentina a few very confused seconds to realize that Nicola was actually Nico, the pop star whose songs were all over the radio.

Why was Nico here?

Who were "the boys"?

And what were they celebrating?

Had Smith mixed up his plans? Had she just accidentally walked into some sort of celebrity orgy?

But, as she followed Nico—or Nicola, as she'd introduced herself—through Smith's foyer to the kitchen, it sure didn't look as if she was dressed for an orgy. Not in skinny jeans and a hip-length sweater.

Smith looked up from behind the blender with a smile that set her heart to pounding even faster.

"Valentina," he said, savoring her name just a little too much for her comfort. "Perfect timing. I can see you've already met Nicola. This is my brother Marcus."

If she hadn't only had eyes for Smith, she would have noticed the man standing next to him. Marcus was also extremely easy on the eyes, if a little bit older than Smith. As Nicola tucked herself under Marcus's arm and leaned into him, he brushed his knuckles down the side of her face as if she never stopped pleasing him.

Valentina's chest squeezed with something she refused to admit was longing. She was trying not to stare, but it was hard to look away from such deep—and pure—affection.

"It's very nice to meet you," she said, feeling awkward and out of place at this small family gathering in the suit she'd been wearing all day on set. Everyone else was casual in jeans and sweaters. Smith had kicked his shoes off and she was disgusted to realize she even found his bare feet sexy. And when he reached up to hold the top of the blender in place and it whirred to life, the sheer sensuality of watching the muscles and tendons flex slightly in his arms held her momentarily spellbound.

It should take more than a dozen inches of skin

showing on each of his arms to set her heart to racing and the heat pooling low down in her belly.

Really, though, it was ridiculous for a man's arms to be that sexy.

And she was being even more ridiculous by making a complete twit of herself—as if she'd grown up in some weird puritanical household where she'd never seen a man's bare arms before.

Marcus's smile was warm as he said, "It's nice to meet you, Valentina."

Knowing that her cheeks were still flushing, she was glad for the distraction of Smith handing out the margaritas. She hadn't been planning to have anything to drink tonight, not if she wanted to keep her head perfectly clear, but she didn't want to be the sole party pooper for whatever it was they were celebrating.

Smith remained by her side as he turned his focus back to his brother and Nicola. "I'd like to raise a toast to your engagement. I couldn't be happier for both of you."

Valentina's eyes widened as she realized what she'd just walked into. Not an orgy, but a family celebration. No wonder there was such obvious love between Marcus and Nicola, and that both of them were absolutely glowing with happiness.

"Thank you," Nicola said with a pretty smile. "After all, Smith, you were the one who gave Marcus and me a place to spend our first night together. Even if," she said with a wicked little glance at her new fiancé, "your brother wouldn't do anything more than give me one teeny tiny little kiss, no matter how much I begged."

Valentina felt her eyes go even wider despite herself. Nicola had begged Marcus to do more than kiss her their first night together? And he'd resisted?

"Really?" Smith said, drawing the word out with pure curiosity as he leaned forward to coax more dirt from Nicola about his brother. "Tell us more."

But before she could, Marcus covered her mouth with his. When they finally pulled apart he murmured, "Good thing I know how to keep you quiet with my teeny tiny little kisses."

He certainly did, Valentina thought, because Marcus's kiss had quite clearly made Nicola lose the train of her earlier thoughts. The sparks between them were practically singeing her from across the kitchen island. She could tell just how much in love the two of them were.

She hoped they knew just how lucky they were to have found each other.

"Congratulations," she said. "I'm so happy for you both."

Nicola's eyes were a little glassy as the four of them lifted their glasses and clinked them together. Valentina was amazed by how right it felt in that moment to be there with them. And how surprisingly normal it all was, considering two of the people in the room were bona fide celebrities.

So normal, in fact, that as they all took a sip and Nicola's hand flashed with brightly colored jewels,

Valentina couldn't resist saying, "Your ring is beautiful."

Nicola all but leaped around the kitchen island to show off her engagement ring. It wasn't a standard diamond solitaire, but a stunning grouping of multicolored stones in a unique hammered-gold setting.

Clearly, Valentina thought as she admired the ring, Sullivan men did nothing by halves.

What, she suddenly found herself wondering, would it be like to belong to one of them? And to know that a strong, beautiful Sullivan would always be there for you?

It was far harder than it should have been to shake the silly questions out of her head as she and Nicola finally rejoined the brothers. Surely, she thought as she reached for her glass again, a couple more sips wouldn't make her lose her head.

Only, when she realized Smith's dark eyes were on her as she took a sip, she suddenly knew that if anything was going to make her lose her head, it wouldn't be the drink.

It would be *him*.

She was about to put her glass down and excuse herself from the impromptu family celebration out of sheer self-preservation when Nicola asked, "How are you liking San Francisco?"

It was a perfectly easy question, one that should have been simple to answer. Only, with Smith standing mere inches away, his eyes holding a tight focus on her as he waited for her response, simple became nearly impossible.

Valentina could feel her heartbeat fluttering against her pulse points, along the inside of her wrist and on the side of her neck, and knew her skin had started to flush with the heat she always felt when Smith was close.

She hadn't wanted to sense his interest, had told herself she didn't want it directed at her, but after their conversation in his trailer the week before, and the way she'd caught him looking at her on set with a dark, hungry gaze, she could no longer deny it. Nor could she deny that it felt as though he was trying to see beyond her conservative clothes and tied-back hair, that he wanted to look deeper into her than she wanted him to see.

"I love San Francisco. Although it's been warmer than I expected." The sun had just set, but she suddenly felt so overheated in Smith's kitchen that she had to unbutton her suit jacket and slip it off her shoulders.

"You and your sister must have brought the sun with you, because last month we were all wearing our ski gear to go get the mail in the thick fog," Nicola said with a laugh that lit up her already stunningly pretty face.

No wonder Smith's brother was smitten. Not only was Nicola talented, but she was clearly a very nice person, as well.

"I'm all for fog," Marcus said as he pressed a kiss to his new fiancée's cheek, "especially if it means it's up to me to keep you warm."

Valentina didn't know much about the music business, but she guessed that at Nicola's level of pop stardom, it wasn't too different from being a movie star. And yet, somehow she'd managed to find love with a man who clearly didn't want her for anything other than herself.

Why, Valentina wondered, hadn't her mother been that lucky with any of the actors she'd dated? If only one of them had had a heart of gold, everything would have been different. Better.

Unfortunately, the only gold had been in the rings on their wandering hands when they thought her mother wasn't looking. Valentina had learned a few simple but effective defensive moves in her early twenties. At the very least, she'd learned how to take care of herself and her sister.

"What parts of the city have you had a chance to see so far?" Marcus asked.

Valentina shook off her thoughts as she smiled and said, "Just the best movie set in the world."

"Smith knows this city better than all of us," Marcus told her. "He'd be a great tour guide."

"Tell me, Valentina," Smith said so smoothly she almost wondered if the three of them had scripted the setup before she walked in, "what San Francisco landmark would you like to see most?"

During the past few minutes, Valentina had realized that the problem with seeing Smith being so easy, so comfortable with his family, was that she almost forgot to keep her walls up around him. It reminded her of the way she was with her sister.

Good thing she'd locked her heart up tight

against actors a long, long time ago. And it was with maximum-security prisons in mind that she gave him her one-word answer.

"Alcatraz."

Only, instead of getting the very clear message in her response and backing off, Smith's eyes were full of laughter. Neither Nicola nor Marcus did a great job of hiding their own laughter behind a couple of choked coughs, either.

In the end, even Valentina found herself unable to hold back her own smile.

Which was when she knew she needed to leave. Immediately. Because she was getting too comfortable with Smith and his family, feeling too warm and cozy and *right* with them.

"Thank you so much for including me in your celebration," she said with a warm smile for Marcus and Nicola, "but I should probably be going. I'll let Tatiana know that we're rescheduling our meeting, Smith."

But before she could lift her bag back onto her shoulder, Marcus was saying, "Actually, we were just dropping in for a few minutes to share the good news with Smith. My mother is expecting us for dinner tonight."

The next thing Valentina knew, she was shaking the happy couple's hands, they were both hugging Smith good-night and she was standing all alone in his kitchen as he walked them out. The sound of the front door closing caused her heartbeat to quicken once again.

There was no reason to panic just because they were alone. And if the fact that he was so close to his family and so happy for his brother had softened her a bit, well, she could handle that softness.

Couldn't she?

Four

After that first day on set, when Valentina had pulled Smith into his office and warned him not to mess with her sister, she'd made sure to steer clear of him, and had been perfectly polite when they met in a group to discuss an issue with the script or wardrobe or Tatiana's schedule. Even when she was watching them shoot a scene, she held perfect focus on Tatiana.

Too perfect.

But if her plan had been to try and fade out of his sight, she hadn't succeeded. It didn't matter how many times he reminded himself that he didn't have time to focus on anything but his movie.

He just couldn't get Valentina out of his head.

It wasn't just because of her incredible legs or exotic beauty. In Hollywood, a great figure and pretty face were a given. But after seeing her with Nicola, and the genuine pleasure Valentina had shown over the stunning engagement ring and their happily-ever-after, he was reminded of just how much family meant to her. She was all business on set—and with him—but as soon as her sister needed her for anything even remotely emotional, she immediately stopped being a business manager and transformed back into a sister. One whose love ran so deep that she didn't hold anything back.

"My brother is one seriously happy guy," Smith remarked as he walked back into the kitchen and found Valentina standing with her glass in her hand, staring out the window at the city lights.

"They both are," she said as she turned her beautiful gaze back to him. "It was very sweet to see."

"I wasn't sure about the two of them at first," he admitted, knowing he hadn't exactly been encouraging in the early days of his brother's relationship, "but somehow they've made the age difference and the demands of both their careers work."

"Is Marcus also in the entertainment industry?"

"Nope." Not even close. "He owns Sullivan Winery."

"Wow, I wish I'd known he was behind some of my favorite cabernets. I would have liked to thank him for all the hours of pleasure he's given me."

She was clearly surprised by Marcus's profession, and yet again Smith loved the fact that she knew next to nothing about his life, when any fan could have recited his siblings' names and careers by heart. He also loved the way she spoke of pleasure...even if she was giving his brother the credit for it.

"Now I get what you mean about the demands of

both their careers," she said. "They really do live in different worlds, don't they?"

Smith refilled their drinks and carried them into the living room. "I don't think it's always easy to juggle her tours and his busy seasons in the vineyards, but they clearly love each other enough to make it work."

When he set their drinks on the coffee table, he could see her surprise at finding a half-finished jigsaw puzzle on it.

"I *love* puzzles," she exclaimed. "Tatiana and I used to do them together all the time before we got so busy."

She immediately sat down on the plush couch, picked up a puzzle piece and clicked it into place. Smith moved beside her and slid a piece into the corner of one of the dogs' ears while she filled in the nose on another. He was glad to see her forget to keep the distance she seemed to think was so damned necessary.

This easy companionship was precisely why he'd brought her over to the coffee table, where the puzzle of three silly dogs was halfway done…and it was yet another reason why he loved his brother Gabe's soon-to-be stepdaughter Summer so much. The eight-year-old girl had taken the picture of the three dogs sitting crookedly with their ears blowing in the breeze and had turned it into a puzzle for him. His twin sisters had been great when they were eight, too. Heck, they'd been great at every age, and even if it sometimes seemed like his sister Lori—aka "Naughty" to Sophie's "Nice"—grew to be more and more of a pain in the butt with every passing year, he wouldn't have given them up for anything.

"Some picture, isn't it?"

He loved the sound of Valentina's laughter. "The absolute best. Where did you find it?"

"Two of the dogs belong to my brother Zach and his fiancée, Heather. The huge one," he said, pointing at the Great Dane, "and the little one—" he popped a section of the Yorkie's shoulder into place "—fell in love first. Zach and Heather weren't far behind them, though."

"What about the poodle puppy?"

"The poodle belongs to my soon-to-be niece. Summer is eight years old and she brilliantly maneuvered her single mother and my brother Gabe together. They're getting married on New Year's Eve in Lake Tahoe. It's where they fell in love last year."

"Oh," she said with a little sigh, "that's just lovely." Her eyes, her mouth, were soft as she practically brimmed over with emotion.

Smith had lit a fire earlier, and now, as they sat together working on the puzzle, it hit him that this was the first time in his life he'd ever experienced something this warm, this sweet, with a woman. Heck, now that he thought about it, this was actually the second time he'd tried to put this puzzle together. The last time it sat unfinished, the woman he'd mistakenly brought home had thought it would be sexy to swipe it off onto the floor so that he could do her on top of the coffee table. A while later, when the woman had gone to the bathroom to straighten her hair and clothes before he sent her home, he'd immediately picked up the pieces.

Doing a woman he'd picked up at a Hollywood event on top of his coffee table was something a movie star did.

Making a puzzle in front of a fire was something a couple did.

"Your family sounds incredible," Valentina said, her words tinged with wistfulness as she reached for another puzzle piece and popped it into place. "Your parents must have had a perfect marriage for everyone to turn out so well."

"They did seem to have a pretty great marriage, although to hear my mother tell some of her stories about my father, he had his moments." Smith winced slightly at the tug in his chest that nailed him whenever he spoke about Jack Sullivan. Smith didn't miss him every day, but when he did, the sense of loss could be overpowering. "He died when I was thirteen."

Her eyes widened at the information, giving him even more confirmation that she hadn't spent one moment of her life reading about him in a magazine or looking him up on the internet.

"I'm sorry," she said, "I didn't know."

He was amazed by how much it meant to him, this possibility of building a relationship with someone where they both started from the same place, so that they could both uncover and discover each other's stories at the same time that they wrote their own story together.

"My father," she said so softly he had to focus on her lips to hear the words as her eyes closed and she sucked in a breath, "died, too."

It was pure instinct to cover her hand with his over the loose puzzle pieces. "How old were you?"

Her breath shook slightly as she said, "Twenty-two. I know I should be over it by now, but—"

It wasn't enough to simply hold her hand; he needed to wrap his arms around her. It didn't surprise him when her long, lean limbs fit perfectly against his.

"I used to think the same thing, that one day I'd wake up and I'd be over it. That I'd be able to think of him without it hurting." He took one of her hands and put it over his heart, as if to soothe the ache. "It hasn't happened yet."

When she instinctively moved her hand over his to try to comfort him, his chest squeezed tight at just how good it felt to have her touch him with such innate sweetness.

"I miss my father so much," she admitted. "Everything changed after he died."

"I know exactly what you mean." And he did. Because even though his mother had been amazing as she stepped up to the plate to parent eight kids by herself, and even with his brothers and sisters all banding together to take care of one another, it had still sucked to lose his dad. Really, really bad. "That first year, all nine of us—" the nine that their father had left behind "—were all trying so hard just to be normal. But how could we be when nothing was normal anymore?"

"Normal," Valentina echoed the word in a hollow voice. "I would have given anything for normal. Especially for Tatiana."

"How did your sister and mother deal with losing your father?"

"Tatiana is beautiful, but resilient," she told him. "A lot like her character in your movie. She seems so fragile and gentle, but she's actually tougher than most of us."

Impressed with her insight into the character he'd written, he told her, "My sister Sophie is a lovely, soft-spoken librarian." He shook his head as he thought of all the times people had underestimated his quiet sister. Especially the man who had recently become her husband. Jake should have known he never stood a chance. "She also has a core of strength that any warrior would envy. I thought a lot about her when I was writing Tatiana's character. It helped that Soph was pregnant at the time so I could easily picture her in the role if I needed to."

Valentina had relaxed against him by degrees as he'd spoken about his sister. He left her hand where it was still resting on top of his, even though he knew it probably wasn't fair to take advantage of her momentary vulnerability.

"Do you have any other siblings apart from Tatiana?"

"No." She paused before adding, "It's always just been me and her."

No question, there was something more behind that statement. So much more that he said, "What about your mother? How did she deal with losing your father?"

Valentina jolted back from him as if he'd burned her. She blinked at him from across the couch, looking as though she had abruptly surfaced from a dream. One that had surprised her—and scared her—in equal measure.

A beat from reaching for her again, Smith realized it was exactly what he couldn't do. Not unless he wanted her to run. But just because he knew that didn't mean it was any easier to shift his attention back to the puzzle and pick up one of the pieces.

His entire adult life, when Smith had seen something he wanted, he'd taken it. In many cases, it was given to him before he even had to reach for it. But he knew without a doubt that Valentina wasn't like anyone else he'd ever wanted. If he wanted her to trust him, he'd have to earn that trust moment by moment, truth by truth, smile by smile.

"Everyone has always said how well my mother dealt with losing my father," he said slowly. "And she did. She has." He slid another piece into place without even really seeing the picture before him. "But she's never let herself love anyone again. She's never even been with another man, as far as I know, in all these years."

Valentina picked up her drink and drank it all

down in one long gulp that had his eyebrows going up with surprise.

"Funny," she said, "my mother's just the opposite. She's slept with every single man, every *actor,* who so much as looked at her or said she was pretty." Her words were sharp now, with pain she wasn't bothering to hide. "But you know the funniest part about it?" She looked straight at him as she said, "I don't think she loved any of them."

When he saw pain in her clear, beautiful eyes, nothing could have stopped him from reaching for her again.

Nothing but the ring of the doorbell that had Valentina jumping entirely off the couch this time. Her face flushed with guilt as she looked between him and her empty margarita glass.

"I'm sorry, I never should have said any of those things to you. Especially about my mother. Please don't say anything to Tatiana about—"

He took his final chance of the night to slide his hand over hers. "I promised you I wouldn't hurt your sister, and I won't hurt you, either."

She stared at him, her pupils dilated again so that her eyes were entirely green for a moment, and he wasn't sure if she believed him. And maybe she was right not to, because even though he now had an inkling of why she was wary about trusting a man in his profession, it was still so easy to imagine coaxing her upstairs to his bed, stripping off her clothes layer by layer, tangling her hair in his fingertips and taking the rest of the night to explore her. To learn her most sensitive curves and hollows, to experiment with touching and tasting her until he knew precisely what would have her begging for more. Begging for *him*.

The doorbell rang again and he had to all but force himself to walk away to let her sister in. But throughout the rest of the night, as the three of them worked through promotion timelines and interview requests, with Valentina sitting as far from him as she could without raising her sister's eyebrows, Smith couldn't force away his desire for her…or the memory of just how good it had felt to hold her in his arms in front of the fire, his heart beating against their linked hands.

Five

Holding her cell phone up to her ear as she rang her sister's agent, Valentina looked out the small window in her trailer-slash-office on the *Gravity* set. She'd expected winter in San Francisco to be cold, but from the way the heat of the sun was eating up the morning fog, it looked as if it was going to be another perfect day outside.

She was hit with the urge to forget about work for a few hours and get out on the water in a kayak, or up in the mountains on foot to enjoy looking out over the gorgeous city they were working in. Over the past few years, Tatiana had taken acting jobs in beautiful cities all over the world, but Valentina had never considered moving to any of them. Until now. It helped, of course, that the house they were temporarily renting in the Noe Valley was incredibly cute. Regardless of how early she headed to the set, or how late she returned from it, someone was always out walking a dog or riding a bike. For a big city, San

Francisco managed to be a perfect combination of a cosmopolitan city and a small town.

George Kauffman picked up. "Val, great to hear from you. Fill me in on everything. Especially the incomparable Smith Sullivan. Because if he's as gorgeous as he was the last time I saw him, I honestly don't know how anyone is getting a damn thing done on set."

Valentina liked Tatiana's agent a great deal. While he was incredibly slick when he needed to be, and was a master of negotiation, he didn't feel compelled to wear his agent hat all the time. More than once the two of them had gotten a little tipsy celebrating one of Tatiana's successes. The fact that he was gay helped, too, if only because Valentina knew she'd never need to worry about whether her sister was safe with him. It was a large part of why she herself had let her guard down with him several years back.

Unlike, she thought with a wry twist of her lips, the way she constantly felt she had to add new layers to her protective walls whenever Smith was near.

Valentina was as sensual as the next woman, and she certainly enjoyed sex when she found the time and the right man to have it with, but she'd never brought her sensuality into the workplace. Ever. Only, it seemed that whenever she and Smith were in the same room, no matter how hard she tried to focus on business, she couldn't stop the heightened awareness that took her over one cell at a time, from her heart that beat too fast to the tips of her toes that curled in her shoes every time he so much as said her name.

"Filming is going fantastically well," she told him. "And Smith has been a dream for Tatiana to work with."

George made a sound of approval over the line. "Of course he has. That man is a dream, period. You know," George added in a thoughtful voice, "he wouldn't be a bad choice."

"For what?"

"To break your extremely unfortunate dry spell."

The phone almost dropped from her hand. "You're crazy."

But she'd said it too quickly, too forcefully. She who doth protest too much, and all that.

She could all but see George's smile as he said, "He's always had good taste in women. Unfortunate for me," he said with a playful grumble at Smith's sexual orientation, "but good for you. And from what I remember about our casting meeting, his eyes kept circling back to *you*."

"Don't be ridiculous," she said in as light a voice as she could manage, as if they were joking about something that would never, ever happen in a million years.

"Well," George said after a pause that was just a little too long for her comfort, "I think we both know that if the beautiful and talented and filthy rich Smith Sullivan is smart enough to try to stick his hands up your skirt, you won't stand a chance."

She hated knowing her friend and colleague was right, hated it so much that as she grabbed a stack of notes on her desk, she tried to put a stop to all of his nonsense by saying, in her sternest, most businesslike tone, "If you're done speculating over whether or not Smith Sullivan wants to stick his hands, or any other body part, up my skirt—or if I have strong enough superpowers to resist him—perhaps we can now discuss the details of Tatiana's recent commercial offer."

A creak from her office doorway made her finally lift her gaze from her paperwork…to stare straight into Smith's amused eyes.

Oh, God.

Oh, no.

Could he have heard what she'd just said? About her skirt, and his hands, and…

Yes, she realized with a hard thunk of her heart as it careened down to the bottom of her stomach. Of course he'd heard every last word of it.

Why else would he look so amused…and, quite possibly, delighted?

"George, I'll need to call you back in a few minutes."

"Oooh, you sound tense. And more than a little breathless. A movie star must have walked into the room." George was obviously giddy over it. "Why don't you just leave your phone on speaker so I can hear his voice—just in case he says all those naughty things I know we're both hoping he'll say."

She hung up on Tatiana's agent and immediately stood up so that she and Smith would be on even ground. Well, as even as they could be, given the six or so inches he had on her even in her heels.

"You didn't need to hang up so quickly for me,"

he drawled in a voice that didn't try to be sexy. It just *was*.

"I know how busy you are," she replied. And it was true. As star, director, producer and screenwriter of *Gravity,* she wasn't sure how he'd managed more than a handful of hours of sleep a night since production began. And yet, he didn't look the least bit tired. Instead, he looked even more handsome than he usually did.

Clearly, he wore smug well. Because she knew damn well just how smug he had to be feeling after what he'd heard her say to George.

Even worse, though, than the mortified flush that still hadn't left her cheeks, was the fact that she had to clasp her hands tightly in front of her as she asked, "What can I help you with this afternoon?" It was either grip her fingers tight enough to leave marks on her palms or give in to the urge to reach for him... and find out if the dark shadow on his chin felt as deliciously sexy against her fingertips as it looked.

He moved from the doorway into the trailer, which suddenly seemed tiny with the two of them in it. A vision hit her of Smith backing her up against her desk and putting one leg between hers to open her up to him before he slid her skirt up and—

"—asked for your number so she could thank you herself."

His voice finally penetrated her too-vivid daydream and she found herself blinking up at him. She had barely heard a word he said.

When had he moved even closer?

Her heart raced at his nearness, and as she inhaled a deep breath to try to pull some oxygen into her lungs, she accidentally took in his scent instead. Pure, clean and so male that her heartbeat only ratcheted higher, to the point where she was sure that he would be able to see the pulse racing beneath her skin if he looked.

Which, she suddenly realized when she caught the direction of his gaze on the pulse point at the side of her neck, was exactly what he was doing.

It felt as if the fog outside had come in through the trailer window to wrap around her brain. She couldn't remember what they'd been talking about, had barely heard what he'd said. But she still had enough sense to realize that if she didn't say something soon, there wasn't going to be much room left for talking anymore. Not when he looked—and smelled—so darn good.

"Someone was asking for my number?" she asked him in the crispest voice she could manage under the circumstances.

She'd been cursed—although some women would probably have felt blessed—with a voice that made men think of sex, even if her conservative outward appearance gave the opposite impression. It had taken years of practice for her to school the huskiness out of it, much the way British actors often erased their accents to play American roles. But when she was nervous—or worked up—that huskiness would creep back in.

"Nicola called. She and Marcus just received the

arrangement of purple tulips you sent them at his winery as an engagement gift. She'd like to thank you directly rather than just through me. Could I give her your number?"

"Of course you can."

She couldn't read his expression as he continued to look at her. "Forever love—" his eyes darkened with the heat that was so much a part of him she was surprised the whole trailer hadn't already gone up in flames "—is the meaning of that flower."

Valentina tried to ignore her rapidly beating heart. "It seemed appropriate for them."

"It is." Smith leaned one shoulder against the wall and crossed his feet at the ankles as if he had all the time in the world to chat with her. "I was surprised to hear that you'd sent them an engagement gift."

"I've always thought that real love that comes without any strings should be celebrated."

Where had that come from? She didn't need to be discussing love with Smith Sullivan. Especially when something told her that if she gave him even the slightest bit of insight into who she was, he'd find a way to take advantage of it.

"I agree with you," he told her, "especially given how many strings people try to knot together in this business. It's one of the reasons I wanted to make this movie, even knowing people will try to write it off as a simple love story."

She was surprised by just how well they agreed with each other on that point. Surprised, and frankly frightened at the prospect of how many other things they might agree on given the chance...

And yet, she thought as if watching herself from a distance, it seemed that once she got going on a roll with all of her opinions about what love should and shouldn't be, she couldn't find a way to stop herself from spouting, "I've always wondered why love has to be so full of conflict and strife. Why can't love be simple? Why can't it just be as pure as two people who realize that they can't live as well, or as happily, apart as they can together?"

Smith's eyes grew even more intense with every word she spoke. When she finally managed to close her mouth, he said, "I spent months struggling with the screenplay for *Gravity* before I could find the heart of what you just said so eloquently. That love doesn't have to be hard. And passion can exist without the need to fight. I see it with each of my siblings who have found love, the way safety and desire can be one and the same."

His words were so gentle and warm that she felt as if she was stepping into his strong arms even though they were still several feet apart.

"Marcus and Nicola are part of the reason I have to make this movie. Because, as you just said, love without strings should be celebrated." When his mouth curved up, his beautiful smile worked almost like gravity and she needed all her willpower to resist being pulled into his force field. "Nicola also called me to make sure that I knew how great she and Marcus thought you were, just in case I was stupid enough to miss it." His smile turned unabashedly sensual. "I assured her that, for all my faults, stupidity isn't one of them. Come out on a date with me, Valentina."

Panic swamped her in an instant, the key scenes of any "relationship" they might possibly have playing out as clearly as any of the dailies she'd watched just that morning. If she let herself be wooed into a date, and then his bed (because how could anyone possibly date Smith without begging him to make love to her?), she had no doubt that despite hating everything about the spotlight and media and fame that came with his life, she'd foolishly fall head over heels for him...mere moments before he moved on to the next movie, the next set, the next woman who presented a challenge.

All of which was why she made sure her answer was as direct as his question had been. "No."

Any other man would have taken her refusal for what it was: a negative response that she had no intention of altering. Ever.

Smith, of course, wasn't like any other man she'd ever met. So instead of giving her a hurt look and walking out of her trailer with his tail between his legs, he moved closer yet again, all but pinning her against the window.

"From the first moment you and I met, there's been something between us."

She wasn't foolish enough to argue with him. Not when his statement was stupidly on point...but not as stupid as acting on those obvious sparks and letting them turn into flames that would burn her heart to ashes.

"You're a very attractive man," she admitted, "but since ten million other women are also attracted to you, I figure there's no point in making a big deal out of it."

"Only ten million?" he teased her.

Valentina honestly didn't know whether to laugh or slap the arrogance out of him. Nor would she take the third—and most obvious—option of melting at his feet the way pretty much any woman alive would be doing right now.

Why couldn't he just get mad like a normal guy would when his attentions were being denied? All his teasing did was make her want to tease back. "Okay, probably more like a hundred million. But the end result is the same." She paused to make sure he understood her very clearly this time. "I'm still not interested in going out on a date with you."

"Why not?"

"I don't date actors."

He nodded as if it was a very wise decision. "Me, either."

She did a terrible job of hiding her surprise from him. More like shock, actually, given what was printed about him on a regular basis in the entertainment magazines.

Then again, hadn't she been in the business long enough to know that what the entertainment press dished out to the public really was a crock most of the time?

"How about this?" he said in a voice that was far too reasonable for her comfort. "When I'm with you, I'll be a director. Or a producer. Even a screenwriter, if it makes you happy."

She shouldn't have laughed at the laundry list of titles, but how could she not? And it was true—Smith Sullivan was much more than just an actor.

Still, that didn't change anything.

"How about I clarify my position?" She mirrored his reasonable tone perfectly. "I don't date anyone in *the business*."

There, that should do it. How could he possibly argue with that?

But when he didn't look the least bit daunted, her stomach clenched. She told herself it wasn't due to need, or desire or the sparks that kept leaping and growing between them.

"I'm also a brother." He moved closer. "A son." Closer still, so close that she could almost feel his breath on her upturned face. "A friend." She was mesmerized by the color of his eyes, so dark now that the blue was almost black. "And I hope to be a father one day, too."

She couldn't keep the breath from whooshing out of her lungs as his comment hit her right in the center of her softest spot. She could have defended herself against cocky or sexy or confident.

But how could she protect herself against family?

"Why me?" She wasn't asking to fish for compliments. She truly was confused. "You could have any woman on set. Any woman on the street. Any woman anywhere."

"You're smart. Beautiful. Great at your job. Devoted to your sister. You have a knack for solving puzzles and I like you, Valentina." He paused before adding, "I want you, too. Very, very much."

His honesty floored her. But so did the knowledge that at least a dozen actors had likely said similar things to her mother in the years since her father had died. And every time her mother had given in, what had it left her with except an increasingly broken spirit…and heart?

Valentina told herself she was being just as honest as she said, "You can't have me."

Because she knew that if she was stupid enough to actually go out with Smith, that if she was even stupider about letting herself fall for him, she would only be setting herself up for complete and utter emotional destruction.

Case in point: Smith and Tatiana would be filming a love scene together in a few weeks. It was going to be hard enough to watch her sister bare herself to the cameras like that. But if Valentina were foolish enough to let Smith into her bed and her heart during filming, she couldn't even begin to imagine how difficult—how *impossible*—it would be to sit quietly in the background and watch Smith kiss, touch, caress another woman. Especially when she still hadn't been able to forget how it had felt to be in his arms for those few minutes when they'd talked about their families in front of the fire in his living room.

A shiver ran through her as she took a step away from the window, and from Smith. When she felt there was enough distance between them for her head to remain clear, she said, "We're going to be working together for the next few months. I don't want to make things difficult for anyone on set, especially my sister. It will be hard on her if she thinks you or I have a problem with each other." She wasn't teasing him, wasn't trying to be a challenge he couldn't resist as she asked, "Can't we just be friends?"

At last, she could feel his frustration rumble through the trailer. It seemed he was no longer the perfectly in-control man he usually was.

Oh, why did witnessing that brief loss of control have to make him even more appealing? And why did she want to see it again—only next time they would be talking less…and kissing more?

"Of course we'll be friends," he said in a soft voice that caressed her just as well as any touch of his hand would have. "We already are."

Her pleasure at that statement came swift and warm through her veins. So, unfortunately, did the instant disappointment that he'd given up so easily. Of course, it was what she wanted. And yet, evidently a part of her had been hoping for more.

Both her pleasure and disappointment were short-lived as he held her prisoner with his dark gaze. "But just because I'm your friend doesn't mean I've stopped wanting you, too."

Even worse, she thought as he made an exit as

good as anything he'd won an Oscar for, it didn't make *her* stop wanting *him*.

And as Valentina sank down into her office chair, she realized—too late—the extent of her mistake.

She should have grabbed seduction, desire, with both hands.

Seduction would just have been her body. Desire would simply have been two people making each other feel good in bed. She could easily have written off a roll in the hay.

But friendship involved her heart.

As she buried her head in her hands, all she could think was, *Why couldn't I have been smart and just slept with him?*

Six

As filming kicked into high gear, the hours on set grew longer for everyone. There weren't action scenes to choreograph and memorize. There weren't digital effects to render. Nor were there hours spent in makeup and wardrobe.

But there was emotion.

So much emotion came from Smith and Tatiana as they played two characters who loved and lost, then learned how to love again. Just watching them act out their parts over the past week left Valentina drained and empty at the end of each day.

How, she wondered for the hundredth time, *did they do it?*

And yet, a part of her envied them that freedom to yell and laugh and cry and love all in the course of a workday. For all her hard work on set, Tatiana was always able to shake off the strong emotions within minutes of the director saying, "Cut." For her, it almost seemed as if her day had been akin to a cleansing therapy session.

These past weeks, Valentina had been turning more and more to her own secret project as a way to deal with the emotions churning around and around inside her. Tatiana was the only person who knew that Valentina was working on a screenplay about a female writer who woke up one day and found herself actually living out the story she was writing…including falling in love with the fictional hero she had created.

Tatiana had been trying for months to convince her to send it out to some of their contacts. Even though Valentina knew this was a logical next step in the Hollywood career of someone who loved the stories but not the limelight, she'd also known her script wasn't quite ready. Amazingly, it was after going through Smith's screenplay backward and forward with Tatiana at least a dozen times that Valentina finally realized where the holes were in her own work. And she knew that the changes she'd been making were good ones. Really good ones. Because she'd been lucky enough to learn from Smith what it took to make a truly emotional, impactful film.

And as she sat with the crew and watched Smith play his part of the harshly powerful yet disturbed and guilty businessman, her heart squeezed tight in her chest. When the movie was released in theaters, the audience would see every single one of his emotions in his eyes, in the set of his mouth and the lines on his forehead. And they would know without a doubt that the girl on the street he'd pushed down and stepped on had haunted him more and more with every day that passed.

* * *

Again and again, he'd gone back to Union Square, to the corner to watch for her, to wait for her. More than once as he'd been standing in the middle of the rushing crowds, a call had come in on his cell phone from a brother. A sister. His mother. But he'd never picked up those calls.

And the young woman had never come back that way again.

As the months had passed, the man's shoulders had stayed just as broad, his face just as handsome, his company more profitable than ever. But he'd grown more and more hollow, with more one-night stands, and wilder parties with acquaintances and colleagues that meant nothing. In the hours that were left between women who didn't matter and work that seemed to matter just as little, he drove himself even further into the ground with 5:00 a.m. runs and midnight swims.

But still, he couldn't forget the girl's eyes.

Or what she'd screamed at him before she ran off.

Until, finally, he found her working at a coffee shop. He recognized the pink streaks in her hair first, darker now than they'd been so many months ago, and her face was even prettier than he'd remembered.

A play of emotions moved across the businessman's face. Relief. Hope. Along with determined, unstoppable intent.

She was helping a customer, and unlike the day he'd crashed into her on the street when she'd been so pale, her skin glowed and her hair shone. For a moment, the man's mouth began to move into a smile. The first he'd worn in a very, very long time.

At that moment the girl moved, shifting away from the register...and he saw her belly.

Her extremely pregnant belly.

Now he was the pale one as all color leached from his tanned skin. He had to grip the back of a chair to keep his balance, and more than one customer shot him a concerned look as he stopped cold in the middle of the coffee shop.

All it took was an instant to calculate that she'd already been pregnant when he'd knocked her down... and his foot had landed hard on her stomach.

Bile rose in his throat at what he might have done to her, to the life she carried, that day.

His own hands went to his middle as his eyes squeezed shut for a split second. She could have lost her baby because of him.

There were so many things he had to make up to so many people. But for now, she was his only focus.

He would make this up to her.

He would protect her and the baby.

And he would make sure she never hurt again.

He was just moving toward her when she laughed at something a coworker said. Again, he was hit hard with emotion

Straight in his heart.

Her eyes met his just then, and as their gazes locked, her glowing skin paled. The cup in her hand was forgotten as she backed away from him, card-

*board slipping from her hands as steamed milk hit
the floor and splattered all over her shoes and pants.*

*It was as if the warm splash of liquid brought her
back to life. With a brisk smile that never even came
close to reaching her eyes, she brushed off the concern of her coworkers, who were checking to make
sure she hadn't been burned, and picked up a nearby
mop to clean up the mess she'd made.*

*The businessman walked toward her and stood
silently behind the counter, watching as she calmly
finished mopping up, then put away her cleaning sup-
plies. Her hands were steady as she washed them in
the sink.*

*At last, she turned to him, her chin up, her beauti-
ful eyes shuttered. "What can I get you today, sir?"*

*For months, he'd thought of her as frail. Now, he
realized just how strong she really was, partly because of the set of her mouth as she waited for his
response, partly because of how well she carried the
child inside of her.*

He would help both of them. No matter what.

"I'd like to talk to you."

*Her mouth tightened, that flash of fury he'd re-
membered so well coming back into her eyes as she
replied, "The special roast this month is from Ja-
maica, if you'd like to try that."*

*He nodded. "Fine." But even as relief began to
loosen her shoulders, he said, "I'll wait here until
your next break."*

*Barely veiled irritation informed her movements
for the next thirty minutes. She sighed as she untied*

her apron. Her long cotton top floated over her belly now, making her look even younger.

She knew the man was waiting for her, but she had no intention of dealing with him. Even if a part of her was curious about why he wanted to talk to her. And especially because he was even better looking now than he'd been that awful day when he'd pushed her down on the sidewalk and actually stepped on her.

She didn't owe him anything.

She turned and disappeared into the cramped back area where the employee lockers were. The last thing she expected was for the man to push in through the door a moment later.

Working to ignore the way her heart was pounding, she said, "Only employees are allowed back here."

"I'm sure Joe would be happy to make an exception for me." At her confused look, he explained, "My company funded the owner's expansion."

"Fine," she said, mimicking his earlier tone. Not wanting to draw this out, she asked point-blank, "What do you want?"

Instead of giving her a direct answer, his gaze moved to her stomach. She barely resisted the urge to try to cover herself with both hands.

"You're pregnant."

She all but snarled, "Obviously."

His wince was there and gone so fast she almost thought she'd imagined it.

"Are you—" She was amazed to see him falter,

even for a split second. "Is everything going okay with the baby?"

"Yes, the baby is perfect."

"Where do you live?"

She gave him a look that clearly said she thought he was crazy. "You don't even know my name. Do you actually think I'm going to tell you where I live?"

"Jo." Her eyes widened before he reminded her, "Your name tag was on your apron," and then, "My name is Graham."

She looked down at the cheap watch on her wrist. "My break's just about up now, and since the baby is sitting on my bladder, I've got about thirty seconds to get to the bathroom before I'm needed behind the register again."

If she'd expected him to be bothered by talk of bodily functions—or to finally get the picture and leave—she was disappointed. Still, she really did have to go, so she walked into the bathroom. After taking care of business and washing her hands, she stared at herself in the mirror, schooling herself in what she needed to say to the man. To Graham.

She took a deep breath to steel herself for it, then stepped into the back room where she knew he'd still be waiting for her.

He was too big for the small area.

And too darkly handsome for her peace of mind.

"I'm fine." She held her hands out from her body so that he could really see her and her huge baby bump. "That day on the street, what happened was an accident." One that had infuriated her into actu-

ally yelling at a stranger. "I shouldn't have lost it on you." He watched her silently. "Now if we're done rehashing all that, I have to get back to work."

But as she tried to walk past him, he said, "I own a two-bedroom condo that I haven't had any luck renting out. It's in a good neighborhood and one of the women in the building runs a small day care on the ground floor."

Whatever she'd expected him to say, it wasn't this.

"I already have an apartment." In a crappy neighborhood where she honestly didn't like the idea of having a newborn.

"Please, Jo, let me do this for you."

He'd said please, but even then she could hear the steel in his words that told her he wouldn't take no for an answer.

But she had just as much steel in her.

"Thanks for the offer, but you'll have to find another tenant."

She walked out and got back to work, knowing all the while that victory was only temporarily hers... because the odds of a determined man like Graham taking no for an answer were next to nil.

As the cameras stopped rolling, Valentina realized her face was wet. What she was watching wasn't real, but even surrounded by lights and cameras, it was almost impossible to remember that.

Surreptitiously, she bent her head and used the tips of two fingers to wipe her tears away while reminding herself not to feel foolish for having gotten caught up in the emotion of the scene. After all, no one was paying any attention to her, and they were filming a truly beautiful story.

But when she lifted her head, she saw that she was wrong.

Smith was paying attention…and his eyes were full of something so sweet that she couldn't quite tamp down the response of her body that came from nothing more than one look from him.

It seemed like forever since he'd sought her out in her office and caught her saying embarrassing things to George on the phone about his hands up her skirt. For the first few days after their conversation, she'd been edgy, anticipating how Smith might make his next move.

But as each day passed into the next, she became more and more certain that, despite what he'd said about not giving up, he'd decided to take her refusal to date him at face value.

She was happy about it. At least, she tried to be happy about it, if for no other reason than the simple fact that she *should* be happy his attention had come and gone so quickly. It meant she could relax and keep her focus where it belonged—on her sister—rather than on a man who was too seductive, too damn alluring, for her own good.

An hour later, after double-checking that her sister had everything she needed for an *Elle* fashion shoot the following morning, Valentina yawned behind her hand and headed back to her on-set office to collect her laptop. Tatiana wasn't the only one who'd be on the beach the next morning at sunrise for the photo shoot. Fortunately, no one would be taking Valentina's picture, so that meant she could put in a few more hours behind the computer tonight without anyone giving her grief about the dark circles under her eyes come morning.

She opened the door to her office and the fresh, delicate scent hit her first.

One perfect lily of the valley was laid across her laptop. The little white flowers that ran up the length of the stem were so beautiful her breath caught in her throat.

There was no note attached…but that didn't stop her from understanding that she hadn't been forgotten at all, because she was all but certain that the flower had come directly from the patch in Smith's front garden.

And judging by the ragged stem and the way a couple of the blooms at the bottom were slightly crushed, he'd picked it for her himself.

Jo, the heroine of *Gravity,* had a dream of owning a flower shop, and there was enough of the language of flowers in Smith's movie for Valentina to know what the meaning of this particular flower was.

Sweetness.

She didn't bother to try to convince herself that Smith had given her just any random flower. No, she'd spent enough time lying to herself lately, and she was too tired right now to do it yet one more time.

Smith, she knew with a certainty that sent a fragile warmth moving through her chest, knew exactly what he was doing. He could have sent her any message in that language, could have given her a yellow rose for *friendship* or a pink rose for *desire*. Even, perhaps, a red-petaled impatiens to signify that he, too, was losing patience.

Instead, he'd given her a flower that spoke to something else entirely, to hopes and dreams she hadn't ever allowed to become a reality.

It would be safer, better in the long run no doubt, to put the flower in the trash and let the overnight cleaning crew take it.

Carefully, Valentina lifted it and inhaled deeply. No one had ever given her a flower before.

And she couldn't possibly throw away something so beautiful.

Seven

The next day, after Tatiana's photo shoot wrapped, Valentina got on a plane to Los Angeles for a meeting with George and the Japanese fragrance company to iron out the final details of her sister's upcoming trip to Asia.

George had clearly intended to prod her further about Smith, but when he saw that she was too tired to rise to the bait, he dropped it and kept on track with business instead. Four hours flew by and when she rose to pack up her papers and head back to the airport, George put an arm around her as they walked out to the limousine.

"Reports from the set have been fantastic."

"Tatiana is brilliant in the movie, George. It's definitely going to be her big breakout role." She smiled at him. "Get ready to start working even harder."

"It looks to me like you're already working too hard."

"I just didn't get enough sleep last night," she countered.

He raised his eyebrows. "Is there something you need to tell me about a certain hot star…and my favorite business manager?"

"Absolutely not!" Valentina said with a little too much heat.

"You're a terrible liar, you know, Val."

"I've been so careful not to encourage him, but he's—"

She clamped her mouth shut as she realized, too late, that she'd just confirmed George's suspicions.

"If you ask me, you most definitely *should* encourage him. I know I certainly would."

She was afraid to open her mouth again—who knew what she might admit to this time?

"You did a great job raising Tatiana," he said softly. "So good that she's a remarkably kind and reliable movie star." George was one of the few people who knew their family situation. "But now you need to take some time for yourself, too."

She couldn't admit just how off-kilter his words made her feel. It wasn't a sacrifice to manage her sister's business affairs, not by any stretch of the imagination. Besides, lately her brain had started a disturbing pattern of filling in the few gaps she had with Smith. His laughter, the dark eyes that always seemed to zero in on her in the middle of a crowd, the easy way he had with everyone on set, from the camera operator to the cleaning crew.

"Actually," she said slowly, "I have been taking some time for myself." She took a deep breath before saying, "I've written a screenplay. And—" Oh, this was harder than she thought it would be. For all that she thought she wasn't afraid of rejection, maybe she was. Just a little bit.

"And?" She could hear the barely repressed excitement in George's voice.

She smiled at her friend. "I'd like you to read it."

He clapped his hands together like a happy child. "Finally!"

She raised an eyebrow. "What do you mean, 'finally'?"

"Tatiana swore me to secrecy, and she'll kill me if you let on that she told me." He looked at her with big, puppy-dog eyes. "Please don't tell her I blew it. Besides, she only told me because she loves you. She said it's great." He didn't waste any time asking, "Do you have it with you?"

Valentina realized that once she actually gave George her screenplay, the ball would start rolling whether she was ready for it or not.

Forcefully reminding herself that she'd only told him about it because she finally believed that it was ready, she said, "I'll email it to you as soon as I get back home." She clicked her leather bag shut, then pressed a kiss to George's cheek before sliding into the backseat of the airport limo. "And thank you for always being such a great friend."

Fortunately, she was too tired during the flight back to San Francisco to worry too much about her conflicted feelings over Smith or about sending her screenplay out into the world. Her eyes and brain were blurry as she finally got home, stripped off her clothes and made herself send the screenplay to George before she fell into bed.

The next morning, she let herself sleep until the last possible second and felt worlds better when she walked onto the set. Her stomach growled, and she knew she was going to be cranky without her daily hit of morning sugar, but losing half a day to travel meant she needed to get the ball rolling on high-priority items before she dropped by craft services to get something to eat.

A few minutes turned into three hours of email and phone calls and she missed breakfast altogether. With the Japanese fragrance deal in the crucial final planning stages, she had a feeling it was going to be one of those long days. She headed back to her office to continue to work and was so focused on the items on her mental to-do list that she was seated behind her computer before she noticed the plate and cup on her desk.

Her stomach growled in immediate response to the fluffy cinnamon bun, dripping with sugar, that sat in the middle of a beautiful green hand-thrown plate. Telling herself there wasn't a person alive with the willpower to resist the treat, especially when presented so beautifully, she pulled off a piece and popped it in her mouth.

Her eyes closed as the hit of sugar, perfectly spiced with cinnamon, hit her tongue, and a low moan of pleasure escaped her lips. It was decadent. Full of too many empty calories.

And exactly what she needed.

She didn't know how she'd missed the aroma of freshly brewed coffee before now, but when she reached for the mug the liquid was still warm as she greedily drank it down. She admired the ongoing beauty of the lily of the valley she'd put in a blown-glass vase she'd found in the kitchen the night before.

She was just putting down the mug when she finally saw the note.

Valentina,
The color of the plate and mug made me think of the green in your hazel eyes. I missed seeing them—and you—on set yesterday.
Enjoy your breakfast.
Smith

Valentina stared at the note for a very long time before carefully folding it up and slipping it into her purse. And then she ate every last piece of the cinnamon bun with more pleasure than she'd allowed herself to feel in as long as she could remember.

By the time Valentina finally emerged from her office to say thank you to Smith for both the flower and breakfast, she was frustrated—and more than a little relieved—to remember that he had an off-site meeting with his investors. He didn't need to share these kinds of details with her and Tatiana, but he obviously believed an informed team worked better than one kept in the dark. It was yet another factor that set him apart.

"Honey!"

Valentina turned with surprise to see her beautiful mother walking toward her with her arms outstretched. Even though she was a good six inches taller than Ava Landon, and hadn't been a child for a very long time, as Valentina stepped into the familiar arms and was enveloped by the expensive air of perfume, she suddenly felt two decades younger.

"I'm so glad I could make it here today. You know how much I love being on set."

She loved her mother enough to momentarily forget to be wary about Ava's reasons for the sudden visit to San Francisco. "You look great, Mom."

Ava Landon lit up the way she always did at compliments, before turning her gaze to her daughter. "You've lost weight. You know how much better you look when your figure is fuller."

Valentina stifled a sigh. "I think Tatiana has a small break before they need her again on set. I'll take you to her trailer."

But her mother was looking over her shoulder. "Here I am, baby!"

A good-looking man who couldn't be too much older than Valentina was walking toward them. Her mother leaned in closer and said, "Isn't he just too beautiful? I'm so in love with him."

Trying not to wince at her mother's too-free use of the word *love,* and glad the question was clearly rhetorical, Valentina shook the man's hand as her mother made the introductions.

"David, this is my eldest daughter, Val."

Valentina saw the slight surprise flash in his eyes as he saw just how different she looked from her mother and sister.

"Val, David is just *the most* talented actor."

Valentina felt her lips tighten as the wariness she'd momentarily forgotten grabbed her with a hard shake. Didn't her mother remember how "deeply" she'd been "in love" with the last dozen actors like David?

And how could it possibly be that easy for her mother to fall for someone...or at least fool herself into believing the desperation, the painful longing for something real and lasting, was love?

"That's great," Valentina said with a smile for David.

It would break her heart when he broke her mother's heart—as each and every good-looking actor always had—but she'd learned early on that there was no use trying to protect her mother from the men she chose to date. At the very least, David didn't look like the type to try to grab her ass when her mother's back was turned.

Valentina tried to be grateful for small mercies.

Unfortunately, now that they'd appeared from out of the blue, on top of everything else she had to take care of today, she'd have to make sure that her mother's big plans for David's acting career didn't annoy anyone on set. Thank God Smith was out for the afternoon. What a disaster that would have been otherw—

"Good afternoon, Valentina."

She would have groaned at her terrible luck were it not for the way Smith's low, warm voice always affected her. In less than a millisecond, anticipation—

and a rush of desire that came despite knowing she could never act on it—knocked the wariness out of her.

There simply wasn't enough room, she was amazed to find, for both Smith and anything else.

"Smith." She liked the feel of his name on her lips too much. "I'd like you to meet my mother."

He smiled as he picked up her mother's hand and pressed his lips to the back of it. Her mother was all but squealing with joy as he said, "You have two remarkable daughters, Mrs. Landon."

"Call me Ava," her mother said in that breathy voice she always used with good-looking men. All men, actually. "Your mother didn't do so badly herself, Mr. Sullivan."

Valentina cringed inwardly as he said, "Call me Smith, please."

At her mother's sharply expectant glance in David's direction, she said, "And this is David." She knew she'd never hear the end of it if she didn't say, "He's an actor."

Smith's expression was just as friendly as it had been from the moment he'd walked up to them. "Nice to meet you," he told the other man with a handshake.

"Big fan of yours," David said, and to his credit, he sounded as if he meant it rather than simply saying it to suck up to the big movie star he hoped would get him a job.

"Thanks," Smith said with genuine gratitude before turning his focus back to Valentina. "Hope you don't mind if I tag along if you're heading over to say hello to Tatiana?" he said without a trace of guile.

Of course her mother put her hand on his arm, her perfectly shaped and manicured pink nails contrasting in a totally feminine way with his tanned skin.

"That would be absolutely lovely, Smith. It's so much fun getting to know my daughter's costars. Tell me all about yourself."

And as her mother dragged him off, Valentina was both mortified and grateful to know that he'd be there to help her deal with her mom—the one person who always tied her up in knots, no matter how hard she tried to stay untangled.

"I'm sorry about that," Valentina said to Smith after Ava Landon and her boyfriend had left. "My mother doesn't mean to hurt anyone. It's just that when she's with one of her men, she sometimes forgets to think about how anyone else might feel. It's like they're all she can see for a little while."

He heard the *sometimes,* the *doesn't mean to,* the *little while,* and knew all of those qualifiers were simply Valentina being kind. Her mother was a nice woman and she clearly loved her daughters. But he could see that she'd hurt them, too. Especially Valentina.

The need to comfort her had him reaching out to stroke her cheek, then slipping his fingers beneath her chin and tilting her face up to his.

Her skin was soft. So incredibly soft. Yet again, Smith was surprised by how much he wanted her.

He'd never let a woman distract him from his work, and he had never had any trouble keeping a woman inside the boundaries he'd set for her. Especially now that he was at the helm of his own picture, it was too important to him to afford to lose focus because of a woman. And yet, even with all the valid reminders echoing in his head—*You're too busy for this. For her. For anything other than making this movie*—it didn't take more than a look, a smile and now the softness of her skin against his fingertips for him to want her.

"She loves you. And you love her. Anyone can see both of those things, even if your relationship isn't perfect." He continued to stroke his thumb over the soft skin of her jaw as her lips opened slightly in surprise at his words. "You were right when you said that love shouldn't have to be a battlefield. When it's with the right person, I've seen love be easy. Sweet. And perfect."

He'd never wanted to kiss anyone as badly as he wanted to kiss her right then. One hot kiss was all it would take to make her forget her mother's visit, and he could almost justify it to himself that way.

Only, he'd never seen her this vulnerable before, as if the armor she was so careful to put on every morning before coming to the set had been stripped away in one fell swoop by her mother's unexpected visit.

It would be the easiest thing in the world to take advantage of her vulnerability.

Easy…and wrong.

Fortunately, Smith knew Valentina well enough by now to know that in the same way a kiss would have helped her forget her churning emotions over her relationship with her mother, so would getting back to work.

"Do you have a few minutes to discuss a request that just came in for a photo shoot with Tatiana and myself?"

She blinked at him in confusion for a few seconds, clearly surprised by his sudden shift. But then, the next time she blinked she was the same cool, calm businesswoman he'd seen for the first time in that meeting months ago and had been unable to forget.

"Absolutely. What are the details?"

He'd been so focused on turning her thoughts from her mother that, too late, Smith realized he might not have picked the best thing to discuss with her. Then again, perhaps her reaction might actually end up telling him more about her true feelings than she was willing to admit to his face.

"They'd like the two of us to play our characters, wearing clothes, makeup, even the props from the movie."

"That sounds fine," she said, clearly wondering why he'd felt the urgent need to discuss it with her right then. "Did they give you any other details?"

He tried to keep his voice easy as he explained, "The photo editor wants to do a pretty tight focus on the characters as a couple."

He was pretty sure Valentina's step faltered right before she said, "How tight a focus?"

"They want to portray the intimacy of the couple's connection."

She stopped in the middle of the lot, the fierce

protector again, her cheeks flushed as she informed him, "I'm not okay with Tatiana being dressed up and photographed as some sort of nubile sex kitten."

He wanted to smooth away the hard lines at the corners of her mouth. Not with his fingertips, but with his own mouth. With a kiss that would heal as much as it would arouse.

Soon, damn it. He needed it to happen before he lost his mind entirely over wanting her.

"Neither am I," he said softly before clarifying, "From the conversation I had with the photo editor, I believe their goal is to highlight the romantic elements...not the sexual ones. And that's the direction I'm pushing them to go in, too—for romance rather than sex. We see plenty of sex every day in magazines and on TV. But romance will stand out."

He watched her long, smooth throat move as she swallowed. "Romance." The word slipped from her lips with equal disbelief and longing. "That sounds—"

Her words faltered now just as her step had a short while before, not because she was worried about her sister being photographed with too few clothes on, but, he hoped, because she didn't like the image of her sister being romantic with him. And there was only one reason that would bother her: if she wanted him for herself.

Finally, she got out the words, "You two are going to look great together in the magazine."

Unfortunately, while he was glad to see she wasn't nearly as immune to him as she tried to pretend, he hated hurting her in any way.

"Valentina, if you have any reservations at all about it, you need to let me know."

But she had already stuffed the emotional woman away and was back to being all business. "I think the photo shoot sounds fantastic. People are going to see it and rush to the theaters to watch the two of you together on-screen. And they won't be disappointed." She turned away to head back to her trailer. But then she stopped and faced him again. "Thank you for being so kind to my mother and her boyfriend."

Frustration ate at him as he let her go back to her office, climb the stairs and shut the door behind her. It had been a really, really long time since Smith hadn't gotten exactly what he wanted, exactly when he wanted it. Not just because he was a movie star. Not just because he was wealthy enough to buy anything he wanted.

But because of the man he'd always been.

Smith knew how to focus, how to channel every last bit of his energy into his work. For the first time ever, even though the timing couldn't be worse, he was considering turning that focus on a woman.

Hell, who was he kidding? It was pure need that was driving him to it, not some logical decision he was making. Because the truth was, he wanted Valentina so badly that the want, the need, was tearing at his insides. And it was a need only made worse by the sure knowledge that he could have already taken her, could have easily stripped her down and lowered her to the small leather couch under the window of her office for his pleasure...and hers.

Once upon a time, her beautiful body would have been enough for him. And when he was younger, he would have believed that the easiest way to deal with the need would be to use his charm and looks to persuade her to have a hot, but very casual, film fling.

But now, something told him that uncovering her sensual side wouldn't be nearly enough. Not just because it would only fuel his need to know more about the rest of her…but also because he knew that if he risked touching only her body, she'd write off her heart entirely.

What the hell was happening to him?

He pushed one hand through his hair as he pulled his cell phone out of his pocket with the other. He hit speed dial on the number at the top of his list. Just hearing his mother's voice had him smiling again.

"Hi, Mom."

"Smith, honey, how are you?"

"The movie's going well."

"I'm so glad to hear it." She paused for a moment, and he knew she hadn't been fooled by his reply about the movie and not himself. "And how is everything else?"

For as long as he could remember, Mary Sullivan had had laser-sharp radar when something was bothering one of her kids. She never poked, never prodded, but was always there when they were finally ready to come for help and advice. Smith knew he'd called her because it was long past time for him to admit that he knew *exactly* what was happening to him.

"There's a woman."

"So I've heard," his mother said softly. "Marcus and Nicola said Valentina is very pretty. Very sweet, too."

Smith immediately thought back to the tears on Valentina's cheeks during filming the previous day. She'd been so moved by the love story he'd written that the sweetness of her response had tugged at him, right in the center of his chest. It was why he'd given her the flower and the cinnamon bun—because they were both sweet, and both reminded him of her.

"She is sweet," he confirmed to his mother. "And beautiful, and smart, and strong." He blew out a hard breath. "And she won't let me take her out on a date."

Jesus, it was like being fifteen years old again and pouring his heart out over his mother's chocolate chip cookies in the kitchen. Smith loved his brothers and sisters, but only with his mother had he ever admitted just how difficult his extreme fame had been for him from time to time, especially when it reached a point when he could no longer go where he wanted, and was left feeling trapped under a magnifying glass. It had taken years to learn how to deal with it, and to find ways to make sure he lived his life according to his own terms, while still managing the demands of his fans and the media. Just like today, when he'd needed someone to talk things over with, Mary Sullivan had been the only person he could think of calling.

"Did she tell you why?"

"She doesn't trust actors." He had to admit, "And I don't blame her. There're a lot of scum in my profession."

"You've worked together for long enough now that she would know you're not one of them," his mother told him with perfect certainty. "But sometimes it's harder to admit to ourselves that we want love in our lives than it is to keep living without it."

Smith was suddenly hit with the realization of how close this situation between Valentina and himself was to the relationship between Jo and Graham in his film. In *Gravity,* both the hero and heroine were stubbornly convinced that love was the hard part, when the truth was that love should be the easiest thing of all.

He'd written the damned movie, and yet he'd needed his mother to point out the obvious to him: there was no point trying to fight an attraction that knocked him off his feet—it was time to fight *for* it instead.

"Have I told you lately how smart you are?" he asked her.

"So are you," she said, and he could hear the smile in her voice now. "You're one of the smartest men I know. Smart enough to know a good thing when you see it and to do whatever it takes to make sure you don't let it go." She was as serious as he'd ever heard her as she said, "And if it turns out that she's the one, no matter what, remember who you're fighting for—even if it feels like you're the only one fighting sometimes."

Over the course of her life, his mother had gained the wisdom that came with having a loving husband and a family to call her own. Smith had learned all his important life lessons from her, and after watching Valentina and Tatiana with their mother, he would never take Mary Sullivan for granted for a single second.

"You know how much I love you, don't you, Mom?"

"Oh, yes, honey," she said in a voice that was slightly thicker now, "I do know. But it's always nice to hear it one more time."

Eight

Valentina woke with the same sinking feeling in her stomach that she'd had when she had gone to bed last night. She'd been so flipped out over the thought of Smith and her sister posing for "romantic" pictures in a magazine—even though they would be completely in character, clothes and all—that she'd fled without remembering to thank him for the flower and breakfast. And that was on top of her completely unprofessional minimeltdown over her mother's visit.

She dropped her head into her hands as she sat on the side of her bed. For so long she'd been able to push these kinds of feelings away. Why was she having such trouble doing that now?

And why did she have a sinking feeling that the answer had Smith's name written all over it?

Even worse, why was it starting to feel as if he might also be the cure for her swirling, conflicting emotions?

With mechanical precision she showered, brushed

her teeth, dried her hair, applied her makeup and slipped on one of her suits. No matter what happened today, she'd be professional. And she would keep her emotions off the set and away from Smith Sullivan.

Once on set, she headed into her office to put down her bag and was planning to turn right around to finally say a polite thank-you to Smith for the flower and breakfast when she found something new on her desk.

Maybe she should have been prepared. After all, it was the third morning in a row that Smith had put something special on her desk for her to find when she arrived at work.

But how could she have possibly prepared for this?

With trembling hands she put down her leather bag and reached for the wooden frame. The black-and-white picture wasn't big, but it was beautiful.

She and Tatiana were laughing together on the set. One of her hands was on her sister's shoulder, while Tatiana had one around Valentina's waist. They'd always been so easy with their affection, had been curling up together under the covers to watch movies, and giggle, and comfort each other since her sister was a baby. Valentina had never thought twice about how natural it was to reach for her, to hold her, to laugh with her.

Their closeness wasn't something she took for granted, but seeing it captured so beautifully made her see it anew for what it was.

Yet again, Smith had made sure she saw the gift

first, his note second. She didn't put down the frame
as she picked up the sheet of paper with her free hand.

Valentina,
This picture was one of the candids Larry has
been taking of the cast and crew. You and Tatiana are so easy. Sweet. Perfect.
    Looking at how happy you are in this picture
makes me smile.
Smith

Just as she'd done the previous morning when she'd
found the breakfast he'd left for her, she reread the
note several times, until his words were imprinted
on her memory.

No wonder he'd been able to write such a beautiful screenplay, if he could capture so much with so
few words. Words that were so perceptive. Words
so right that all the things he had said he believed
love could be were captured in this one simple picture. Neither she nor her sister were posing, and
both of them looked confident in their love for each
other.

The love between them just *was*. And the deep,
intrinsic knowledge that nothing would, that nothing could, ever pull them apart made it even more
precious.

A few moments later, it wasn't the photo that she
lifted to press to her lips as she took a shaky breath
and worked to clear her gaze. She didn't know how

it was possible, but the short, beautiful note even smelled like Smith: clean, sexy man.

She knew how powerful actors usually behaved. She'd seen enough of them ply her mother with diamond bracelets and expensive trips—and even a car. One call to an assistant and each of those gifts were dispatched, much to her mother's joy.

And yet, the flower, breakfast and now a black-and-white photo that she'd treasure forever meant so much more than glittering jewelry or any other expensive toy ever could.

She knew Smith was balancing a dozen responsibilities on this film, between acting, producing and directing. She'd heard him talking on the phone with more than one member of his family during quick breaks, especially his pregnant sister Sophie, whom he checked in on every single day.

And yet, somehow in the middle of more pressure than any person should be able to withstand, he was thinking about her, too. She put in long hours and got in earlier than most of the crew, but his hours made hers feel borderline lazy.

He didn't have the time to waste on her. Because that's what it had to be in the end, didn't it?

A waste.

Yes, if she gave in to his wooing, they would likely end up having hot sex. Her entire body tingled at the thought of just how hot sex with Smith would likely be.

But even while she schooled herself to get over the crazy fantasy of a night with him, a voice in her head forced her to listen as it whispered that being with Smith wouldn't just be hot…it would also be easy. Sweet.

And perfect.

Though it was already open, Valentina knocked on Smith's trailer door. She valued her privacy enough to value everyone else's, too. Especially that of a man who rarely seemed to have any himself.

"Come in."

With his deep, inherently sensual voice rasping up her spine, her first thought was the same one she always had when she saw him.

Gorgeous.

Followed immediately by *sexy.*

And then *want.*

But close on their heels was another.

Tired.

For the past few weeks, Smith's energy hadn't flagged, hadn't waned, nor had she ever once caught him complaining. But for the very first time, he looked worn down.

Her protective urges jumped to the fore. "Is everything okay?"

He got up from his desk to pour her a cup of coffee. "Much better now that you're here."

God, it was so hard to keep fighting her feelings for him. Because she liked him. Wanted him, too, with a desperation that was breaking her down, slowly but surely, every second he was near.

And even when he wasn't.

"I know how busy you are," she began, but she was sick and tired of stalling around him. She'd always prided herself on being direct. Forthright. And appreciative when someone was kind. It was precisely what she'd taught Tatiana. And, she knew, what her mother had taught her before that.

Valentina moved closer to him this time, rather than farther away. "I forgot to say thank you yesterday for the flower. For breakfast. And, especially, for the photo. You didn't have to." She smiled at him as she said, "But I can't deny that I'm glad you did."

When his smile came, it took away some of the exhaustion stamped into his nearly perfect features. "It was my pleasure, Valentina."

He handed her the drink and their fingertips brushed as she took the mug from him.

Only, it wasn't coffee she wanted as the word *pleasure* zinged around inside her head and body like a pinball.

"How do you do it?" she asked him before she could stop herself. "How do you keep all the balls in the air and give so much of yourself while still keeping it all together?"

"Keeping it all together?" He gave a slightly harsh laugh. "Jesus, Valentina, can't you see that it's killing me?"

"Directing, producing and acting all at the same time is a tough order," she agreed.

His eyes grew darker as he said, "I can handle all of that."

She could feel the quicksand pulling her in, deeper

with every word tossed out between them, with every moment she spent with Smith in his office. That quicksand had to be the reason she couldn't leave. The reason she couldn't even consider it.

Her lips felt dry, too dry, and she had to wet them before asking, "Then what's killing you?"

A low groan left his lips as his gaze dropped to her mouth for a split second, then back up to her eyes.

"Not doing this."

His mouth was on hers before her heart could pound out its next beat and even though she'd come here to thank him for his thoughtful gift—*not to kiss him!*—somehow she was in his arms and they were kissing as if he'd been away to war and had finally come home to her.

No one had ever kissed her like this. With such warmth. With such need.

And with such perfect, sweet passion.

All the things she'd ever heard about the earth spinning too fast and blood rushing and limbs going numb—they were all happening to her. The kiss grew hotter, deeper, more and more intense with every second that their lips and tongues collided.

Never. She'd never felt desire this intense from a man...or from herself. And yet, even as their mouths took them into more and more dangerous territory, Valentina knew it was just one more piece of the puzzle they'd been building together. Because even in this one kiss, right alongside need and heat were all the other things that connected them: family, laughter and an easy compatibility that she couldn't remember having with anyone other than her sister.

For the first time in her life, Valentina gave herself over entirely to a man. Not only because Smith's kiss demanded it, but because she wanted nothing more than to feel.

Everything.

Everything she'd dreamed of for so long.

Everything she'd longed for in the secret hours of the night when her defenses came down.

Smith's mouth moved over hers, his hands cupping her hips and pulling her in tighter before making a slow path up her back to her shoulders and then into her hair. Valentina finally let herself embrace the freedom to feel, to desire and be desired…and, most of all, to pretend for a few short moments that there were no consequences to this kiss.

Smith had thought about kissing Valentina so many times, had come close enough to her mouth on enough occasions, that he'd already decided how she would taste.

Sweet like spun sugar, with just the slightest kick of exotic spice.

As a connoisseur of women, he was good. Good enough that when his lips finally met hers, and his tongue had slid against hers on a groan of deep-seated need, he found out just how right he was.

But not nearly accurate enough, because Valentina tasted better than any of the sweetest, most succulent treats he'd ever had.

So much better, he thought as he cupped the back of her neck to pull her in closer to brush his lips over hers again and again. He loved each and every one of the little gasps and moans she made as he found the sensitive corners of her mouth with the tip of his tongue, and then the fullness of her lower lip with the very edge of his teeth.

As long as he could remember, he'd been in complete control. With women. And roles. Even, once he'd adjusted to the demands of fame, with the press and his fans.

But in the span of one kiss with Valentina, his passion and desire spiraled the second his mouth touched hers and his hands met the curves that were so much softer than he ever would have guessed. He was no longer in control, not even for a second. And he didn't want to be.

One kiss had been all it took to confirm not only how deep her passion lay, but also that neither of them had a prayer of fighting this, even if he was the only one who accepted that truth.

When they finally drew apart to drag much-needed oxygen into their lungs, he let himself appreciate the few precious seconds he had left of Valentina still being soft in his arms, her eyes cloudy with stunned pleasure.

Smith didn't claim to always understand women, but he wasn't as clueless as some guys. Valentina had wanted that kiss…just as much as she hadn't.

He wouldn't let her regret it. But he couldn't let her overthink it, either.

She kept her hand flat on his chest, almost as if she was bracing herself while her eyes cleared little by little. But then they clouded over again, this time with alarm.

She was pushing against his chest and saying, "Smith, I didn't—" when he gently cut her off.

"I have something else for you."

He forced himself to release her even though the caveman inside him told him he needed to finish claiming his woman before she could get away. During the past two decades, it had been easy to put love and relationships on the back burner. Even his longer, more serious relationships hadn't ever been with someone he would sacrifice everything for, and they had been nothing like what his parents or brothers and sister had in their relationships.

But Smith knew chemistry. After all, it was his job to create it with each and every one of his costars. Yet, even to him, the chemistry between him and Valentina was extraordinary. And—whether she was ready to accept the truth of it or not—inevitable.

He had never acted out a part with her, and he would not do so now, which meant he couldn't force the easy smile he knew would help as he said, "I was going to give this to you tomorrow morning, but now seems like a better time."

Smith could see the gears in her brain working, questioning why he'd sidestepped their kiss altogether…and, possibly, why he wasn't asking for another one. Or to take things to the next level.

"I can't accept any more gifts from you," she said,

the sensual quality of her voice that she always tried so hard to hold back in full force after their kiss.

What, he couldn't stop himself from wondering even though it only made his unfulfilled desire for her more excruciating, would she sound like as she came apart in his arms, her neat and tidy hair messy from his hands and spread out across the pillow?

All of the blood that hadn't already rushed south took a trip in that direction as he imagined the heat of her skin, the sexy rasp of her voice, as she lay sated and sweet beneath him in the few moments he'd give her to recover before he took her again.

He picked up a white envelope from his desk. "Let me give you one more, Valentina."

She sucked in a sharp breath as if he'd just asked her for another kiss rather than request she open the envelope to find out what was inside. And maybe that was why she finally took the envelope from him, because it was the lesser of two evils: the gift or his mouth back on hers.

She slid open the flap and pulled out two tickets. He saw the surprise first, and then the pleasure she couldn't hide.

"Alcatraz? When I called they said all the tours were sold out for the next two months." She looked back down and read the fine print. "These tickets are for tomorrow night."

"I haven't been to Alcatraz since my fourth-grade field trip."

She gripped the tickets tighter. Again, he watched her gears churn. Up, down. Forward, back.

Finally, she said, "The fourth grade was a long time ago."

"It sure was. My memory is pretty fuzzy now."

He didn't want to force her to ask him to accompany her, but he sure as hell wasn't going to turn her down when good manners dictated she do just that.

With the grace and poise she radiated everywhere from the boardroom to the set, she finally asked him, "Would you like to see it again?"

"I sure would."

He thought she gave a small sigh of resignation before she said, "Okay, then. Why don't you join me?"

He didn't have to force his smile this time. "I'd love to."

"I should get back to my office." But instead of moving toward the door, she said, "About that kiss."

"It was a great kiss, wasn't it?"

She flushed, but didn't try to deny that he was speaking the truth. "Yes," she said in that innately supersexy voice that put him right back on the edge of grabbing her for another one, "it was a great kiss. But—"

"I want to kiss you again, too, Valentina."

She made a sound of frustration and even that had his body reacting. "Whether you or I enjoyed the kiss is irrelevant. I can't kiss you again." Before he could do anything more than raise his eyebrows at her emphatic statement that they both knew didn't do a darn thing to erase the heat between them, she said, "And you know why. We've already talked about this."

"We did," he agreed, "but why don't you tell me again why you won't go on a date with me."

"You're an actor."

Smith had been telling stories for long enough to know a thing or two about pacing. The time had been right earlier to take a kiss they'd both needed, and then, on the heels of all that heat, to push her for the invite to Alcatraz. He figured he had just a little more wiggle room left.

"After that kiss, I think you'll agree that I deserve another reason, one that doesn't lump me in with a bunch of self-obsessed scum."

"You're one of the biggest movie stars in the world, and people are dying to know anything they can about you, including whom you choose to date." She shook her head. "I can't imagine anything worse than being in the spotlight. And if I were to go out on a date with you, that's exactly where I'd end up."

Of all the problems Smith had with finding the right woman these past few years, this hadn't been one of them. The women in his world always loved the spotlight, so much so that he wondered if he'd ever find one who wanted him for any other reason.

But he didn't doubt for one second that Valentina was telling him the truth. Especially not when she'd said, *I can't imagine anything worse than being in the spotlight* with such vehemence.

"Look," she said in a much gentler tone, "we have to work together for the next few weeks. If we're going to go see Alcatraz together tomorrow, I don't think it's a good idea for you to be under the false assumption that this—" she gestured between the two of them "—is ever going to happen again."

At thirty-six, Smith had fame, he'd made a fortune, he'd traveled and partied and thrown himself into his work for two decades. Now he was ready for what came next: to be with a woman he not only desired, but with whom he could share his life, his dreams. A woman with whom he could grow old. He was also ready for kids—to play with on the beach, to throw balls with in the park, to let loose with their cousins at a family party.

So even though he'd heard Valentina's reasons loud and clear, and even though he couldn't deny that his life came chock-full of spotlights, Smith refused to give up. Not when something told him that she might very well be *the one*...and that if he didn't fight like hell for her, he'd never stop cursing himself for a fool.

"How about this? I won't kiss you again until you ask me to."

She barely hesitated before saying, "I'm not going to ask you to kiss me again."

"Yes," he said softly, "you will."

She blinked at him. Once. Twice. Three times before saying, "I still don't understand why you're trying so hard when I've given you every reason to let me go."

He wouldn't kiss her until she asked, but he'd said nothing about putting limits on touching her. He moved closer again, close enough to reach for the tip of her ponytail and run his fingers through her long, soft hair.

"Ask me to kiss you again, and I'll remind you of one of the reasons."

The look she gave him said, *Nice try,* even as she said, "You must have shared plenty of hot kisses with other women."

"Not that hot. Not even close." He paused just long enough to let his fingers slide from her hair down to the exposed skin above the collar of her fitted wool jacket. She shivered beneath this barest of touches. "And neither have you."

Nine

Valentina had never been so thankful for Smith's busy schedule or her sister's popularity. It meant that they'd been interrupted in his office before one kiss could turn into any more, and that she could go straight back to her own office and bury herself in her workload…with Smith only edging into her mind every other second, rather than every single one.

Because even as their kiss led them into increasingly deep and dangerous waters, she could feel his patience, and how tightly he'd been holding on to his control.

With a heady shiver of anticipation she knew she shouldn't be feeling, Valentina could no longer deny the absolute certainty that Smith's patience was going to run out soon.

And that hers would, too.

Even though she'd tried again and again to keep her distance, she hadn't been able to keep from getting closer to him instead.

With every word he spoke, she could feel her defenses crumble just a little bit more. Had he chosen that moment before the knock came at his office door to reach for her, she would have gone to him, with him, without a protest, without a care in the world.

Just as Valentina was trying to complete the impossible task of dragging her focus away from Smith's kiss and back to her email, Tatiana popped her head in.

"Got a second?"

Valentina immediately got up from behind her computer. "Always." She put her arms around her sister and gave her a hug hello. "What's up?"

Her sister's gaze sharpened on her. "I actually wanted to check on you."

"Me?"

"Is everything okay?"

Dozens of responses flew to the tip of Valentina's tongue: *Smith kissed me. Or I kissed him. I honestly don't know what happened. Only that it was good. So good that I can't seem to find my center again.*

But even though she badly wanted to talk to her best friend in the world about her twisted thoughts and feelings, she didn't dare. Not when Tatiana was working so closely with Smith. Her job as lead actress on a major feature film was hard enough on her. The last thing she needed to be worrying about was whether or not her sister was getting along with her all-powerful costar.

"George asked me the same thing," Valentina said

with a smile. "I think I'm officially too old to get away with missing a few hours of sleep."

Tatiana rolled her eyes. "You're not old, you just work too hard. And because that's entirely my fault, I'm treating both of us to a spa day on Saturday."

Valentina almost moaned aloud at the thought of getting a massage and then sinking into a spa. "You know I love working hard. But I'm certainly not going to say no to a spa day with my favorite person in the world." Just then a text came in on her phone from George. She read it aloud to Tatiana. "Your esteemed agent has just asked me when you'll be up for a conference call to talk about your commercial in Japan."

"Would tomorrow work? I was actually going to head back to the house soon to go over my lines a few more times."

"Okay, I'll tell him," Valentina said, and then, "Do you want me to run them with you?"

Her sister shook her head. "No. I mean, I know them cold. That's not really the problem."

She always did, thought Valentina. Even when she was a little girl, her sister had never flubbed her lines. She'd left it up to the less prepared adults to do that.

"I guess I'm just a little nervous about shooting tomorrow's scene. I mean, I know how to pretend to be in love, or how to act scared, or happy…but I've never been in labor before."

"Thank God for that," Valentina teased, glad when her sister smiled. "You don't need to overthink it."

"I know I shouldn't," Tatiana agreed, "but I just really want to do the scene justice for all the mothers out there who've gone through so much pain for their kids." With clear hesitation, she said, "I talked to Mom about it."

Valentina felt a sharp pang in the center of her chest as she forced out, "That was smart. What did she say?"

"She was actually pretty helpful."

Valentina bit back a sarcastic, *She was?*

"She told me all about her labor with each of us, about how it hurt so bad that Daddy refused to let go of her hand for even a second. Eighteen hours," Tatiana said softly. "That's how long he held her hand. Until he could finally hold us."

Valentina exhaled a shaky breath as she reached for her sister's fingers and gripped them tightly. "I miss him so much sometimes."

"Me, too," Tatiana said. Even though their mother wasn't there with them, they knew she had to miss him most of all.

Her sister was just getting up to leave when Tatiana spotted the black-and-white picture. "Oh, I love this picture! When did you get it?"

"This morning. Smith found it in the candids Larry has been taking on set and gave it to me."

Her sister's eyes flickered to hers. "That was nice of him."

Valentina nodded and carefully said, "He's certainly setting the bar high for your next costar."

Tatiana stared at the photo for another few seconds before putting it down. "I was thinking about ordering pizza and chasing it with some ice cream to help put myself in a pregnancy-craving mindset. Any interest in joining me?"

"Are you kidding?" Work could wait. A night with her sister was precious. She grabbed her bag and her phone, but purposefully left her laptop on her desk for once. "Pizza and ice cream sounds almost as good as a spa day. In fact, if we pair it with *Pretty Woman* I may not need the spa at all to put a spring back in my step."

"What is it," her sister asked as they headed for the parking lot, "about a prostitute and a billionaire falling in love that's so darn perfect?"

Valentina shrugged. "Who knows?" After all, the last thing she had a clue about was love, fictional…or otherwise. "Some things are just perfect," she said as she found herself thinking about Smith again, "even when they don't make any sense."

And some things, like her relationship with her mother, would never be perfect no matter how badly she wanted them to be.

The next day, feeling much more relaxed after a night of gorging on junk food while reciting all the lines in *Pretty Woman* to each other, Valentina sat back with the rest of the crew and watched Smith and Tatiana as they stood with their heads bent over the script, talking through the nuances of the scene one last time before they started shooting.

Most of the movie had been filmed in order so far. It wasn't always like that, but Valentina liked it when the story arc made sense. Heck, she liked it when things made sense, period.

Yesterday they'd filmed a handful of montage scenes of Smith's character, Graham, slowly wooing Tatiana's character, Jo.

First, he gave her baby booties, soft and pink and so pretty that she hadn't been able to refuse them. When Jo had said, "I haven't asked to know the sex. It might be a boy," Graham's eyes had clouded over.

"It's a girl." And then he'd walked out, leaving Jo frowning, still holding the booties.

The next time he came to the coffee shop he was carrying a small silver bag with more pink inside. Only this time he didn't stay to watch her pull out the tiny baby clothes, pretty little dresses that everyone exclaimed over. She ran from the coffee shop and caught him halfway down the sidewalk. Her thank-you came first, her admonishment not to keep bringing her gifts came second. But all he said in response was that she needed to be more careful about running down a crowded sidewalk in her condition.

Jo found the brand-new stroller and newborn-baby seat inside her apartment the next afternoon when she arrived home after an early-morning shift. She ran her hand over them admiringly even as she decided that Graham had gone too far. Not just because the gifts were way too expensive and it would take her forever to pay him back, or because she was touched despite herself at the fact that he'd clearly done his research about the safest baby gear. But because he'd not only figured out where she lived, he'd also figured out a way to get the stroller inside without asking her permission.

It was easy to look up Graham on the internet and find out where he worked. Or, rather, the name of the building he owned in the financial district.

Jo knew she looked horribly out of place with her big belly and bright maternity clothes and pink-streaked hair on the busy street full of tense people in dark suits all rushing as they spoke into earpieces. Five months ago it might have bothered her the way people stopped and stared at her, wondering what the heck she was doing so far out of her environment, but with her entire focus on giving the businessman— or, as she'd just learned, billionaire—a piece of her mind, she simply didn't care.

The glass in the front of the building was so clean and clear she imagined people walked nose-first into it every day. Pushing the heavy front door open, she had to stop to take in the high ceiling, the polished granite floors, the quiet reverence to money that the building—and every occupant in it—exuded.

Irritated with herself for being impressed, she marched up to the security desk. "I need to see Graham."

To his credit, the man didn't blink an eye. Not at her youth. Her clothes. Or her belly. "Name, please."

"Jo. I don't have an appointment." She lifted her chin. "But he'll see me."

The guard studied her for a long moment and she stared back as calmly as she could. Finally, he *picked up the phone. "Angie, I have Jo here to see Mr. Hughes." Whatever the receptionist said caused a flicker of surprise across the man's face.*

He put the phone down and stood. "I'll escort you up personally, Jo."

She worked to keep her cool as they rode up in the elevator. And when he said, "Congratulations," she was the one lifting her head in surprise this time.

Her hands automatically went to her stomach. She started to feel a little sick. Well, not sick exactly, but the twinges she'd been having in her back had definitely gotten worse.

It was yet another reason she needed to make him back off. She didn't want anything to distract her from the baby.

And Graham was definitely *a distraction.*

"Thank you," she said, and then it was time to step off the elevator and onto the plushest, cleanest carpet she'd ever seen. Even in a showroom, she mused, it couldn't look so brand-new.

Struck with the irrepressible urge to kick off her shoes and bury her toes in the soft fibers, she was stunned to see shiny black shoes come to stand right in front of her scuffed silver ballet flats.

"Jo."

Every time he said her name, it sent a shiver through her. Today, the lie she told herself was that it was fury that caused the trembling.

She didn't care who heard her say, "I asked you to stop giving me things."

She expected him to herd her into his office, to

close the door and make sure what was said between them stayed private.

He didn't move an inch. "You need them."

She wanted to yell at him. But she found herself lowering her voice as she accused him, "You broke into my apartment."

"The stroller and seat would have been stolen if they'd been left outside. And I didn't want you pushing them all the way home from work."

The fact that he was right about both of those things did little to mitigate her fury.

"Look," she began in as patient a voice as she could muster, "I know you still feel bad—"

A sharp pain to her midsection turned her words into a cry.

For the first time since that day on the sidewalk in Union Square, they touched each other, her hand flying out to his arm to brace herself against the brutal pain.

Jo's eyes were closed too tightly for her to see the panic fly across Graham's face.

"Tell Ellis to be outside with the car in sixty seconds," he told one of his assistants without ever looking away from Jo. To the other he said, "Call California Pacific Medical Center and tell the doctor to have the birthing room ready for us in fifteen minutes."

The pain finally having broken, Jo realized his hand was on the small of her back as he moved them into the elevator.

"What are you doing?"

"Taking you to have your daughter."

She opened her mouth to argue, to tell him she could take care of herself, when another pain hit her, even worse this time.

Graham's voice was low, soothing and incredibly gentle. "Breathe, Jo. In first, slowly." She managed to suck in a breath, though it felt as though her small frame was being torn in two. "Good. Now let it out, just as slow." She did as he directed, and he praised her again. "You're doing great."

When the elevator opened on the ground floor, she was actually glad to have his strong arms around her.

"Not too much farther until you can lie down in the backseat of my town car."

Her eyes widened with alarm at the idea of going anywhere with him, but she was still weak from the last contraction and had a feeling the next one was going to be even worse.

He slipped her hands into his as he helped her gently onto the seat and barely flinched as she rode out yet another wave of pain by gripping his hand so hard his fingers cracked.

His encouraging murmurs helped her until she collapsed back against the soft leather, just lucid enough to ask, "How do you know just what to say?"

His strong, hard mouth trembled as he said, "My sister." Just as quickly as the grief had come, it went.

She wanted to ask him more, but before she could push the question from her lips, a new shock of pain ripped through her. While her wail reverberated off the walls of the town car, Graham tugged her closer and held her tightly against him as if he could take her pain into himself instead.

Sweat soaked through her clothes as he gritted out a harsh command to his driver. "Faster. We need to get to the hospital. Now."

"Yes, sir."

When they finally arrived at the old stone building, he lifted her out of the backseat as if she weighed nothing and pushed carefully in through the front hospital doors. He didn't stop at the front desk; instead, he just walked with her in his arms to the room that was now ready and waiting.

Two nurses and an obstetrician entered the private birthing room and began to take blood pressure and other vitals, while the doctor asked Jo in a gentle, very calm voice if she could examine her to see how things were progressing.

Throughout it all, Graham held her hand.

And refused to let it go.

As they shot the hospital scene several more times from different angles, all Valentina could do was stare at Smith and Tatiana's hands linked together. But it was her mother and father's hands that she was seeing, both of them young, and so hopeful for the future with the family they had made together.

Her throat felt tight as Tatiana and Smith finally broke out of character many hours later and the lights dimmed. Her sister shook out her limbs and laughed as she released the tension, while Smith immediately walked off the set and headed toward the wardrobe department. After a while, Valentina finally rose from her seat and took in a deep breath of air to try to clear the tension from her body, too.

When she opened her eyes again, Smith was standing in front of her, already back in his street clothes.

"Ready to head to the Rock?"

Ten

Smith looked as fresh as if he hadn't been giving his all to the camera for the past eight hours, while Valentina felt like a limp noodle simply from the vicarious experience of watching all that emotion. She'd forgotten all about Alcatraz during filming, but with a rush the nerves—and reservations about being alone with Smith for so many hours—came back.

"I should check in with Tatiana first."

But when she turned to look for her sister, she was laughing with one of the crew—Jayden from special effects. Clearly, she was just fine, and she already knew Valentina and Smith were heading to Alcatraz. As Tatiana was off to Los Angeles for an event later that evening, Valentina simply gave her sister a quick kiss on the cheek and said she'd see her in the morning.

Which meant there weren't any good reasons left to draw out their departure.

"Need anything from your office?"

"Just my jacket." She'd worn long pants and a sweater to the set today knowing they were going to be out on a boat and on an island in the middle of the bay tonight.

They walked in silence to pick up her coat, and fortunately everyone was so used to seeing the two of them meeting for one reason or another, that no one thought it the least bit strange that they were heading off together in Smith's car. He didn't put his hand on her back as they walked, didn't stand too close, and she appreciated his discretion.

After all, this wasn't a date. He was simply acting as a friendly tour guide for a few hours in his native San Francisco. The fact that he was a ginormous movie star and could easily have hired a whole staff of people to show her around town was irrelevant. Of course, she could only imagine how happy the tour operators had been to hear from Smith Sullivan. They probably couldn't get him the two tickets fast enough.

It wasn't until she slid into the passenger seat of his Jaguar that she realized they'd never been in such a small space together before. The roar of the engine had her heart racing. Or, maybe it was the way he turned and gave her a sexy grin right before he drove out of the lot and onto the busy San Francisco streets.

With every mile he covered, the memory of the kiss they'd shared loomed bigger and bigger, to the point where her lips actually started tingling as if it had been a minute rather than a day since she'd pressed her mouth to his.

"Valentina." Her name on his lips had heat rushing through her as she slowly turned her gaze to him. "Look at that moon."

She'd been staring down at her clenched hands so hard that she was surprised when she looked out the window and realized a full moon was rising over the water, the blue bay turning a deep purple.

"It's beautiful."

So beautiful that it suddenly didn't make any sense to be nervous. She'd never forgive herself if she forgot to soak up the wonder of the experience just because she was so worried about what Smith wanted from her.

He'd promised he wouldn't kiss her until she asked, hadn't he? And she wouldn't ask him, so that meant they could just be friends.

At least, she hoped they could as she turned back to him and said, "You were great today."

He kept his eyes on the road as he smiled at her compliment. "Thanks, it felt good. Of course, your sister makes it easy."

"You should have seen her when she was ten. She'd be doing a commercial with a bunch of pros, and by the end, pretty much everyone knew she was the reason they'd shone so brightly."

He pulled into a gated parking lot by the water, and when she stepped out of the car, the wind blew hard enough that she needed to put on her coat.

"Let me," he said as he slipped it over her shoulders.

Warmth moved through her, and not just because of the wool. He hadn't copped a feel, hadn't touched anything but her coat, but even from where he'd been standing behind her, heat had radiated from him.

What, she found herself wondering, would happen if she let herself lean into his warmth, his strength, just for a few moments?

It was harder to shake the crazy question out of her head than it should have been. Grateful for the cold rush of air that blew past—on the hopes that it could blow the forbidden desire away, too—she reached into her pockets for her gloves, but they were empty.

Smith finished putting on his jacket just as she shivered. He was frowning as he said, "Are you warm enough?"

"It's just my hands. I forgot my gloves."

He slid his fingers through hers. "Does this help?"

She knew she should pull her hands away. But, oh, he was so warm. And her hands always got so cold.

She looked down at their linked hands, but when she looked back up, the "Yes" she'd been about to say got lost in the need in his eyes. The same need she knew had to be mirrored in her own. All she could manage was a nod.

Her heart momentarily stopped beating as his gaze dropped to her mouth. Her memories of the sweet pressure of his lips on hers made her want it again so badly that, in that moment, she couldn't bring herself to care that he was about to break his promise to her. Only, instead of kissing her, he simply lifted her hands to his lips.

He didn't press a kiss to either of them, just held

them against his mouth for a long moment before he said, "Why don't we go see what the moon looks like from the boat?"

Valentina stared at the yacht in confusion. "I thought you had to take a ferry to get to Alcatraz."

"Usually you do," he said, "but they made a special exception for you."

"Not for me," she said with a shake of her head. "For you." Suddenly, she turned to him with a frown. "We aren't going as part of the regular group tour, are we?"

The wind blew a lock of her hair into her mouth and he reached out to slide it away, letting his fingers linger on her cheek for a moment.

"No, we're not."

His captain for the evening came out on the dock to greet them, and when he introduced Billy to Valentina, Smith didn't miss the approval in the other man's eyes. He helped Valentina on board, and even though her eyes widened a little at the luxurious interior, she didn't make a fuss about it. Probably because she simply didn't give a damn about his money or possessions. In any case, she and Tatiana had been to Hollywood events on even bigger boats than this.

Yet again he was surprised by how nice it was not to have to explain his life to her. It was why so many people in the entertainment industry ended up together. No one else could really understand what it was like unless they'd lived through it themselves. Yes, she'd said she didn't like being in the spotlight, but the fact that she'd helped Tatiana deal with the paparazzi for so many years meant Valentina would also be adept at avoiding them. She'd know exactly where to look for them, how to outwit them and, when there was no choice, how to gracefully give in to them for an hour or two.

"What can I get you to drink?" He gestured to the fully stocked bar.

"Sparkling water would be lovely, thank you."

He poured two glasses and joined her where she was standing at the rail staring out at the dark water. Just then Billy got them under way and the sudden movement jolted them enough that she fell back into his chest. Finally getting to hold her, it struck him yet again how surprisingly soft and curvy she was against him.

"Steadier now?"

She didn't answer for a long moment. Finally, she nodded. "I think so."

"And are you warm enough?"

"I am now."

He wanted to bury his face in her hair to breathe her in, wanted to lower his mouth to the sweet curve of her neck, wanted to taste her soft skin. Instead, he reminded himself that one hand on the small of her back, the other holding hers to keep it warm, would have to be enough for now. Until she asked for more.

In silence, he held her as the boat sped across the bay toward the infamous prison.

A national park official stood on the island's pier as they docked. "Welcome to Alcatraz." The gray-haired man, who introduced himself as Sam Maines, had a deep, commanding voice that gave extra gravity to the historic maximum-security prison. He was a man who looked as comfortable on the rocks as the prison guards from a half century ago must have.

As he helped Valentina disembark from the yacht, Smith made a mental note to get Sam's contact information for the next time he needed a strong, steady, gray-haired man in a film. Not to mention the fact that the man's eyes hadn't so much as flickered when he'd realized who Smith was.

The night, he thought as the wind blew across them and Valentina instinctively leaned in closer to him for warmth, was just getting better and better. He loved the fact that she didn't make even the slightest move to pull her hand from his as they followed the guide up past the officers' club toward the south entrance.

"Alcatraz was cold," Sam told them. "Harsh. Unforgiving. And it was also home to the families of the guards who kept it running."

Smith had always been interested in history, especially one as colorful as this. But tonight he was far more interested in the way Valentina ate up the stories Sam told them about the way Al Capone made several attempts to con the warden into giving him the special privileges he'd had at other prisons...but was denied at Alcatraz.

Smith didn't know if she realized it, but whenever she heard something really interesting, she gave his hand a squeeze.

After thirty minutes or so, Sam led them into the

cell house building. When they came to the main block of cells, known as Broadway, all three of them stood in silence as they took in the forbidding bars, the cement cells.

"I'll leave you two to explore for a few minutes."

As soon as they were alone and walking together down the middle of the cells, Valentina said, "Can you hear them?"

Yes, he could hear the same echoes in the silence that she obviously did. "It's like the men were here yesterday instead of fifty years ago."

She read the plaque on the wall where they'd stopped. "Three men plotted their escape right here." She let go of his hand as she moved into the cell, to get a closer look at the hole in the cement. "Just think, they spent months whittling away at the cement. Everyone told them it was impossible." Smith moved in behind her as she turned to ask him, "Do you think they made it, after all?"

"That water is pretty cold. What do you think happened?"

"I'm sure they belonged in prison, and that the crimes they'd committed were wrong, but I still can't help but hope they made it out of the water alive." She gave him a crooked smile. "And that they made the most of the years they'd stolen back for themselves."

Smith knew most people would be surprised to find out that Valentina was a secret romantic. But he'd known it about her almost from the start. That first day on set when he and Tatiana had stopped filming and the two of them had immediately dropped out of character, Valentina's eyes had stayed soft and clouded over with emotion long after the cameras had stopped rolling.

Without warning, the prison cell doors slid shut behind them. Valentina automatically jumped into his arms as she let out a surprised—and slightly panicky—laugh.

"Did you know Sam was going to do that?"

"No." But he had just decided to give Sam the tip of a lifetime for coming up with this brilliant plan. Smith looked down at Valentina. "Puts a whole different spin on things when the doors close, doesn't it?"

Her eyes were bright, and so damn beautiful, as she stared up at him. "Yes," she breathed. *"Different."*

He'd never break a promise to her in a million years, but that didn't mean he could stop himself from lowering his face to hers. Her cheek was so soft against his. He barely stifled a groan as she reached up to wind her arms around his neck.

"How long do you think he'll keep us locked up?"

Her whisper against his ear had him harder than he'd ever been in his life. He slid his hands slowly down her back until they rested just above the curve of her hips.

"Not long enough," he answered with perfect honesty.

She shifted against him so that she could stare up at him and he held his breath as he took in the clear desire on her face.

Lord, he wanted to kiss her. She was fire in his arms, heating up the cold cell with the press of her curves against him. Her lips opened and he was sure that she was just about to ask him for a second kiss when the heavy sound of footsteps broke the heady silence.

Before Valentina could pull out of his arms, he lowered his mouth as close as he could to hers without touching it and whispered, "Not even close to long enough."

Eleven

A short while later when they stepped out under the full moon, Valentina's breath caught as she took in the incredibly romantic, and unexpected, scene. Water crashed on the rocks just below a table set for two, with four portable heaters ringing the white tablecloth.

A vase in the center of the table held a single pink rose.

The meaning of the flower he'd picked was loud and clear as he extended his hand to her: *desire and passion.*

"Hungry?"

She nodded, knowing there was more than enough moonlight for him to notice that if he looked closely he would see she was hungry for far more than food. He held out her chair, and when he sat down opposite her, the table was small enough that their knees bumped underneath, making her smile through the nerves that her attraction had brought front and center. He poured a glass of cabernet from Marcus's winery and handed it to her.

He lifted the covers off their plates and her stomach grumbled in appreciation at the lobster and crab before her. She had no idea how he'd managed to get such delicious food delivered to the island. Their tour guide had left them alone again and there was no chef or waiter around as far as she could see.

"I agree with your stomach," he teased, and picked up his fork to dig in.

Valentina took her first bite and a small moan of pleasure slipped out. "So good."

She didn't see that Smith had stopped with his first bite halfway to his mouth, his eyes dark, hungry, as he watched her.

But she couldn't miss how hoarse his voice was suddenly as he said, "I'm glad you like it."

When was the last time she'd eaten a really good meal? She honestly couldn't remember, and it was no surprise given the long hours she'd been putting in since filming began.

She took another bite and her eyes closed on their own. "I forgot how much I like good food." She tried to tamp down on the greed racing through her veins as she turned her focus back to him. "This is amazing. Your boat. The private tour. Dinner." She reached for his hand without thinking. "Thank you."

He slid his fingers into hers. "I'm glad you invited me to come with you."

She couldn't keep the smile off her face, not when

he'd gone to all this trouble for her and it had been such a wonderful night already.

"Well," she teased, "I could see how much you wanted to see Alcatraz again. Do you have some story ideas kicking around in your head about it?"

"Maybe. You?"

She was surprised by his question. Surprised enough to say, "I can't stop wondering about the women on the island."

"Makes sense that the only women on the island were married."

She nodded. "It does, but who says they were all happily married?" At his raised eyebrow, she explained, "What if one of them was in love...but not with her husband?"

His eyes lit. "Are you asking, what if one of them fell in love with one of the prisoners?"

"Yes," she said as the excitement over her brandnew idea took even deeper hold. "And what if he'd fallen in love with her, too, even though both of them knew there was no way they could ever be together?"

Smith didn't say anything for a long moment and she wished she'd never said a word.

"I love the idea, Valentina." His thumb slid across the sensitive skin on her palm as he said, "Tatiana told me about the script you've been writing."

"I'm going to kill her." It was one thing to tell George when they'd known him practically forever. It was another to spill her secret project to a man she'd been trying so hard to keep as an acquaintance. Even if he was getting closer every day.

"You know how little sisters are," he agreed, though it was clear that he loved Tatiana spilling Valentina's secrets to him. "I'd like to see it."

"My screenplay?"

"Yes. Tatiana told me what it was about and I have a feeling I'm going to like it. A lot."

She shook her head, pulling her hand from his. "No."

"You love to say no to me, don't you?" he teased, but there was an undertone of frustration beneath it. "Do you think I'm doing a good job with *Gravity?*"

"Of course I do. You've got us more on track than any of the other movies Tatiana has worked on."

"Then why won't you let me see your script?"

"Because I don't want you to think that's why I'm here with you tonight."

Smith's free hand was warm as he brushed it across her cheek. "I would never think that, Valentina. *Never.*"

God, it was so tempting to lean in closer to him.

No.

She. Would. Not. Ask. Him. To. Kiss. Her. Again.

Trying to turn her focus from anything but his shockingly seductive mouth, and how much she wanted to feel it pressed against hers, she asked, "What else has my darling little sister told you?"

"Are you sure you want to know?"

Her heartbeat kicked up. Even in her weakest moments, she hadn't told her sister about her feelings for Smith, about the way he turned her inside out.

"Always so worried," he murmured. "You know

Tatiana loves you too much to ever hurt you in any way."

Of course Valentina knew that. But she'd been hurt by family before, by a loving mother who had all but disappeared after their father's death when her daughters needed her the most, and then had returned as another woman entirely.

"Besides, it's not Tatiana's fault that she spilled the beans. I was grilling her for anything she would tell me about you."

"What else did she spill?"

"How you were a total Bon Jovi fanatic as a teen-ager."

Valentina had to laugh at herself. "Their songs are really quite intelligent and poetic if you listen to the lyrics."

"I agree," he said with a grin. "I'll make sure to tell Jon about his beautiful fan."

"You know him?" she asked before muttering, "Of course you do. Just so you know, I may have to smother my sister with a pillow tomorrow night. Sorry you're going to have to find a new costar this late into filming."

Smith was the one laughing this time, but then his expression shifted into a more serious one. "She also told me how you dropped out of college to manage her career."

Valentina couldn't stand Smith's thinking she'd been living a life of sacrifice for the past ten years. "I've loved every minute of it."

"I know you have. It's what makes the two of you

such a great team. You both love what you do—
Tatiana in front of the camera, you behind your laptop."

She picked up her fork, determined to enjoy the
rest of the incredible meal. "Now that you know some
truly embarrassing things about me, it's your turn to
share your worst." She pointed her fork at him. "And
don't cheat by telling me something I could find in
an interview."

He gave her a look filled with pure innocence. "I
would," he said as he also picked up his fork, "if there
was anything embarrassing to share."

"So you're perfect, huh?"

He raised his eyebrows as though he was hurt.
"You don't think I am?"

She couldn't hold back her laughter. "No." She
shook her head as she took a bite of scalloped po-
tatoes, then washed it down with a sip of the very
smooth cab. "I definitely don't."

When he didn't laugh with her, she thought for a
moment she'd insulted him. But then she realized he
didn't look upset.

He looked pleased.

"You never see me as a movie star, do you?"

She could sense just how serious his question was.
And how much her answer meant to him. Maybe a
day, a week, ago she could have brushed it off with an
answer to placate him. But she'd come to respect—
and like—him too much to do that.

"You surprised me the first time we met." She
twirled the stem of her wineglass in her hand and

tried to find the right words to explain. "I've met so many actors over the years, between the ones my sister has worked with and…the ones my mother has dated." She pushed away the twinge that thinking about her mother always brought to keep her focus on the man sitting across from her. "I thought I knew exactly what to expect from you. After all, you're more famous, more successful, than any of them."

She shook her head, remembering sitting in his San Francisco production office that first day they'd met. Just looking at him had made her warm all over, especially when he held her gaze with his dark eyes and she'd felt the crackling attraction between them even with George and Tatiana in the room.

"Your phone rang, and when you saw who was calling, you got the biggest smile before you excused yourself to answer it. I wanted to think you were one of those people who thought he was so important he could take calls in the middle of a meeting." She looked up and met his warm gaze. "But you were talking to one of your sisters, asking her how she was feeling, if the doctor had told her anything else about the size of her babies." And Valentina had started falling for him right then and there.

Still, she needed to make one last gasp at saving herself, didn't she?

Fortunately, she knew exactly how to do it: with a pointed reminder of what he did for a living.

"You're right that I haven't seen you as a movie star since that very first day we met, but this—" she gestured at the table, the yacht moored off the pier

"—isn't the kind of magic an ordinary man can pull off. Thank you for a fairy-tale evening," she said softly. "It's not one I'll ever forget."

"Me, either," he said, and as his eyes dropped to her mouth for a split second, she thought for a moment that he'd forget his promise not to kiss her. But then, instead of kissing her, he said, "How about dessert?"

Her desperate brain turned the word *dessert* into *a kiss* and she nodded with enthusiasm. "Yes, please."

He reached down for a pink box and Valentina's hands shook, not with nerves but with nearly unbridled lust, as she reached for the box top and uncovered dessert.

Desire tangled with joy as she looked down at the two oversize cupcakes on the plate. One of the cupcakes had a frosting picture of Smith behind prison bars, gripping them tight with a cute but pleading look on his face.

The other had a cartoon version of Valentina made out of frosting, dangling the key to his cell with one finger, a wicked look sparkling in her eyes.

Valentina didn't ask for a kiss, couldn't have possibly wasted another second with words, as she got out of her chair, reached out, slid her hand around the back of his neck...and kissed him.

Twelve

Valentina's kiss made Smith forget to move slowly. He couldn't think beyond his need for more of her mouth against his, and for the chance to discover the secret sweetness of her curves, always so well hidden beneath her tailored suits. Only knowing Sam and Billy were waiting for them kept him from throwing his coat down on the rocks and making love to her right then and there.

"I want you in my bed," he told her. "Tonight."

And when she said, "I want it, too," Smith knew every good deed he'd ever done had just been rewarded.

Taking her hand firmly in his, he pulled her up from the table so that they could get on his boat and back to his house as soon as was humanly possible, but she tugged back.

"Wait." She picked up the box with the cupcakes in it. "You promised me dessert."

Sweet Lord, the sensual look in her eyes when she said *dessert* made him a greedy bastard as he took her mouth with his again while the cold air whipped up on the bay and blew over them. He felt her shiver in his arms and forced himself to pull back. Their guide waited for them as they made their way across the rocks and cement to the pier.

"Thank you for the wonderful tour, Mr. Maines," Valentina said, her smile wide and genuine. "I'll never forget my visit to Alcatraz."

"It was my pleasure." Clearly, Sam was utterly charmed, his ruddy complexion coming not only from the wind but also from the pleasure of being complimented by a beautiful woman.

They shook hands and then Smith helped Valentina climb back onto his yacht. This time, instead of taking her out to the deck, he brought her inside the warm living room. His boat had a master bedroom suite, and Lord, it was tempting to take her there. If he had been the one piloting the boat for the evening, he would have anchored out on the dark water and done just that.

But even though Billy was utterly discreet, Smith didn't want another man within a half mile of Valentina when they finally made love. He wanted to possess her wholly, completely, wanted to know he was the only man who would hear the sweet sounds she made when he kissed every inch of her skin from top to bottom, back to front, and then started all over again with her beautiful mouth.

They settled in on the plush leather couch as the engine turned over and the boat started back across the water. Knowing he'd be lost if he started kissing her again, Smith forced himself to have the patience to simply gather Valentina into his arms and hold her.

Of course, she didn't make it easy for him to keep his hands off her as she nuzzled closer to him, her breath warm on his neck, her lips soft as they roamed lightly over his skin. His fingertips stroked over her face, down her neck, then just into the seam of her shirt so that he could brush against her collarbone. Against his skin, he could feel her gasp of pleasure at his gentle touch.

He'd known from the first time they'd kissed just how responsive she was, but he found himself stunned all over again by the way she reacted to his touch, as if he was the first man who had ever stroked his hands across her beautiful skin.

But even touching her shoulder was making it too hard for him to remember that Billy was only a dozen feet away upstairs at the helm. Smith forced himself to slide his hand from Valentina's skin and into hers instead.

Only, if he'd thought that would cool the fire raging inside him, he was as wrong as he'd ever been about anything. Because just holding her hand, turning her palm upward so that he could stroke his thumb across her skin, was the hottest foreplay of his life.

She lifted her eyes to meet his and the unmasked desire he saw on her face nearly undid all of his good intentions to wait until they got home. He couldn't trust himself to kiss her, but he had to brush his other thumb over her lower lip.

Her eyes closed on a soft moan of pleasure, similar

to the way she'd appreciated their dinner, only this time she wasn't working to hold him at bay anymore.

No, this time she was pure, sensual woman against him.

And when the tip of her tongue slipped out to lick the pad of his thumb, he was the one groaning and pulling her even closer, until she was all but sitting on his lap.

Beneath the blanket he'd draped over both of them, his hands moved lower to cup her hips, and just as he'd known she'd be, Valentina was a perfect fit in his palms. He loved having one of her hands held in his, the other splayed across his chest, over the heart that beat hard and fast for her.

"We'll be docking soon," he said to try to remind himself that he could make it. He'd never wanted a boat ride to end so quickly. He realized he was holding his breath, waiting for the moment when they approached the dock.

"Good," she said in an equally breathless voice. "Until then maybe we should talk."

He nodded. "Talking's good." But his mind was empty of everything but her.

"Tell me about the rest of your family," she suggested. "I know about Marcus and Nicola. And you've told me a little about Sophie and her pregnancy. But I don't know much about the others yet."

His siblings' names and faces all mixed up in his head for several seconds. Finally, he pulled a name out of thin air. "Chase." Smith forced himself to concentrate. "He's a photographer. He's married to Chloe. They have a baby. Emma."

He knew his words were coming out staccato, that he wasn't putting any color whatsoever into his description, but damn it, it was all he could do just to keep from pushing Valentina down onto the couch and ripping off her clothes.

"How old is their baby?"

"Three months."

Valentina's eyes lit up and went soft all at the same time. "She must be so beautiful."

God, if he hadn't already fallen for her, right then and there he would have known just how beautiful her soul was, just by the way she reacted to the thought of a three-month-old baby.

"She is. None of us can get enough of her."

Valentina's eyes moved to his mouth, then back up to meet his gaze, and he could almost taste her lips before she quickly said, "Tell me about everyone else."

Damn it, she was right. They needed to keep talking, to keep doing anything but making out again. Because this time if they started, neither one of them was going to be able to stop.

"Sophie's a librarian and has been invaluable, not only with this film but with helping me research my roles for the past ten years."

"I'm sure she loves to help," she murmured.

"Zach is into cars. He just got engaged to Heather. She trains dogs."

"The dogs from the puzzle, right?"

He nodded. "Plus Summer's poodle. My brother

Gabe is going to be her stepfather soon, when he marries Megan on New Year's Eve. Gabe's a firefighter."

"I love the fact that you and your siblings all do such different things," she said, and then, "I've chatted with Vicki a few times when she's come to drop off another new sculpture. She's engaged to your baseball-playing brother, isn't she?"

"Ryan and Vicki are the newest engagement in the family." He had to reach out and brush a lock of hair back from her forehead, for no other reason than that he couldn't resist touching her.

"Is anyone else but you free?"

Free? He wasn't even close to free, and was only now realizing that he hadn't been since the day he'd first seen her, first talked to her, first tasted her lips and held her in his arms.

"Just Lori. She's Sophie's twin. A great choreographer. We call her Naughty to Sophie's Nice."

Valentina grinned. "Naughty, huh? What does she think of that?"

He grinned back. "She loves causing trouble and making sure she lives up to it every day of her life."

"Of every one of your siblings, I think she's the one I'm jealous of." Valentina looked down to where her hand was still splayed out over his chest before lifting her eyes back up to his. "Getting to be naughty, knowing it's okay just to let go, sounds so wonderful."

Oh, hell. He'd known there was passion simmering just beneath Valentina's cool and collected surface, but hearing her say it aloud sent him all the way to the edge of his control.

The gentle jolt of his yacht as the engine was turned off stopped him less than an inch from her mouth. "I've got to help Billy dock up," he said in a voice raw with the passion he was trying to keep from unleashing for just a little while longer, but Lord knew he could barely move his arms from around Valentina to go and do it.

Her eyes were full of so much sensuality as she said, "I'll help, too. Just tell me what you need me to do."

His body responded immediately to the idea of Valentina letting him take charge, and he couldn't resist dropping his mouth to hers for a quick, hard kiss in the few seconds before they made it to the dock.

"I've never seen you take orders from anyone."

She nipped at his lower lip before murmuring, "That's because no one has ever had the guts to give me any before now."

His entire body responded to her way-too-tempting challenge as she shimmied past him and out onto the deck.

Working quickly and efficiently—or as efficiently as Smith could, given that watching Valentina tie a perfect sailor's knot made his fingers slip on the ropes more than once—the three of them brought his boat in and secured it to the dock. And then, finally, they were saying good-night to Billy and were back in Smith's car.

He was gunning out of the parking lot when Valentina said, "I think we need to set some ground rules before we get to your house."

Her words still held that note of sensuality that had been present ever since she'd kissed him earlier, yet he could tell she was completely serious. Smith had never liked being constrained by rules. He knew when to respect them, whether he wanted to or not… and he also knew when it was absolutely imperative to break them.

So even though he was beyond desperate to get her into his bed, he pulled over on a dark street and turned the engine off. "All I want is to give you pleasure, Valentina. More pleasure than you've ever imagined." But that wasn't enough. He knew he had to offer her more than just pleasure. "I promise I won't do anything, not one single thing tonight, that you don't want."

She blinked at him, her gaze full of a mixture of longing and lingering worry that tugged hard at his heartstrings. And when she said, "I know you won't," her softly spoken response pulled them even tighter.

"Whatever happens when we get to my house—" he paused, knowing he couldn't let either of them hide from what was about to happen "—and to my bed, I don't want either of us to regret tonight." *Or any of the nights that I know will come after that.*

Her pause was longer this time before she said, "I won't regret it." She slid her hand over his. "I want tonight just as much as you do." She paused again before adding, "But only tonight."

Her thumb brushed over his palm the same way his had across hers on the boat, as if the gentle touch of her skin could in some way soften the fact that she'd just made her intention to spend one night with him, and one night only, perfectly clear.

He lifted her hand to his lips, knew that was as close as he could get to kissing her again until they were behind the locked doors of his house—unless they wanted to get arrested for indecent exposure in his car.

As sure as Valentina was that this couldn't go past one night, he was even more sure they were going to end up in it for the long haul. Just like his siblings and their mates. Just like his mother and father.

Thirteen

As soon as they were parked in his garage, Smith jumped out of his car, yanked open Valentina's door and scooped her up into his arms.

"Don't forget the cupcakes." The fact that his brain was barely getting enough blood by that point made it hard to understand that she actually still wanted dessert. Until she whispered, "As soon as I saw them, I pictured us eating them in bed…naked."

Jesus, he thought as he paused only long enough for her to reach down and grab the box of cupcakes. He was as close to losing it as he'd ever been, despite the fact that they both still had their clothes on and they were a good hundred feet from his bedroom.

But as much as he wanted her in his bed, naked beneath him as he made love to her the way he'd been dreaming of for too damn long, he couldn't keep his mouth off hers any longer. Not when he was finally holding her in his arms, and she was looking at him with such heat in her beautiful eyes, a flush of sensual anticipation staining her high cheekbones and coloring her unpainted lips a dark rose.

Standing holding her in the middle of his living room, Smith lowered his mouth to Valentina's in a kiss so soft, so sweet, it was more a breath than a meeting of their lips. Low down, his gut twisted tight as he tasted the exotic spice of her with a long, slow swipe of his tongue over her full bottom lip. Her soft moan of pleasure at the sensual touch had him tightening his hold on her, and his lips pressing deeper against hers. When her tongue found his and stroked against it, it was his moan sounding in the room.

Finally, he was getting to kiss her, hold her. And as she stroked one hand over his jaw while opening herself up even more to his kiss, and kissing him back with unabashed passion, she was so much sexier, so much sweeter, than he'd dreamed.

Again and again he tasted every inch of her mouth, the sensitive corners, the curves and contours of the Cupid's bow at the top of her upper lip, then back yet one more time to nip at the fullness of her bottom lip before laving over the small hurt with his tongue.

On a gasping breath, Valentina whispered his name. "*Smith*. You're making my head spin."

"Good," he said before he kissed her again. He wasn't even close to having his fill of her mouth as he pulled back just far enough to tell her, "Because it's what you've done to me from the very first moment I saw you."

But even as his words sounded against her lips, she was licking out against him, making him even crazier to have her, and this time when they kissed, gentleness gave way completely to greediness, to the need to turn desire into possession.

"Please," she begged on a rasping breath when he let her free for just long enough to try to catch her breath.

"Tell me," he urged her even as he had to steal another taste of her lips. "What do you need, Valentina?"

"More."

Her confession nearly took him all the way over, without anything more than their kisses to get him there. And yet, this anticipation, the shockingly sensual dance where they drew out each other's pleasure with simple kisses, with gentle caresses, was too good to turn away from just yet.

"Yes," he agreed as he dropped his mouth to hers again and drank in the pure sweetness of her response. "I could keep kissing you forever."

As they'd kissed, her hazel eyes had dilated until the brown had been edged out almost completely by green.

"Everywhere."

The one word from her lips was full of so much need, so much desire, that what was left of the blood flow to his brain crashed in one big wave toward the hard-on throbbing behind the zipper of his jeans.

"I need you to kiss me *everywhere*."

Immediately rewarding her with kisses along her jawline, and then against one earlobe, as he pulled the very sensitive flesh between his teeth and she shuddered in pleasure, he was even more amazed by how well she covered up her sensuality on a day-to-day basis. Especially when it ran this deep, when her response to every kiss, to every touch, floored him… and made him desperate for more of her.

Hovering on the precipice of taking her on his living-room rug, Smith forced himself to mount the stairs to his bedroom instead. She held on to him with one arm around his neck, the other holding the dessert box dangling from her fingertips.

Every time he'd imagined making love to her, he'd envisioned making her lose control. But when he finally stood at the foot of his bed with the one woman he desired above all others in his arms, Smith finally understood that he'd gotten it backward. Because with nothing more than a handful of kisses, Valentina had taken complete charge of his body, his arousal.

Still, as he lowered his mouth to hers in another soft kiss, and she trembled in his arms, he loved knowing that maybe, just maybe, he wasn't the only one losing all semblance of control.

He lowered her to his bed, and when the dessert box finally slipped from her hand onto the covers, he slid his fingers through hers. They stared at each other for several long moments, and he swore he could hear the beating of her heart, and his own, racing with each other.

Fast.

Dangerous.

And so damned right.

Finally, he leaned his weight into hers, and held her

steady beneath him as he took her mouth again and again, her taste more and more addictive with every kiss. Just as generous with her kisses as she was with everything else she did, she held nothing back as she pressed into him, wrapping her jeans-clad legs around his hips to bring him closer.

Hotter.

Sweeter.

More, he thought when he couldn't get enough of her mouth, or of the sleekly sensuous curves moving beneath him.

"Too many clothes," he murmured against her neck as his fingers found the hem of her sweater, her stomach warm and sensitive even under the cotton shirt that still separated his fingertips from her bare skin.

Even as he reached for her, she was running her own fingers beneath his shirt, and over the muscles of his abdomen, which rippled beneath her touch.

"Yes," she agreed with a nip to his earlobe, "too many."

He had to take her mouth again, their tongues swirling together until he needed to draw away for a split second to pull her sweater and shirt all the way off. Her breasts rose and fell with each breath, and when he looked at her again, he saw that she wore the simple black bra better than any supermodel could have.

"Thank God," he said as he reached out and ran one finger over the swell of first one breast, and then the other, "you're finally here with me."

Again, she trembled beneath his barest touch, and

he loved watching her lose control so much that even though he was dying to taste her again, he held back long enough to brush his fingertips over the incredibly soft skin at the swell of her breasts one more time.

Barely a heartbeat from ripping off her clothes and just taking her with absolutely none of the finesse or gentleness that he usually gave to his lovers, Smith tried to force some rational thought back into his brain. Maybe, he thought with more than a little desperation, putting her on top would save them both from moving too fast this first time.

A moment later, he was pulling her over him so that she had to brace her hands on his shoulders to steady herself. Her hair came down around them like a curtain of honey-colored silk, her gorgeous breasts nearly slipping free of her bra.

Ah, yes, he thought, it was the perfect position for him to lie back and really appreciate, to take the time to savor Valentina's beauty.

Only, when she smiled down at him, a sensual lift of her gorgeous lips that had his breath catching in his throat and his entire body heating up at least another ten degrees, he realized his mistake.

He'd need to be locked up in a cell with the key thrown away and the bars reinforced with extra steel before he would ever truly be able to keep himself from moving too fast with her. Because with her torso bared to his hands, how could he keep himself from stroking, from touching, from shifting his erection up against her jeans-clad thighs as she ground down onto him?

But it didn't truly hit home just how far gone the idea of slowing things down was until she lifted her hands from his chest and reached behind her back to unclip and toss aside her bra.

Holy hell.

She was gorgeous.

Never in his life had he seen such beautiful breasts, just full enough for his hands when he cupped her, and so sensitive that when he stroked his thumbs over the taut peaks, her nipples tightened and drew his mouth straight to them.

"Oh, God," she gasped as his tongue circled the tip of one breast before his teeth lightly teased her damp skin, "that feels so good." When he moved to the other side of her chest and did it again, she moaned the words, "So, so good."

"Do you have any idea how long I've wanted to taste you like this?"

She didn't do anything but shake her head, but he hadn't expected her to answer, not with his lips and tongue and teeth teasing her until his head was spinning with the exotic taste of her.

"You taste so good, Valentina. *So damned good.*"

Each word he spoke was more raw, and full of need, than the word that came before, as twenty years of sexual experience, of other women, fell completely away. The softness of Valentina's skin against his fingertips, the taste of her on his tongue, was all that remained.

"Everyone thinks I've been obsessing about the movie, but all I can think about is you." He pressed his face to the curve of her neck, then inhaled. "What your skin smells like." He ran his hands into her hair. "What your hair feels like flowing between my fingers." He rocked his hips up into hers. "And what sounds you're going to make when you come."

"Oh, yes." She threaded her hands into his hair to take his mouth back to her breasts. "Make me come."

Sweet Lord, he knew he'd been falling for this woman for a reason. Just as bold in the bed as she was in the boardroom, she had him mesmerized. Hypnotized.

He had to call on every ounce of control he'd ever possessed to keep his hands from shaking as he undid the button on her jeans and pulled down the zipper. Even then, he still shook with need that didn't have a prayer of being contained as she lifted her hips so that he could slide the denim, and the lace beneath it, off her hips, then down her smooth thighs. After she'd kicked off her shoes, then used her bare feet to push her jeans and panties off the rest of the way, he pulled her back down on his lap, her legs straddling his again.

"I don't think," he told her as he stroked his hands down over her naked back, to the soft flesh of her hips, all while drinking in the most beautiful sight he'd ever had the pleasure of seeing, "I've ever been this happy in my entire life."

He loved the way she moved under his hands with a soft purr; loved the fact that she wasn't the least bit reserved in her nakedness; loved that once she'd made the decision to be with him tonight, she'd given herself all the way over to their lovemaking.

And he loved it even more as she said, "You're making me happy, too," then put her hands on either side of his face and leaned down to kiss him in her innately seductive, yet incredibly sweet, way.

Just that fast, sweet shifted to sultry as they moved together on the bed, their hungry bodies twisting up his sheets even further as he laid her naked body back against the pillows and levered himself up over her on his hands so that he could stare again.

Her skin was awash in gold, with just the slightest hint of rose behind it. Her breasts were full, the perfect size not only for his hands, but also for her slender frame, as were her softly rounded hips.

"I—" He could hardly speak, hardly think. "I need a second." He worked to draw in a breath, and when he mostly failed, with what little oxygen he had left, he told her, "You're so beautiful."

Thank God he didn't need to be able to get his brain to work to run hot, wet kisses over her mouth, her chin, the curve of her neck, her shoulders, the sweet swell of her breasts and then beneath where her skin turned out to be even more sensitive. He made his hands keep pace with his mouth, kept them from venturing down too far, too fast. Every new place on her body that he discovered, he wanted to touch, to taste, to breathe in, all at once.

Her stomach was flat, but soft, too, as the muscles beneath her skin rippled at every press of his lips. Intoxicated by her, desire wrapped so tightly around him that he didn't think to slow down now as he moved lower down her body to the soft curls that covered her sex.

Smith breathed her in as he slowly cupped her with his hand and felt her wet and hot against his palm. He now knew the taste of her mouth, her breasts, the taut skin over her stomach.

But he needed to know *more*.

On a sound of deep, desperate need, he covered her sex with his mouth, slicking his tongue slowly over her, once, twice, three times. He felt her hands move into his hair, pulling his mouth down tighter against her even as she arched up to take his tongue deeper inside her. And when her inner muscles gripped him, and her cries of ecstasy started to ricochet off his bedroom walls, Smith's own pleasure at having his mouth on her, his hands under her soft hips, made it almost impossible for him to keep from losing it.

In the aftermath of her climax, Smith couldn't bring himself to move his mouth, to take his tongue from her soft, slick skin. For several minutes, as Valentina lay loose and panting against the covers of his bed, he gently kissed and licked and nipped at the skin on her inner thighs, and then her hip bones and back up to her belly button, realizing he'd never get his fill of her.

Somehow, some way, he was going to have to figure out how to turn this one night she'd given him into many, many more. But for now, he could barely think beyond the need to have her.

And to keep making her his, any way he could…

Fourteen

Valentina looked down to find Smith staring up at her, his eyes even darker than normal, and so intense that her heart skipped a beat in her chest.

She could see the desire on his face, knew hers matched it in equal measure, and yet past the desire was something that tore at her heart—a longing, a need she'd worked so long and so hard to hold at bay. Something that went far beyond making love.

She imagined cold nights wrapped up together under a blanket on the couch.

She saw her tears dried by someone she knew she could trust with her deepest, darkest secrets.

And perfect afternoons on rocking chairs holding hands while grandchildren played at their feet.

Tenderness rose up in her just as swiftly as the pleasure had and she pulled him back up over her to give him a kiss that was even sweeter than any that had come before. Just as sweet was the next warm rush of pleasure as his hands explored her naked skin from curve to curve while his tongue teased hers. She could taste herself on him and shivered at the incredibly potent memory of Smith between her legs, lapping at her as though she was the sweetest treat he'd ever been given.

She wasn't surprised by wanting him, not when Smith was so incredibly desirable, and sexy. But she was surprised by just how deeply her need for him ran…and by the fact that she already wanted more, even before she'd had all of him.

So much more.

Which was why, even though she'd barely come down from her first orgasm, when he slid one hand down over her breasts, then down to the vee between her legs, it was the most natural thing in the world to open her legs for him, and to lift herself into the wonderfully deep strokes of his fingers inside her.

"God, Valentina." He licked at her neck, before sucking her skin between his teeth and lips. "You're so wet. So damned wet, and hot, for me."

With every thrust of his hand, his palm rocking over her sensitive flesh, he took her higher and higher. So incredibly high, she found herself actually bracing for it to all come tumbling down around her. Because how could she possibly fly so high without knowing for sure if she'd make it back to earth in one piece?

"Smith."

She didn't know what she was trying to tell him. Didn't know if she was begging for more, or pleading with him to have mercy on her. Her eyes fluttered open and she knew what she saw in his gaze—the hunger, the emotion, the desperation that was there in her own for him to see.

"I'm right here," he said when he felt her tense, soothing her with his touch, even as he sent her flying higher and higher into uncharted territory. "Come for me, Valentina. Let me have all of you again."

And, oh, how she wanted to be completely his, if only for one perfect night.

Just that quickly, her defenses dissolved beneath his touch, his mouth on hers, the slick of his tongue against hers. And as waves of pleasure crashed up and over her again, she was surprised to feel neither emptiness, nor the slightest shame at the way she writhed against him, as purely sexual a being as she'd ever been.

Just as he had after her first orgasm, Smith took her all the way through, then past the delicious peak of her climax. Safe, yet oh-so-heady warmth surrounded her as he rained kisses over her breasts, then across her ribs, over her stomach, then down past her sex to press soft kisses on the inside of each leg. At the same time that his mouth roamed her, his large hands stroked down over her muscles, down the length of her arms, her back and then both legs, making her so incredibly relaxed.

It had been fun, sexy, exciting, to be naked beneath him, over him, while he'd still been fully dressed. But an ever-growing need to have all of him, too, made her impatient and she was soon pulling off his shirt with little care for the buttons popping off or the sound of one sleeve tearing.

She loved the way their hands looked together as he helped her unbutton and unzip his jeans, his big and tanned, hers slender and pale. That simple image showed what she'd always felt around him, more feminine, more sensual, than she'd ever allowed herself to be with anyone else.

Not, of course, that she'd *allowed* herself to be that woman with him, not even tonight. Smith had simply *demanded* that sensuality from her from the first moment they'd met.

Valentina wasn't promiscuous, but she hadn't been a nun for the past decade, either. And yet, being with Smith felt like making love for the very first time. They were more than a man and a woman who couldn't resist coming together—they felt like a miracle.

Or, at the very least, she thought as he threw his shirt onto the floor, kicked off his jeans and grabbed a condom from a drawer in the bedside table, *he* was a miracle.

Because she'd never seen such a beautiful man in all her life.

She'd known his face was near-perfection, but the breadth of his shoulders, the lean muscles that rippled over his arms and across his stomach, his strong hips and thighs, all wrapped in tanned skin…

"I need a second to appreciate *you* now," she told him as he came back to stand over her.

Lifting a hand that trembled with both need and excitement, she ran the tip of one finger lightly down the deep line at the center of his abs. Tilting her face up to press a kiss to his skin, with her lips and tongue, she went back over every inch of perfection that she'd just touched.

His muscles flexed and jumped under her hand and mouth as she whispered, "I might even need two."

"Take as long as you need."

His voice was raw with desire, and she loved knowing she'd done this to him. She would never be his physical equal—no one would—but she could match him passion for passion, need for need, kiss for kiss.

Only, her ache for him went even deeper, so deep that her hands shook as she ran them down over his torso until she couldn't take any more time at all and had to pull at the waistband on his boxers to drag them over his erection. Thank God, a moment later Smith had a condom on and then he was back over her, her hands in his on either side of her head.

He didn't move, didn't push inside her, didn't even kiss her again. Instead, he simply stared into her eyes as if there was an answer he'd find if he only looked hard enough for it, and had the patience to draw it from her.

"Valentina."

The way he whispered her name with such desperate hunger had her closing her fingers tightly over his, and lifting her head so that their mouths could meet in a beautifully brutal kiss, both of them biting, sucking, taking from each other what they needed, and giving just as much back.

She couldn't get over her amazement at finally

feeling the heat of his skin, the dark hairs on his chest, his muscles moving against hers...and to know that all those secret fantasies she'd had about him since the day they'd met were finally coming to life.

And, oh, she'd never felt so alive as she did when she opened herself to him and he finally came into her. The stretch of her inner muscles over his thick, hard length made the pleasure so intense that her eyes fluttered closed, and her hips lifted automatically to take him deeper, her ankles linking together behind his hips to bring him closer.

Completely connected now, she could practically feel his heart beating inside her as he said her name again, and it was almost enough to have her coming apart around him. But before she could make even the slightest sound to let him know just how close to the edge she was, his mouth covered hers in a kiss so heartbreakingly sweet, so gentle, even as continually rising passion drove her to wrap her legs around his hips tighter still.

And moments later, when he finally lifted his mouth from hers, everything inside of her rebelled at letting him go.

For weeks, she'd pushed her feelings for Smith into the shadows. It had been a secret she was trying to keep from everyone, especially herself.

Tonight, carefully guarded secrets were no match for desire.

Valentina threaded her hands into his hair and pulled his mouth back down to hers. She wasn't just offering herself for one night anymore...she was demanding he take everything from her. It had never been like this for her. She had never been this ravenous, this insatiable.

In perfect sync, they moved together, her hips colliding with his, her body begging for every deep, hard thrust. Sinfully sweet became beautifully dirty as they both spiraled out of control in each other's arms.

Valentina couldn't remember ever feeling so good, so languid, so satisfied, even though Smith's heavy weight was pressing her into the mattress, and the tangled sheets were bunched up under her calf.

"We made a mess of your sheets," she murmured against his neck, licking at the salty sweat just below his ear. "They're all tangled now."

"Good."

She couldn't miss the deep satisfaction in his voice, nor the fact that all it took was feeling the vibration of his chest through hers as he spoke to bring her sated body back to life beneath him.

Knowing she was safe as long as the night still surrounded them, and wanting to make the most of every single one of the stolen hours, she said, "I'm ready for dessert now."

Smith lifted his head and smiled down at her. "I thought that *was* dessert."

She pressed her mouth to his and loved getting lost in his kiss. "No, that was just to make sure we worked up an appetite for cupcakes."

She loved the sound of his laughter, loved even more knowing that she'd pleased him. Because, oh, my, how he'd just pleased her. Again and again, with every touch, every kiss, every stroke of his body against—and into—hers.

"The cupcakes are over here," she reminded him as he walked beautifully naked across the room to his dresser. He opened a drawer and pulled something out of it.

As satisfied as she'd felt just seconds ago, Valentina's heart was now beating hard and fast as she wondered what Smith had planned for her. Especially when he said, "Close your eyes."

"Why?"

He grinned at her. "Trust me, you're going to like it."

His easy use of the words *trust me* had her quickly sitting up in bed, her gut clenching. She could give her body so much more easily than she could give her trust to a man.

But as she looked up into Smith's eyes and saw the careful way he was watching her, she was amazed— shocked, actually—to realize that she did trust him. At least for this one night, when she could be absolutely certain that nothing, and no one, would come between them.

On a long exhale, she let her eyes close, and a moment later, she felt something soft being wrapped around her eyes. Before she could ask him why he was blindfolding her, Valentina smelled sugar and chocolate.

"Take a bite."

She bit into the cake pressed softly against her

lips and every one of her taste buds came completely alive. *"Mmm."* She started to lick at the frosting she could feel on the corner of her upper lip, but Smith's tongue beat hers there.

"Delicious."

He moved the chocolate back to her lips and she took another bite. Dessert had never tasted so good before and she was more than ready to feel Smith's mouth on hers again when he surprised her with the sensation of something cold across the tip of one breast and then the other a beat later.

"Did you know there was filling inside the cupcake?"

She was so lost in the heady anticipation of what he was about to do that she could barely get out the word *no*.

"I can't tell what flavor it is. Maybe you can help me?"

"Smith. Please."

He'd reduced her to begging yet again, but she didn't care, not when she could feel his warm breath on her skin and then his tongue moving over her as he licked greedily at her incredibly sensitive nipples. She clutched blindly at his shoulders as he moved to clean off her other breast in the same powerfully seductive, wickedly perfect way.

Only when every last drop was gone did he move his mouth to hers and kiss her again. When she was completely breathless, he said, "Tell me, Valentina. What flavor was it?"

Love.

He tasted like love.

The forbidden four-letter word popped into her head unbidden, not just once but twice, startling her as she went stiff in his arms.

Instantly sensing her distress, he pulled the tie he'd used as a makeshift blindfold from her eyes and ran his hands slowly down her arms. "I promised I wouldn't do anything you didn't want me to do tonight," he said in a soothing voice. "Was it the blindfold?"

It wasn't, of course. She had liked that part very, very much.

She reached for him and wound her arms around his neck. "You didn't do anything wrong."

And he truly hadn't. She was the one who was going to have to work like crazy to protect herself again come morning. Which was why she should be glad for the small slip. It was the perfect reminder that even as she gave him her body, she needed to hold back her heart.

Trying to recapture the playfulness from just moments before, she said, "But I do feel kind of sticky now."

His dark eyes held hers for a long moment, until her prayers were answered and he'd let her strange behavior go. He swept her up into his arms and carried her into his bathroom.

As he started the water running, his hands roamed over her skin, his mouth playing at the curve where her neck met her shoulder. She arched into him and there was barely twelve inches of water in the bottom of the tub when he said, "I need you again, Valentina."

"Yes," she said as she slid with him into the shallow water. "Again."

Somehow he found a condom and had it on just in time for her to come down onto him at the exact moment that he plunged inside. She'd have thought this second time would be wonderful, but not anywhere near as special as their first time.

And yet, when he pulled nearly clear of her before driving in again so deep and fast, she had to cling to him more tightly. She cried out with pleasure at the gentle bite of his teeth and the sweet pull of his lips over her breasts, along with the tight hold he had on her hips with his big hands. Valentina knew in that moment their lovemaking would never become ordinary, nor simple.

Not even if they had decades together in each other's arms, instead of only one night.

Afterward, when they were both clean and dry again, and she felt more exhausted than she ever had before, Smith gently brought her back to the tangled sheets on his bed, tucked her in and pulled her against him.

She had never slept well while sharing a bed with anyone, not even her sister on the nights when Tatiana had had childhood nightmares and climbed in with her. And Valentina's decision to spend the night with Smith hadn't included sleeping like this with him. It was only supposed to be sex.

But with his strong, warm arms around her, and

one of his hands wrapped around hers so that both rested on top of her heart, she simply didn't have it in her to fight the darkness of sleep…or the sweetness of being like this with Smith.

Fifteen

More asleep than awake the next morning, Valentina curled into the warm body beside her and sighed with pleasure. It wasn't until she felt a hand stroke over her hair and soft kisses pressed to her closed eyelids that she finally woke up.

Oh, God, she thought as she tried to keep her body from going instantly stiff against Smith's, what had she done?

No, she hadn't forgotten that she'd slept with him. She'd made that decision with a clear mind and didn't regret it, wouldn't ever let herself regret the most sweetly sensual hours of her life. But as morning light shone in through his second-story bedroom windows, she did regret breaking one very important rule: she'd stayed the night.

She was a flesh-and-blood woman, full of hormones and desires. One hot night of sex was okay. Great, even, especially if it meant she could stop spending all her time and energy wondering about how it would feel to make love with Smith. But now it was time to turn her focus back to real life.

But waking up in his bed, having breakfast, sharing the part of her day with him when she was the most vulnerable…that was most definitely not okay.

Somehow she needed to figure out how to get out of his bed and his house without making a big deal of the one night they'd shared together.

But as he softly kissed her eyebrows, then each cheekbone, the tip of her nose and then her chin, the last thing she wanted to do was leave his bed. Desire rose again, fast and hot, and she wanted so badly to thread her hands through his soft hair and drag his mouth to one of the places she most needed it.

So many rules she'd already broken for this man… and there were so many more she knew she might not be strong enough to keep from breaking. But instead of turning away from him, she turned deeper into his arms, her leg moving to slide against his as she arched into his touch, silently begging him for more.

Until the harsh sound of a cell phone yanked her out of the sensual fog.

Her eyes flew open, her hands going flat on his chest. "Your phone—"

"—can keep ringing."

But the ringing phone reminded her of her sister's schedule and an important interview they had booked for today. Shock hit her that she'd come this close to forgetting. Clearly, making love with Smith had muddled her brain in a serious way.

"Smith, you and Tatiana have a phone interview with *Entertainment* magazine this morning."

The words were barely out of her mouth when Valentina's phone began to buzz with the ring tone that signaled her sister was calling. Tatiana had spent last night at an event for up-and-coming young actresses in Los Angeles, so she wouldn't know Smith had spent the night in bed with Valentina and she definitely wouldn't guess that he was with her right now.

Smith might be able to ignore his phone, but she couldn't. Especially not when it was her sister calling. She scooted out from beneath him and tried not to feel shy about her nakedness as she hurried over to her purse across the room.

"Hey, T." *Please,* Valentina silently prayed, *don't ask me any questions that I'll have to lie to answer.*

She all but dived under the covers with her phone to her ear, as Smith watched her with still-hungry eyes.

"I've got Beth from *Entertainment* magazine on hold," her sister told her. "She keeps asking me when Smith is going to call in. Did he say anything about canceling to you last night when you were at Alcatraz?"

"No, he didn't say anything about not being able to do the interview. Maybe he's just running a bit late. I'm sure he would never put you in an awkward position with a journalist because he didn't show."

Right then, instead of leaning over to pick up his phone, Smith put an arm around her waist and dragged her up against his naked body—his very hard, very aroused naked body—surprising her even further with a soft kiss to her mouth.

A half gasp, half growl left her lips and her sister asked, "Val? Is everything okay?"

"Let me see if I can reach him," Valentina promised her sister before, for the very first time ever, she hung up on her.

Glad for the rush of frustration that was quickly replacing desire, she was about to lay into Smith when he finally picked up his phone from the side table and started dialing.

"Beth, sorry to call in so late," he said when he had the journalist on the phone.

But instead of letting Valentina go so that he could focus on the interview, he pulled her in even closer to him, his arms holding her firmly around the waist, one of his legs a heavy weight over both of hers.

"How's your son doing? Still tearing up the soccer field?"

Close enough to hear the woman's cheerful answers, Valentina tried not to make a sound. God forbid either the journalist or her sister could tell that Smith was in bed with a woman.

Especially with *her*.

He didn't make it easy for her to remain silent as his hand stroked slowly over her ribs, down to her waist and then the curve of her hips. She trembled with the effort to keep from voicing her pleasure at his touch. Especially after a night when she'd been able to let herself go completely—when she simply hadn't had any other choice but to let go.

She'd thought it was just for that one, very special night when all rules—and all worries—were off. But now the sweetness of his touch wasn't enough to combat the brutal reminder of who he was.

Smith Sullivan, movie star.

How could she have let herself forget?

Not that going back to assess the hows and whys mattered much at this point. The point was that she had forgotten. And, more important, she needed to never, ever forget again.

On set, she constantly saw him as a professional in either his producer, director or actor roles. But after hearing him with his family, being with him at Alcatraz and on the boat—and most definitely now that she was in his bed—she saw Smith as simply a wonderful man.

Not to mention the most sensual, most infuriatingly persistent man she'd ever known.

Despite all of the stern warnings and reminders she gave herself during the long minutes that felt like hours as he chatted with her sister and the journalist, Valentina's body continued to heat up by degrees. Smith never came close to touching her breasts, or that sensitive spot between her legs, but that made it almost worse because everywhere he didn't touch throbbed and swelled with need as she prayed for his interview to end.

In her secret heart of hearts, she knew she didn't want the interview to ever end. Not if it meant she had to finally make herself leave Smith's arms.

At long last, when she could have sworn he'd run

his hands over every inch of her skin but the spots that ached desperately for his touch, he finally put down his phone…and turned his entire focus back to her.

"Sorry about that. Now," he said as his fingertips drew a trail of goose bumps over the delicate skin on the inside of her forearm, "where were we?"

She took a deep, too-shaky breath. "I was leaving."

Most men would have been more than happy to let their one-night stand escape. Heck, pretty much any other man on the planet would have been telling her not to let the door hit her too hard on the way out… and any other woman on the planet would have been begging Smith to let her stay.

When the thought occurred to her that maybe that was why they'd always fit together so well—because neither of them behaved as they should—she fought to shove it away.

His hand didn't still on her skin. The same slow stroke of heat warmed her more with every pass he made over her curves as he said, "I don't want you to go," in a low voice that thrummed up and down her spine and over her skin.

"You know what we agreed last night," she reminded him.

"I know what we agreed," he said, "but that was before."

That one word—*before*—and all the memories of the *after* that had included his mouth, his hands, his body over hers forced her to silently acknowledge her own foolishness.

Had she really thought she could get what she

needed from him in one short night to fill her well, scratch her itch and purge the desire from her system? And hadn't she known all along that his kisses, his hands warming her skin, his body pressing down hard and perfect over hers, would be akin to a trap?

One she'd never, ever want to escape from.

She wouldn't deny that somewhere between working together on set and a moonlit dinner on the rocks at Alcatraz, they had become friends. And, oh, to be Smith's lover was truly an extraordinary thing.

But giving her body and laughter and companionship to him was one thing. Giving her heart to him would be something else entirely.

Because no matter how much she enjoyed being with him, regardless of how wonderful he'd been thus far, at the end of the day he was still in the one profession in which *forever* truly meant nothing. Her own mother had wanted to believe in that false forever so many times. But wanting to believe in the fairy tale hadn't ever been enough to actually make it come true.

Even worse, their whole affair would end up captured on film, by photographers and cameramen who worked for a public that couldn't get enough of their stars' private lives.

"Last night was amazing," Smith said as his hands continued to explore her body. And there was no point in acting as if what he was saying wasn't true.

"But that doesn't change who you are. Or who I am." Her crystal clear logic didn't convince him to lift his limbs from where he still had her pressed to the bed beside him and frustration at just how badly she wanted to stay with him had her saying, "You should have let me go during your interview. It wasn't fair that you kept me here."

In a heartbeat Smith had her flat on her back with her hands held above her head—so quickly that the air squeaked out of her lungs.

"Fair? Do you think any of this is fair?" His eyes went almost black just before his mouth took hers in a hard kiss, one that had lost any veneer of gentleness. "Do you think it's fair that I'm falling for a woman who wants nothing to do with me just because of my job?"

He nipped at her lower lip this time, before taking her mouth again in a kiss that had her responding to the heady mix of pleasure and pain. As his free hand cupped her breast, for a split-second she wondered if she should be frightened of a man who had just lost control and was now letting loose his frustration on her. Instead, she arched into Smith's touch with a passion she could not control.

How could she ever be afraid of him? He'd been so gentle, so sweet, with her from the very beginning. He'd held her in his arms when she'd talked about her father. He'd treated her sister like the precious jewel she was. And she also knew that what they'd shared together the previous night could never be misconstrued as just sex...because it had been making love, from the first kiss to the last gasp of pleasure.

Her tongue was tangling with his now as his hand moved lower, over her stomach, then lower still. He lifted his mouth from hers, his eyes blazing with heat and frustration and boundless desire as he stared down at her.

"Is it fair that I can't stop thinking about you for one second when I'm working on the biggest film of my life and shouldn't be thinking about another god-damned thing?"

If he hadn't been holding her hands so firmly above her head, she would have reached for his face to comfort him. Instead, all she could do was shake her head.

"No." She swallowed hard at the raw emotion etched on his shockingly beautiful face, and at the powerful emotions coursing through her, as well. "It isn't fair."

She couldn't make things fair for him, couldn't give him whatever it was he seemed to want, couldn't promise him a future where it didn't matter who he was or how complicated his life and career were.

All she could do was give him herself, and plea-sure, one more time.

Smith was so much bigger, so much stronger, than she was, but passion—and the pain of knowing how badly she had hurt him this morning by wanting to leave so soon after waking—gave her the strength to take charge and tumble them over so that he was on his back and she was straddling him. Her wrists were still in his hand, but now her palms rested flat over his chest, right where his heart was beating fast.

With her thighs opened wide above him, she found his hard length and began to move over him, not taking him inside, but gliding up and down his thick length again and again until they were both panting. All the while, he held her hands over his heart as her belly tightened down and she rocked harder into him. With one hand he gripped her hips hard to help her over the edge of pleasure that was already approaching. She cried out his name as her climax took her over, head to toe, Smith's hard body steady beneath hers as she rode out wave after wave of sweet sensation.

It wasn't until she finally came back to earth that she realized he had reversed their positions again so that she was lying back on the bed. Her body was still vibrating from the incredible strength of her unexpected release when she felt him shift slightly to the side, heard a drawer opening and paper tearing, her entire body clenching tight, then opening again for him, in anticipation of even more intense and heady pleasure.

Smith was a heartbeat from roughly thrusting into Valentina when sanity punched him hard across the jaw.

What had he just done? And what the hell was he about to do to her?

"Valentina, forgive me."

"Forgive you?" The words were soft, and sounded so damned sexy, from lips swollen from his rough kisses. "What have you done?"

Did she really not realize he'd all but tackled her just minutes ago when frustration—and a helplessness he had no idea how to deal with—had finally gotten the best of him?

He lifted one of her wrists and winced at the red marks. He didn't know if he deserved the chance to make it better, but he couldn't stop himself from trying.

"I hurt you," he said just before he leaned in to press his mouth to the sensitive skin at the inside of her wrist. "I never meant to hurt you."

The last thing he expected was for her to slide her hand from his and place it against his cheek.

"No," she said softly, "you didn't hurt me. I'm the one hurting you. And I'm sorry." She lifted her mouth to his and pressed a soft kiss to one corner of his lips. "I'm so sorry for hurting you." She pressed a kiss to the other side before both hands moved to his face. "That's why I tried to leave this morning, because I don't want either of us to get hurt. But," she admitted before her mouth found his with a kiss that stole another piece of his heart, "I didn't want to go." Her tongue swept across his lips. "I still don't." She pulled back enough to look up at him. "Please, Smith, kiss me back."

She'd never gotten around to asking him for a kiss at Alcatraz. She'd simply taken it instead, and he'd loved that she had.

But now, as she finally asked him for his kiss, he prayed it was her way of saying he hadn't hurt her... and that she wouldn't hold anything he'd done this morning against him.

Wanting her more than he'd ever thought it was

possible to want another person, he cupped her face in his palms and turned her soft kisses into the dark, dangerous tangle of lips and tongue and teeth that they were both craving. And yet, even in the swirling darkness, there was such sweetness, a shimmering light rising up over both of them.

"Take me," she begged as she opened herself to him again and wrapped her arms and legs around him. "Please, Smith," she whispered on a soft moan when he lowered his mouth to the hollow of her neck to taste her skin, to try to convince himself that she was real, that she could still want him after he'd nearly crossed the line. "Make love to me one more time."

God, he thought as he kissed her again, he would never get enough of her mouth. Even as he finally moved into her and her hips bucked up into his to take him even deeper, even as he lost hold of anything but how soft and hot and perfect she was beneath him and around him, his lips never left hers.

Sex had always brought him pleasure, but making love with Valentina went so far beyond pleasure. She begged him between kisses to take her harder and deeper until her words blurred together into one long, low moan that merged with his own pleas.

He'd just had more physical pleasure than he'd ever dreamed was possible, but now he hoped for the chance to seduce more than her body.

Smith wanted to win over her heart, too.

Afterward, they lay together, forehead to forehead, nose to nose, mouth to mouth. He wanted to stay like that with her forever, but he was so much heavier that he didn't want to crush her. Shifting onto his side, while still keeping her cradled against him, he stroked one hand over her damp hair.

Unfortunately, too soon, she was saying, "I promised Tatiana I'd have a girls' day with her. We haven't seen much of each other outside of the set."

She offered the explanation as if to try to soothe him, and he was glad to know that despite how clear she'd been about not wanting to date him, his feelings obviously mattered to her.

"In fact," she said, "I really need to get back home before she returns from the airport. If she knew I didn't spend the night at home, she'd wonder why."

A heavy cement block landed on his chest. "You're not going to tell her about us."

She shifted out of his arms and sat up partway on the bed, using the crumpled sheets to cover her beautiful naked skin.

"No," she said softly, "I'm not." She licked her lips. "I don't regret what happened last night. Or this morning." The hazel of her eyes met his, so steady and so beautiful that his entire chest squeezed even tighter. "But I thought you of all people would know how this is supposed to play out."

He worked to keep his expression impassive. "Tell me, Valentina, how is that?"

In her frustration, she sat up higher on the bed, cross-legged so that the sheets slipped to reveal a luscious stretch of hip and thigh. "You're supposed to move on to your next conquest. Everything is supposed to finally go back to normal." Her voice rose a little more with each sentence, until she was practically yelling at him. "Now that we've had sex, you're supposed to be done with me!"

He let her slide out of the bed, closing the bathroom door and locking him out for a few minutes.

Now that he'd had her, he thought as he dragged on a pair of jeans, they were anything but done.

Smith was in the kitchen pouring two cups of coffee when Valentina came out ten minutes later, fully dressed, her hair still damp around her shoulders, her shoes on, her bag in her hand.

"Stay for a cinnamon bun, Valentina."

She looked with surprise at the plate set out in the center of the breakfast table by the window. Her stomach growled even as she said, "Why are you making this so much harder than it has to be?"

"It doesn't have to be hard."

It was what he wanted to show her, what he knew she believed in her heart of hearts—that love didn't have to be hard. He thought again about what his mother had said to him on the phone: *sometimes it's harder to admit to ourselves that we want love in our lives than it is to keep living without it.*

With that sage reminder echoing in his head, Smith took Valentina's bag from her clenched hands and put it down, then pulled out the chair for her. She looked for a moment like she would mutiny until, with a sudden sigh, she sat down.

"You really don't play fair, do you?" She pulled off a piece of the cinnamon bun and popped it into her mouth on a greedy little sound of pleasure. "These truly are some of the best things I've ever eaten. Dripping with sugar, just the way I like them."

He couldn't stop smiling at her as he ripped off a piece for himself. Nor could he stop himself from leaning over to lick off the sugar glistening at the corner of her mouth. "I like it, too."

She opened her eyes and glared at him. "Smith."

He grinned back at her. "Valentina."

She tried to hide the twitch of her smile by turning away and letting her hair fall over her face.

But he saw it.

When she'd finished eating breakfast, had washed her plate, and was turning to say what he knew would be a very polite goodbye, Smith took her into his arms.

"Thank you for letting me love you last night."

He took her mouth a moment later, devouring the hints of sugar and spice that remained on her already sweet lips. When he finally made himself pull back, her big eyes had already gone hazy again with desire, and her skin was flushed with heat. And yet, he could see how hard she was working to fight what she was feeling.

He wasn't twenty-one anymore and life didn't revolve around sex, no matter how great it was. Which meant he also understood that the reason sex with Valentina had been so mind-blowing wasn't because she'd been a conquest. Neither was it because she'd been a mystery he'd been dying to solve.

No, it had been because she mattered to him. On a far deeper level than any other woman ever had.

He'd wanted to find out if she was *the one.*

And this morning he was pretty damn sure he had his answer.

"We can't do this again, Smith. Things could get too messy, too quick. Even now, if Tatiana finds out where I was last night—"

"—she'd be happy for you. And for me."

Valentina lifted her chin. "Yes, she'd be happy as long as we were happy. Until the day came when she had to take sides. She likes you, Smith, so much that it would really hurt her to have to stop being your friend just because we're sisters who always put each other first. I don't want to do that to her and I know you don't, either."

"If I wasn't an actor, if we weren't working together, would you want to be with me for more than just one night?"

He could see how surprised she was by his question, enough to admit, "Yes."

And yet, a moment later, she pulled out of his arms, picked up her bag and coat and headed for the door before adding, "But since I've never had a knack for playing pretend, it doesn't matter what I wish was different, does it?"

For the rest of the day, he couldn't get her expression out of his head. She'd looked determined, and as strong and beautiful as she had always been, but underneath it all she hadn't been able to hide the woman who wanted nothing more than to believe—and to know for herself—that the fairy tale was real.

Smith couldn't wait to prove to her that it was… and that their happily-ever-after would be even sweeter than any flashy Hollywood version could possibly be.

Sixteen

Valentina had barely gotten home, stripped off last night's clothes, and thrown on leggings and a sweater, when she heard the front door open.

Knowing she was most definitely not the actress in the family, she still found herself plastering a stiff smile on her face as Tatiana popped her head in the door. There was absolutely no reason for her sister to think anything had happened between her and Smith beyond a friendly visit to Alcatraz, but she was still worried about being found out.

"Sorry, Val, my plane was delayed. I called the spa and told them we'd be a few minutes late."

Valentina smiled even wider. "Great, I can't wait!"

As her sister ducked into her bedroom to put away her carry-on bag, Valentina felt as if she had a neon sign around her neck that was flashing Liar. Because even though she hadn't actually outright lied to her sister, she couldn't help but feel that omitting to tell the truth was almost as bad.

A few minutes later, when they were en route to the spa in Tatiana's cute little Mini Cooper, Valentina asked, "How was the event in L.A.?"

"Good." Her sister smiled. "I honestly had no idea how much working with Smith would change things for me, though. Everyone kept telling me what a big deal it is that Smith personally chose me for *Gravity*. None of them have even seen so much as a daily yet, but they kept talking about Oscars."

"It *is* a big deal," Valentina agreed. "And since he's told me again and again how much he's enjoying working with you, I bet this won't be the last time you collaborate on a project."

Her sister smiled. "The thing is, even though I know how easy he is to work with, I almost started getting nervous. Although maybe that was just because everyone clearly worships him and they think—"

Tatiana shot Valentina a quick look before suddenly clamping her lips shut.

Valentina worked to keep her voice light and easy as she asked, "What else do they think?"

"Stupid stuff." Tatiana rolled her eyes. "You know how Hollywood is all about imagining costars are jumping into bed with each other. But I told them that he and I are just friends."

Valentina's hands clenched on her lap as she said, "I'm sorry you have to deal with that, T., especially when you're putting in such long hours on set."

"We both knew from the start that costar-romance rumors come with the territory," her sister said in a soft voice. "I can deal with it, because I know the truth. The thing is, if Smith is seeing anyone, I'd hate for her to think that he's not being completely faithful, when he definitely is."

Valentina wished they could talk about something else. Anything else. But she could tell that her sister was waiting for her to say something.

God, she wanted so desperately to confide in Tatiana. But what could she possibly say? *I slept with Smith last night. And then when I started freaking out this morning and tried to run, he half attacked me to keep me in his bed...and I loved it.*

No. She couldn't say that. Couldn't say anything at all to Tatiana about being with Smith. It would be too great a risk on all sides of the equation. And really, what was there to say? It had only been one, beautiful, perfect, sinful night, hadn't it?

One that she would never, ever let happen again.

Finally, she replied, "I suppose any woman who decided to date an actor like Smith would have to decide to trust him no matter what...otherwise, she'd end up going crazy, if the media hounding didn't send her to the loony bin first."

"Hey," her sister suddenly said, "I almost forgot. How was Alcatraz?"

"Fabulous!" Valentina replied in a voice that was just a little too bright. And then, before her sister could so much as ask one more question about her evening, she began to recite the Alcatraz history she'd learned from their guide, Sam.

* * *

"Tatiana, thank you so much for inviting us!"

Valentina was just signing her name on the spa register when she turned and saw Vicki Bennett arrive. Vicki had supplied the sculptures for the movie and she was engaged to one of Smith's brothers. Accompanying her were two women who looked remarkably alike, except for the fact that one of them was *very* pregnant. Not only that, but the two women also happened to bear a striking resemblance to—

"Hi, I'm Lori Sullivan." Valentina's hand was clasped by the twin who moved so gracefully it was obvious she was the dancer in the family. "This is my sister, Sophie."

Valentina worked to keep her panic at bay. It was bad enough that she'd had to keep what had happened last night from her own sister. But now both of Smith's sisters were at the spa, along with his soon-to-be sister-in-law, Vicki.

"It's so nice to meet you both, and to see you again, Vicki." She hadn't seen Vicki since the day they were first introduced when Vicki had been delivering artwork to the set. Valentina really admired her absolutely beautiful sculptures.

Twenty-four hours ago, Valentina would have loved this chance to meet more of Smith's family. Unfortunately, now she was going to be worried about saying the wrong thing the whole time, and accidentally giving away the fact that she and Smith had gotten closer than any of them could possibly imagine.

"Come on," Lori said, "let's go soak in the mineral

baths first. Soph, you can just dip your feet in so you don't boil the babies."

Sophie rolled her eyes in Valentina's direction. "Charming, isn't she?"

Valentina smiled, clearly able to see just how close the sisters were. No wonder Smith loved his family so much. No doubt they had their sharp edges and disagreements like every family, but surrounding all of it was such obvious love.

They'd just changed into their swimsuits and were getting settled into the warm water when one of the aestheticians came to take Tatiana in for her facial, leaving Valentina alone with the Sullivan crew. They all seemed really nice, but she still couldn't keep her nerves totally calm. Of course, they had no reason to ask her about Smith, no possible way could they suspect she'd left his bed just hours before.

Just thinking about what he'd done to her in that bed—and what *she'd* done to *him*—had her feeling even warmer than the water.

Valentina was glad she'd asked Smith to tell her about his siblings the night before, because now she could say, "Your brother said you're an amazing choreographer and dancer, Lori. I'd love to see your work." To Sophie, she said, "He also told me he couldn't do half his research on characters in films without your help. I've been hoping to get to the local library, but work has been crazy lately. There's nothing I love more than spending hours and hours with books."

"I've just started maternity leave to try to get a few

things ready before I give birth," Sophie said in her gentle voice, both hands resting on her belly, "but I'd love to drop by with you just for fun one day soon, if you can take a little time away from work."

How, Valentina suddenly found herself wondering, was she supposed to succeed at keeping her distance from Smith when his family was drawing her in so easily? She truly did want to see Lori dance and to spend an afternoon with Sophie and her books.

"How have you been enjoying working on Smith's movie?" Vicki asked.

Valentina tried to detect whether there was anything behind the other woman's question, or if she could possibly have detected any sparks between her and Smith during the time she'd spent on set delivering her sculptures. But from what she could see on the other woman's face, Valentina knew she was just being paranoid.

"Both Tatiana and I have been loving it. Everyone is working really hard, but they all manage to be relaxed at the same time. That hasn't always been the case on several of the films she's worked on in the past few years."

"Smith's awesome," Lori said, as if that explained it all.

Which, thought Valentina with a small sigh of resignation, was actually true.

Smith was so easy to talk to, so friendly, and yet so in control of the dozens of moving pieces that he automatically inspired everyone's loyalty. Not to mention the fact that he could act rings around the other actors.

"He and I are the only single ones left," Lori told her. "Everyone else in our family—" she nodded toward Vicki and Sophie "—is just so sickeningly happy."

"Now, now," Sophie teased her sister, "is that your bitter, spinsterly side showing?"

Lori laughed and splashed her twin before saying to Valentina, "Do you have any idea what it's like to be surrounded by couples all the time? Especially when I feel like I'm singing that Taylor Swift song on repeat, you know the one about never, ever getting back together with the guy you're dating." She sighed. "And then doing it, anyway."

Sophie frowned. "Wait. I thought you were—"

Lori quickly cut her sister off at the pass by asking Valentina, "What about you? Is there anyone special in your life? Are you falling madly, deeply in love with someone you can't live without like pretty much every Sullivan on the planet has been doing?"

Valentina felt as though everything had gone still, the water from the fountain against the wall slowing down until she could practically see each drop falling, one after the other, into the pool below.

Lie. She needed to figure out how to tell a convincing lie, damn it.

Only, what came out instead was, "Well, there's sort of this guy who's interested, but since I already know it's not going to work out, I've been trying not to encourage him."

She only realized what she'd said after her words came echoing back into her ears a few seconds later. Thank God Tatiana was off getting a facial, or she would surely have been peppering her with twenty questions. Like who the guy was…and why Valentina hadn't so much as mentioned anyone during the past few weeks that they'd been in San Francisco.

Not to mention the fact that Valentina's definition of "trying not to encourage him" clearly needed some work after the night—and morning—she'd spent making love over and over again with Smith.

"Oooh," Lori said as she leaned forward in the water, her eyes flashing with curiosity. "Is the guy cute?"

Valentina couldn't hold back her flush. Or the word, "Yes," even though *cute* was entirely the wrong word for Smith's dark eyes and chiseled male beauty.

More like *devastatingly handsome*.

"But—" Valentina began.

"—you're totally sleeping with him, right?" Lori finished for her.

Valentina's eyes widened at Lori's blunt question even as Sophie kicked water over her sister. "You don't have to answer that," Sophie told Valentina.

"You really don't," Lori said, grinning at her while wiping the water from her face and brushing her damp hair back from her forehead. "Because I can already see from the look on your face that sex with the guy you're 'not encouraging' is awesome." Sophie was clearly about to drench Lori with more water when her twin held up her hands in mock surrender. "Okay, I'll stop. I promise."

But her promise came too late, because a water fight was soon going in earnest, with Vicki and Sophie ganging up on Lori until Valentina had to join Lori's team to keep the battle even. When Tatiana found the four of them after her facial, they were all completely drenched and laughing together like old friends. Tatiana easily slipped into the water with them and joined in on the fun without missing a beat.

Seventeen

Monday afternoon, Smith found Valentina in the set parking lot just as she was about to get into her car. "I'm glad I caught you." He slid into the passenger seat of her Lexus before she could protest. "Tatiana said she thought you were heading out to Union Square. I could really use your help with picking out gifts for the holiday party this week, if you've got a little time to spare."

God, she was pretty, he thought as she turned to face him, her expression clearly wary about the excuse he'd just given her. Saturday morning when she'd been in his bed had been too long ago. He couldn't stop himself from reaching out to touch her in some small way and ran his hands through the ends of her ponytail.

"I'm happy to help you pick out gifts for everyone," she told him in a voice that was anything but happy, "but you and I already know that this—" she gestured between the two of them "—isn't a good idea." The only sign that being near him was affecting her was the slightly breathy tone of her otherwise beautifully modulated voice.

She was right. The two of them weren't a good idea.

They were a *great* idea. And when he slid his hand down from her hair to her arm, then down the soft leather of her jacket to her hands, he could feel just how right he was in the way she trembled beneath his fingertips. He slid his fingers through hers.

"I missed you the past two nights. Badly."

He'd hated sleeping without her each night, hated not being able to take her hand like this today on set. The Sullivan family was an affectionate one and Smith wasn't used to keeping his feelings to himself. Especially when they were this strong.

Valentina sighed. Fortunately, it seemed that her desire was stronger than her will to resist him. So instead of kicking him out, she simply slid her hand from his, turned the key in the ignition and started her car.

Smith settled back into the leather seat, his long legs stretched out in front of him, enjoying just being with Valentina. Her scent, the way the pulse raced at her neck, the fire that leaped in her skin even as she tried to hold it—and him—at bay were all fascinating. There wasn't a part of her that didn't interest and attract him.

A short while later they were walking out of the parking garage and into the heart of Union Square.

Her eyes grew wide as she looked at the holiday lights in the trees and on the buildings that surrounded the square. It all looked so different from when they'd filmed the opening scene of the movie here weeks ago. Ice skaters were making full use of the ice rink at the center of it all, and Christmas music added a festive air to the square.

"It's like a winter wonderland."

Valentina was gazing at a skating couple twirling in each other's arms with such longing that Smith was having trouble resisting the urge to grab her and kiss her beautiful mouth when a group of teenage girls spotted him and ran over.

"Oh, my God, it's Smith Sullivan!"

Their squeals attracted the attention of dozens of other people, all of whom suddenly pulled out their phones to take pictures and text their friends. He wasn't surprised when Valentina moved out of range of the cameras, but when he took a pen to start signing autographs, he greatly appreciated the way she offered to take pictures of him and his fans so that all of them could be in the picture at once. Clearly, she'd been through this more than once with her sister and yet, again, he was glad to know that his world wasn't completely foreign to her.

Couldn't she that if anyone could withstand the unique pressures of dating a movie star it would be her? To his mind, this was a perfect test of how well they would do if this were more than a simple shopping trip, and she was actually his girlfriend.

Ten minutes later, when the last of the crowd seemed to have had their fill, Smith asked her, "Have you ever been to Gump's?"

She gave him such a cute look when she asked, "What's a gump?" that he couldn't resist stroking her cheek, which was flushed from the cold air—and, he hoped, from being with him.

"It's that way," he said with a grin that she, fortunately, couldn't seem to stop herself from returning. "Let's see if we can get out of here before the next group descends."

"I should have rethought my plan to come downtown with you," she said in a slightly apologetic tone, as if it were in some way her fault that his fame had just slowed down the shopping trip. "Although," she said with a wry twist of her lips, "I'm not sure there's anywhere remote enough that you wouldn't be recognized."

"Cities tend to have the most enthusiastic fans. A few months ago I was in a little town in Kansas, and no one even gave me a second glance."

She made a sound of disbelief. "You're very sweet with your fans. I hope Tatiana will continue to be able to deal with hers as well as you do."

He knew what Valentina was doing—talking about his fame to help her remember to keep her distance from him. A street performer was juggling six pins while standing on a rolling board, and while all eyes were on the juggler instead of them, Smith told her in a low voice, "Little doses. That's all fame has to be. The rest of the time, when I'm on set or at home, I'm just like everyone else."

"You're wrong," she said in a similarly low voice that only he could hear as she looked directly at him, her beautiful hazel eyes full of as much desire as regret. "You could never be just like everyone else."

When he thought he heard someone on the sidewalk say his name, he quickly pulled Valentina into the store. The floor manager who greeted them was an old friend of his from high school, and one of the reasons he loved coming to Gump's was because Judy and the rest of her staff went out of their way to make his shopping experience smooth. Even better than that was the eclectic nature of the store.

He enjoyed watching Valentina crane her neck to take in the glass sculptures and Chinese figurines and ornate chairs that shared the space with handmade dog bowls and inexpensive Christmas ornaments.

"There must be one heck of a story about this place."

"Gold rush money," he explained. "The Gump brothers got lucky in the rivers and decided to turn their winnings into this."

"None of these things should fit together, but somehow, they all do. Is there anything this store doesn't have?"

"Let's find out."

They started on the bottom floor and worked their way up. Valentina had an uncanny talent for finding the perfect gift for each member of the cast and crew.

Smith had always prided himself on getting to know the people he worked with on each film, no matter how transient their lives. But Valentina, he now realized, knew his crew members even better than he did.

She might speak of endings and act as if she was prepared for every single beginning to come full circle sooner or later, but right now he saw just how much she wanted to keep that from happening. She was so invested in the cast and crew that she knew all about their spouses and children and what they did in their spare time.

Their gift-wrapped packages continued to pile up when they finally reached the floor he'd been waiting impatiently for. The music was quieter on the fifth floor, the displays even more elegant, the colors softer to complement the very expensive lingerie on display.

Valentina's flush said it all, even before she spoke. "I can't think of anyone who needs something from this section of the store."

He let his gaze move over her flushed cheeks, her full lips, her too-bright eyes. "I can." He moved close enough to slide the tips of his fingers over her hand in the barest of touches. "The next time I see you in silk and lace, Valentina, I want to know that I'm the only man who will ever take it off you."

Pure sensual need hit Valentina at nothing more than the lightest touch of Smith's fingers…and his very sexy words.

Friday night and Saturday morning's pleasure still

felt fresh on her skin, heating tingles that reminded her of just how beautiful every moment she'd spent in Smith's arms had been. She knew he had to be able to see it all on her face, the flush of her skin, the way she all but trembled with passion for him whenever he was near. No man had ever made her feel so feminine before, so aware of her curves, her softness, her warmth.

It wasn't only desire that had her knees feeling weak, though. It would be easier if it were, because then she could write it off as nothing more than a physical attraction that anyone with a pulse would feel for Smith Sullivan.

No, it was the sweet promise in his eyes, in the way he always touched her with such gentleness, and the emotion on his face whenever he looked at her, that had her heart beating so out of control and her words failing her.

Valentina didn't like to think of herself as a coward, even if her heart was pounding faster than it ever had before and she could barely tamp down on the urge to turn and run down five flights of stairs. That, she swore to herself, was the only reason she was going to let Smith have his way in the lingerie section of the strangest, most wonderful department store she'd ever been in.

Not the secretly wonderful thought that out of all the women in the world he could have had—the supermodels, the stunningly beautiful stars—he really had picked *her*.

He collected what seemed like every bra and panty

set on the fifth floor, each one more exquisite than the next, and all of them in exactly her size. How did he know about her weakness for beautiful lingerie?

A weakness only rivaled by her need for a straight shot of sugar first thing in the morning…and her growing, borderline desperate weakness for the man beside her.

Fortunately, instead of saying any more deliciously sensual things to her, things that might very well have tempted her to lose all self-control and drag him into a dressing room, he peppered her with questions instead.

"Did you have a dog when you were a kid?"

"No, but our cat was as big as a dog, and twice as scary to anyone who came to the front door."

"What was your favorite subject at school?"

"Physics."

"I love that you always surprise me," he said with a grin. "Now tell me why physics was your favorite, and not English or history or math."

She shrugged, feeling a little foolish. "At first, nothing about trajectories and acceleration made any sense until, one day, they suddenly did. I guess I felt invincible after acing that class, like there was nothing I couldn't figure out if I just worked at it hard enough and didn't dare give up." Wanting desperately to know more about him, she took her chance by asking, "What about you?"

"I always enjoyed anything where I could get up in front of the class and make a fool of myself. Acting. Dancing. Improv. Glee club. The rest of the time

I was on a soccer field or trying to hit a home run or trying to dunk a basketball. But if I'd known a girl like you was in the lab, physics would have definitely shot straight to the top of my list."

They were in the middle of a store where anyone could see them or take their picture, but despite everything Valentina was afraid of where Smith was concerned, and despite everything she had learned in her physics class, she couldn't find a way to put an end to it all.

Right now she wanted to feel his hands on her waist, his mouth on hers, and she was leaning in closer to do just that when his phone suddenly rang— the one particularly harsh ring tone that told both of them there was an emergency on set.

On a curse, Smith pulled back from her and picked up. When he hung up a minute later, from his half of the conversation, she'd gleaned that one of the lighting rigs that had been giving them trouble from the first day had overheated and taken down half the power on set with it.

"I'll take you back," she offered immediately.

"I want you to finish your own shopping," he replied. "I'll take a cab." He didn't reach for her then, but it would have been easier if he had. Instead, in that low voice that sent thrill bumps running all across her skin, he said, "I enjoyed spending the afternoon with you, Valentina. So much that it will make missing you tonight even harder."

"Don't miss me, Smith. Please don't," she begged him, partly because she hated hurting him, but also because his wishing he could be with her only made her own impossible wishes harder to ignore.

"Would you be happier knowing that I'm waiting for you to come to me instead?"

Waiting? For her?

Oh, God, she didn't know how to respond to that, especially not when he said, "I should warn you now that I'm no good at waiting. Especially not when every single voice in my head is telling me to take what I know is already mine."

Before she could respond, he was gone in another perfectly timed exit that left her feeling as if her heart was hanging by a thread.

A very, very thin one.

Her head was spinning and it was tempting to head back to bury herself in work or a hot bath. But since this was her one chance to get her holiday shopping done, she made herself peruse the rest of the wonders on the remaining floors of Gump's.

Valentina was about to pay for her gifts when she saw the box by the register: a puzzle of Alcatraz.

She hadn't yet bought a gift to give to Smith at the cast and crew holiday party. The puzzle couldn't be more perfect. And as she asked the woman behind the counter to please wrap it up, as well, she suddenly had to wonder—could *Gravity* have as much to do with forever as it did with the first flush of falling for someone?

When she got home a little while later and unpacked the gifts she'd bought, she was surprised yet again—this time by layer upon layer of gorgeous tissue-wrapped silk and lace lingerie. Smith had worked his magic and had the staff at Gump's pack it all in her shopping bags.

Valentina could have quite easily stayed hidden from Smith the next day. She could have stuck near Tatiana, who was filming scenes with alternating trip-let newborns who had been brought in for the movie. She could have buried herself in email, could have even taken her computer home to get her work done in the peace and quiet of their rental house.

But she wasn't a coward, damn it…and she couldn't let Smith keep putting his life on hold while he *waited* for her to come around.

She found him in the screening room, sitting in the dark. His attention was so completely on the screen that she wasn't sure he even knew she'd come into the room, not until he reached out a hand for her and she took it without thinking.

In silence, they watched the scene from the first day of filming. She was stunned to remember that she and Smith had still been strangers back then. Strang-ers until she'd yanked him into his office to warn him away from her sister.

How, she found herself wondering, had there ever been a time when she hadn't known him? He'd be-come so important, so vital, to every single one of her days—and to one incredibly perfect night—that she couldn't imagine not knowing him.

But these questions faded as she got lost in the scene all over again, forgetting everything except the drama playing out before her eyes. When the scene ended and the screen went to black, she had to tell him, "It's even better than I remembered. The two of you are so perfect together."

"Our characters are perfect together. But they aren't real," he reminded her. He tugged her closer to him as she sat in her chair on wheels in the dimly lit room. "You. Me. We're what's real, Valentina. How much longer are you going to make me wait for you?"

It had barely been three days since they'd made love. And yet Valentina knew exactly why Smith had become so frustrated in those intervening seventy-two hours.

Every inch of her skin ached for his touch. He was with her even when she slept. This morning she woke from having a dream in which she was safe and warm in his arms, and her heart broke as she'd reached for him and realized he wasn't there.

"That's why I came to find you," she told him, hating how shaky, how breathless, her voice was.

It was getting harder and harder to get her brain and mouth to work around the desire—and the longing—that was billowing up like an oncoming thunderstorm all around them.

"The lingerie is beautiful. I can't possibly deny that, or lie to you by saying that I'm going to take it back to the store." She could feel her skin flush deeper with every word. "But the fact that I can't re-sist wearing the beautiful things you bought for me doesn't change anything."

He looked as if he was having trouble breathing

for a moment. The storm gathered in even closer as he finally choked out, "You're wearing them?"

Oh, God, why had she told him that? She was trying to push him away, not draw him closer.

Wasn't she?

Eighteen

Neither of them could look away from the other. Their bond, the pull between them, was already too strong. And bigger than either of their good intentions—hers to keep her distance and his to remain patient.

In the end Smith didn't know who moved first, whether he was the one wrapping his hands around her waist to pull her against him, or she was the one sliding her hands into his hair. But it didn't matter who made the first move.

All that mattered was that she was in his arms again.

Her mouth was soft, her lips sweet from the candy she must have been sucking on that morning, her taste even more seductive than he remembered. He needed her too badly to have any thoughts of finesse, but thankfully, even as he pulled her onto his lap, she was crawling over him, her skirt hiking up higher and higher on her gorgeous thighs.

He might have been able to keep it at least partially together if he hadn't felt, then tilted back to see, the lacy edge of a garter. His curse was low, borderline pained, as he traced the lace over her thigh with his fingertips. Her skin was so soft, so warm, as she made little sounds of pleasure at having his hands on her again.

With one quick yank, the rest of his patience disappeared, and he had her skirt bunched up around her waist and his hands cupping her hips.

Holy hell, she hadn't just worn the lingerie he'd bought her…she'd put on the slinkiest, sexiest pair of stockings and panties that he'd given her. Were it not for the punishing workouts he put himself through every morning, his heart would have stopped right there.

"My God, you're gorgeous."

His fingers moved from the lacy edge of her garter, up the soft skin of her inner thigh, to skim the inside edge of her panties. He could already feel how wet, how ready, she was for him as she whimpered softly, then rocked into his hand.

"Show me more." He nipped at the underside of her neck as he begged her to put him out of his misery. "Please, Valentina, I need to see more of you."

She stared at him with big, beautiful eyes. "This is crazy," she whispered. "Completely crazy," she said again, "but I can't stop wanting you, anyway."

With trembling fingers she began to unbutton her blouse, and Smith not only drank in the inch-by-inch reveal of her creamy skin, he also relished her admission of how much she wanted him despite all of her reasons not to. He knew how cautious she was about actors, about the spotlight, and yet here she was, anyway…one more time. Somehow, he needed to make her see that she couldn't live without him… and that the two of them were worth all the irritations and inconveniences that came with his life.

He wanted so badly to taste her, to hear her sounds of pleasure as she leaped off that first peak in his arms, but somehow he managed to hold off until her blouse was open nearly to the waist.

"Valentina."

With one hand sliding into the slick heat between her thighs, he lifted the other to cover the swell of her breast, so gorgeously on display in a bra that just barely covered her nipples. He leaned forward to take one of those luscious peaks into his mouth, cupping one breast even as his tongue slid beneath the lace to slick over beautifully aroused flesh.

Only, instead of sating him, the taste of her made him even hungrier, and so desperate that he couldn't stop his fingers from playing over her arousal, then sliding them into her hard and fast.

Just that fast, with his fingers in her, his mouth on her, she came apart, her arms wrapped tightly around his shoulders, her neck and back arching her breasts into his mouth, her hips rocking into his.

He wanted to savor her, wanted to take hours to pleasure her again and again, to appreciate every inch of her beauty, her sweetness. But the three days—and nights—he'd been made to wait to have her again had been three too long, and just as he'd told her in the store the day before, he didn't have a lot of practice with waiting.

Keeping his head on straight just long enough to pull a condom he'd been praying he'd get the chance to use soon from his back pocket, he unzipped his pants and rolled it on. Valentina's mouth found his just as he lifted his hands back to her waist and positioned her over him. Less than a heartbeat later, she was lowering herself down over him and taking him inside.

Their mouths collided just as fiercely as the rest of them, the pull and thrust of his body against—and into—hers a mirror of the way their tongues were stroking, sliding together. And as she took over their rhythm, her hands gripping his shoulders tightly, her thighs strong and taut as she rocked into him again and again, Smith let go of her waist to cup her breasts with his hands, the lace nowhere near as soft as the flesh in his palms. On a growl, he yanked at the fabric so that his mouth, his hands, could cover her breasts instead.

Just at that moment, his tongue and his teeth found her nipple and she arched back and down, taking him even deeper. As she started to detonate again in his arms, he was right there with her, losing himself completely inside of her.

Valentina's legs shook as she walked back to her office to get her things. They were still shaking by the time she got in her car to drive home.

It was one thing to say she didn't want to be with Smith.

It was another entirely to say it and then immediately melt into him as she begged for more of his kisses.

And it was another still to give herself to him in ways she never had with another man.

Yes, the set had been fairly deserted by the time she went to seek him out in the screening room, but she hadn't thought to lock the door. Anyone could have walked in on them and seen her straddling Smith in the chair, her skirt hiked up around her waist, her blouse unbuttoned and open so that nothing would get in the way of his mouth, his hands or his—

Oh, God, she thought as she pulled into the driveway of her rental house and laid her head down on the steering wheel, *what am I doing?*

Friday night, and then Saturday morning, were supposed to be her one-time-only gift to herself. Even today, before she'd reached for him, she'd justified it by telling herself it was the very last time.

All those years she'd thought actors were the ones who couldn't be trusted.

Now, it turned out that she was the one who kept saying one thing...and then doing another.

The next days passed in a blur of meetings. Important scenes were being filmed and she worked with Tatiana on her lines all the while remembering the secret, frantic, couldn't-possibly-get-enough-of-it sex with Smith.

Somehow, making love with Smith had become an inevitable, and utterly necessary, part of each day.

Every time she saw him, she was more and more tempted to go against what she believed to be true about men in the business. She began to wonder, for the first time, if it wasn't so much that women like her mother were weak, but rather that the pull of these men was too strong to resist?

Every time Smith's hands and mouth touched her, all of her well-thought-out reasons, each one of her careful considerations, every last vow and promise she'd made to herself, disappeared as if they had never existed at all.

When Tatiana asked Valentina to weigh in on her wardrobe for some upcoming scenes she would be shooting with the baby, she shouldn't have been surprised to find Smith there, too. But when Tatiana and Kayla, the wardrobe director, needed fifteen minutes to check out the stash of fabric in Kayla's storage locker, Valentina was surprised by how natural it was not only for Smith to lock the door before pulling her into his arms, but also for her to wrap her arms and legs around him and put her mouth to his as he took them both over yet another brilliant peak.

The next day, she made sure to get in early to make up for the work she'd been too fuzzy to complete after her delightful quickie with Smith. She thought she was the only person on set, but she found him in the kitchen making coffee. The next thing she knew, the door was locked again, the blinds were down and they were making love against the counter, her hands pressed flat on the Formica as she pushed her hips back into his to try to take him deeper, while he gave her everything, absolutely everything, she couldn't help but want. She could have said no, but knowing his touch, his kisses, made her a willing slave to *her desire* every time he was near.

On neither occasion did they talk before or after. Maybe because he knew she wouldn't want to hear what he had to say…or maybe she was afraid of what she might tell him. She knew they couldn't go on like this for much longer, using only the language of their bodies to communicate.

Soon, very soon, what was happening between them would have to be discussed.

And ended.

Friday dawned dark and foggy after a long night spent schooling herself to put a stop to the madness. The weather was a perfect reflection of the way her insides felt. She couldn't keep up with the highs of those stolen moments in Smith's arms, and then the lows of seeing him on set an hour later and having to act like they were strangers. Yes, she knew he didn't want things to be that way, that he would gladly have alerted the entire cast and crew to their budding relationship, but she knew any pain she was suffering now was so much less than the pain she'd feel down the road if she were foolish enough to think of herself as his girlfriend rather than his latest film-fling. Valentina had seen far more women than her mother go through that hell during the past ten years, and she'd always vowed never to put herself in that position. And God forbid that anyone with a camera caught them together. She couldn't imagine seeing herself on the cover of a magazine.

So as she headed onto the set with her gifts for the holiday party, she firmly reminded herself: no matter what, she wasn't going to make love to Smith again.

Smith was known throughout Hollywood for working hard, for holding focus and for always giving his best. But he'd never put in hours like these before, never even knew he had it in him. It was easy to let everyone think his long hours were solely because he was staking so much on the success of *Gravity*.

He alone knew the truth.

Ten minutes in Valentina's arms would fuel him for ten hours, and then when he finally came down from the high she gave him, he missed her so much—and wanted her again so badly—that trying to rest or relax was pointless. Instead, he worked through all those hours of frustration and need, only sleeping when he'd temporarily exhausted her scent, the feel of her on his lips, his hands.

By the time Valentina arrived, most of the cast and crew were already in the space in the big warehouse they'd rented in San Francisco. It was here that they filmed the bulk of their indoor scenes, but now it had been transformed into a holiday party space. Sharing drinks and food and laughter, everyone was having a great time. Despite the noise and the heated discussion between two cameramen about the San Francisco Outlaws' prospect for another Super Bowl that year, he sensed her presence in the crowded room.

Excusing himself, he moved through the room toward her. "I'm glad you're here."

Her beautiful skin was already flushing when Tatiana moved to her side and slipped her arm around her sister's waist.

"I was worried I was going to have to come and disconnect your computer to get you out of your office. You've been working so hard lately. I'm starting to wonder if you've secretly taken on another actor."

Smith could guess exactly how Valentina was spinning her sister's innocent comment as she flushed deeply before saying, "Imagine my trying to keep a secret like that from you." She very purposefully didn't look in Smith's direction as she said it.

He had never been anyone's secret before. Girls, then women, had been proud to claim him, practically from the minute he could walk and talk.

He didn't like being Valentina's secret, disliked it with such vehemence that if he wasn't careful, he was going to completely lose the tenuous grip he had on his patience. Moments of satisfaction had been few and far between over the course of the past week. He was working like hell to keep believing they were getting somewhere…and that that day would soon come when Valentina wouldn't be able to deny their connection any longer.

So rather than pull her into him and kiss her senseless in front of his entire crew, he made himself turn and walk away to play Secret Santa. He let the laughter, the joy, the happiness of the people around him fill him up over the next hours. It was one of the best parts of working on a movie—the way a group of strangers came together and turned into a family over the course of weeks and months. He knew that by the time the taxis were called to take everyone home, many would be pleasantly sloshed, having been able to let their hair down for the first time in weeks. No doubt they'd all be starting work a little later the next morning and Smith knew they deserved this break.

And yet, as he laughed with his cast, as he complimented his crew for the great job they'd been doing, he wanted Valentina with a fierceness that surprised even him. No woman had ever done this to him: made him burn, tore him open, tried his patience to its very limits.

People were dancing all around them as Valentina came toward him, a wrapped box in her hands. "I have a gift for you."

Even though all he wanted was her, he made himself take the present. Gifts had never made him surly before, but he relished the harsh sound of the paper shredding beneath his hands.

Only, when he saw the puzzle, he thought—no, he *knew*—what she was trying to tell him.

Because everything had changed for them at Alcatraz.

"I love it, Valentina."

One word. All he wanted was to change one word. To change *it* to *you*.

He wasn't surprised when she let the dancing crowd pull her in and swallow her up, disappearing before he could say another word. But he knew, with-

out a doubt, that she'd heard what he hadn't said…
and that he wouldn't wait much longer to whisper the
three little words against her lips.

Nineteen

"Valentina!"

She was just sitting down on set to wait for filming to begin when Smith's sister Lori called her name and came to sit next to her.

"It's so nice to see you again," Valentina said, meaning every word. She'd had such a great day at the spa with Smith's sisters a week ago.

"You, too," Lori said, her eyes twinkling with mischief. "I've been dying to get an update on the guy you're having the superhot I-don't-want-this-to-encourage-you sex with. Is he still putting in his best effort to gain your heart? Or has he given up yet?"

Before Valentina could answer—or slap a hand over Lori's mouth—Smith was standing in front of them…looking as if he'd just heard every word his sister had said.

"Hey, Naughty, glad you could drop by," he said as he gave Lori a hug. But his dark eyes were on Valentina the entire time, refusing to let her look away.

"Me, too," Lori said, beaming up at the brother she clearly adored.

Valentina was almost blinded by the beauty shared by the two siblings. Were it not for the kindness in their eyes, and the smiles that so naturally played around their mouths, the Sullivans would have been a very intimidating clan indeed.

Tatiana came by just then to say hello to Lori, which left Smith's focus too much on Valentina for comfort. She tried to shoot him a look that said, *I'll explain what Lori just said later, okay? Just don't do or say anything we're going to regret. Please, can we save this for when it's just the two of us?*

But she could see the frustration in his eyes, the same darkness that had been there after their first night together when he'd pinned her to the bed in the morning and refused to let her leave, the same end to his patience that she'd felt at the holiday party when she'd given him the puzzle of Alcatraz.

God, just the memory of the lovemaking they'd shared had her insides clenching with heat. She could have sworn a hundred times over that she wasn't running just so that he could chase her…but her body disproved that lie each and every time he was near.

"Valentina." His low voice thrummed over nerves stretched taut. "Those files you asked for are in my office."

"Great," she managed in what she hoped was a calm, even voice. "I'll get them from you—"

"Now."

There were no files. And even if there had been,

she certainly could have waited to get them until after he and Tatiana finished shooting their next scene. But something told her it was either follow Smith into his office now…or risk him doing something in front of everyone on set that would have eyebrows rising and tongues wagging.

She could see he wasn't in the mood to wait too long for her to make her decision, so she quickly said, "We'll be right back," to their sisters and led the way to his office. She could feel his eyes on her, the subtle sway of her hips feeling more pronounced beneath the heat of his gaze, every sensitive area of her body already responding to him without so much as a touch.

She'd barely stepped into his office when she heard the door close—and lock—behind them.

"Smith." She slowly turned around to face him. "Lori never would have said that if she knew you were the guy I've been—"

He waited, one eyebrow raised…and her stomach twisted at the sure knowledge that no matter what she said, she was only going to hurt him again.

She couldn't say they were just sleeping together, because she couldn't deny that what they had shared had been more than that. So much more. Even though she'd been trying as hard as she could to convince herself that it wasn't.

"I don't know what to call what we're doing," she said softly. "Actually, I tried to find you this morning in your office so that we could talk." God, she hated admitting it, but he had to know. "I don't know how to handle how fast everything has been moving between us. And even though every day I tell myself it's the last time, things between us just keep getting—"

"Strip."

Words stalled on the tip of her tongue at his rough-edged command.

Day in and day out she watched him dominate his cast and crew on set. However smoothly he did it, Smith was always completely in charge of everything around him. With her, however, he'd invariably been gentle. Even that morning in his bed, he'd been careful not to push her too hard or too far.

Until now.

Strip.

Valentina knew she should be irritated with him for making such a command. Not to mention frustrated at the way he always steered her away from taking measures to shut down their affair.

She should be feeling anything but immediately warm and loose—and desperately wanting—just from the possession in his voice. And from his sure knowledge that she was not only going to obey his sensual command…but was going to absolutely love every single second of it.

So sure, in fact, that he didn't wait for her to start taking off her clothes before he began to remove his own. Unfortunately, he was right about her, because desire grew more and more inescapable as she watched him shrug off his jacket and then undo one button after another on his shirt.

She could barely swallow by the time he reached

for his belt buckle, but somehow managed to croak, "They're going to be looking for you on set soon."

"Then we'll have to make this quick, won't we?"

His shoes and socks were off a moment later and then his pants until he was clad only in boxer briefs that did nothing whatsoever to hide the state of his arousal.

"Our sisters are going to wonder how your clothes got wrinkled," he murmured as he advanced on her.

He was right. If she wasn't going to muster up the strength to leave his office, she needed to get her suit off, and fast. With desire holding her so tightly in its grip that wild horses couldn't have dragged her away, she reached for her jacket with shaking fingers. But Smith was close enough already that he was sliding his hands into her hair and kissing her.

Her hands fluttered from her jacket to his broad shoulders. Right then she should have been saying *no* and pushing him away, but all she could do was say *yes* over and over in her head as she pulled him closer. And then his hands were shoving her jacket off and he was undoing the buttons on her blouse and unzipping her skirt as deftly and efficiently as he'd removed his own clothes.

When she was standing in front of him wearing nothing but her heels and another set of the beautiful lingerie he'd given her, the breath came out of his chest in a heated rush.

"I wish I could spend the next ten hours appreciating you," he murmured as his lips and teeth came down over the tendon that connected her shoulder and neck, "but since we've only got ten minutes…"

Before she realized what he intended, he lifted her onto his desk, not so much as blinking when her hips shoved a stack of papers and a stapler to scatter all over the floor.

"I've never wanted anyone or anything the way I want you. You're making me cross lines, break my own rules, to have you. I need you, Valentina. So damn much it's tearing me apart."

When they were like this, when he was stroking her skin and searing her with his heat, when she could feel just how much he wanted her, she couldn't hold anything back from him. Besides, she was clearly just as messed up as he was, because it was more than just sex that was driving her to be with Smith again and again.

It was the need to be close to him.

To let herself be held.

To be intimate.

To be needed.

These were all the things her mother and father shared…and the loss of them had torn her mother apart after her father died.

But just as she couldn't possibly turn away from his need, there was no way she could deny her own. "I need you, too."

Her admission had him taking her mouth again on a growl of possession as he stepped between her legs. He drew back just enough to say, "Lift your hips," then pulled off her panties. A second later his boxers were gone and he'd found a condom to roll on over his thick length.

The very last thing they should be doing was having sex on Smith's desk while their sisters, and the crew, were waiting on set for him to film an important scene. And yet, as he took her ankles and wrapped her legs around his hips, as she twined her arms around his neck and held on tight, as he thrust into her on a desperate groan, there was nothing in the world she wanted—or needed—more.

They may have had only ten minutes, but what a glorious ten minutes it was as Smith took her over, body and soul, his hips moving in time with hers, his mouth pressing sucking, biting kisses over the upper swells of her breasts.

It didn't matter how many times they made love, she could never get enough of Smith's warmth, his passion, the way he so fully embraced not just life but her, too—sharp edges, soft curves and everything in between as he sent her flying up over another peak of pleasure, before following her over a second later with one more hard thrust that had the desk skidding with a loud screech over the floor.

She was still trying to catch her breath while asking herself exactly how everything had spiraled off so fast from his sister's innocent question—to Smith beckoning her into his lair, then to being thoroughly, and wonderfully, ravished in his office—when he pressed one more kiss to her lips and stepped away to put his clothes back on.

How, she wondered, unable to do anything but stare at his beautiful face and body with helpless longing, was he able to make passionate love to her one second and get back in character again just seconds after? It was one of the reasons she'd never wanted to be with an actor. She couldn't stand the idea of just being part of another scene he was playing to the best of his ability.

Only, when he looked into her eyes, she realized with stunning clarity that although he was again wearing his character's clothes, Smith wasn't the least bit in character. Because instead of the billionaire from the film staring at her, instead of Smith Sullivan the movie star, or even Lori's brother, the man who stood before her was her lover. One hundred percent. *Hers*.

The realization of just how completely he'd given himself over to her left her staggered even as he said, "Since I know my sister's going to want her answer before she's through with you, you can let her know that your guy is *definitely* still putting in his best effort for your heart."

With yet one more possessive kiss, he left her half-naked on the edge of his completely askew desk, still shaking not only with lust, but also with sweet emotion she couldn't keep at bay no matter how hard she tried.

Because, in the end, what amazed her most of all— so much more than the hot, head-spinning sex they'd just had—was that she'd given Smith every reason to give up on her.

But he hadn't.

Valentina's heart was still racing, her legs still trembling, as she put her clothes back on and did what she could to fix her makeup. Without a brush and blow dryer at hand, her hair wasn't nearly as neat as it had been before, which meant that as she returned to the set just as filming was about to commence, she could have sworn that Lori looked at her with a very assessing expression on her face.

Valentina worked to focus every ounce of her concentration on the scene beginning to play out in front of her. Fortunately, it wasn't long before she was completely lost in the story.

Jo sat feeding her baby daughter, Leah, in a luxurious nursery. The walls were bright yellow, the pictures on the walls sweet without being cloying. Six months ago she would have been furious with a man for taking control of her life like this…but pride, she'd quickly learned, had very little place in a mother's life.

Graham had given her and Leah a gift she couldn't possibly have given herself. He'd moved them out of her crappy apartment in a bad part of the city and into a beautiful space across from a park where happy children played every morning and afternoon. If Jo had to work the rest of her life to pay him back for it, she would do so. Happily. And without resentment.

Graham seemed to always be there for her, anticipating her needs almost before she herself could.

Every night, he brought her the most delicious, nutritious dinner any new mother had ever eaten. She was always too tired—and too grateful—that she didn't waste what was left of her energy to turn him or the yummy food away. She was also too polite to turn him away after he was kind enough to give so much of his busy schedule to her and the baby.

And in truth, it wasn't the apartment or the food that she resented.

No. It was something far more insidious, far more potentially dangerous, that had her lying in bed at night tossing and turning when she should have been trying to squeeze in sleep while her daughter finally dozed.

It would have been easier, and so much safer, to hate him. Even to fear him. But everything had changed with the birth of her daughter. And she could no longer deny that in the strange in between of trying to push him out of her life when he would come to the coffee shop every day, up through these nightly meals together in her cozy apartment, the two of them had become friends.

And she wouldn't ever forget the hours when she'd been giving birth to Leah. He'd been there beside her every single second, never letting go of her hand, and it had been instinctive for her to let him hold the newborn.

Graham's gentleness had been so evident. So sweet. So pure. And everything she'd believed to be true about him, everything she'd tried to tell herself was real, was turned on its ear, until she wasn't sure about anything anymore.

Nothing except for how safe she felt with him... and that he was the only other person on earth that she could trust with her daughter's life.

These past weeks, she didn't even try to deny that she looked forward to his visits, especially since he didn't poke at her past and she didn't poke at his. All of it might have continued to be okay—the food, the friendship, the fact that he adored her baby—were it not for one other issue. One even scarier than actually becoming friends.

She was attracted to him. More and more with every passing day. And she wasn't young enough, or blind enough, not to see that he was attracted to her, too.

Neither of them were each other's types. And yet, it didn't seem to matter that she'd always had an unfortunate predilection for rocker types, or that she was the polar opposite of the Amazonian blondes that she'd seen pictured with him the couple of times she hadn't been able to stop herself from going to the computer to look him up.

She opened the front door and Graham's face immediately lit up when he saw that the baby was awake. He wasn't the only one happy, as Leah reached for him with a little gurgle of joy. But he would never take the baby without Jo's permission, and after he'd put the food down on her kitchen island, something bittersweet tugged at her as she made everyone happy by placing her soft bundle into his arms.

Her heart softened more and more with every one of the nonsense noises the powerful man in the expensive suit made to the happy baby as Jo laid out dinner on the small dining table. By the time she'd opened a bottle of beer for him and poured a glass of milk for herself, Leah had fallen asleep in his arms.

Jo reached for the baby, but Graham said, "Eat while it's hot. I'll just go tuck her in."

She knew she should be drawing lines between him and her daughter. But she couldn't justify it, not when he clearly felt nothing but adoration for her. She'd never had a man in her life like that, one who loved her unconditionally. Jo couldn't take that away from Leah.

She asked him about his day during dinner and he made her laugh with stories about the people in his office, the investors he dealt with. He asked about her day, and she told him about her trip to the park so Leah could sit and wobble in the sand and watch the bigger kids play with big wonder-filled eyes. He asked her next about the online horticulture classes she was taking, but even as he got her to share more of herself with him, by what felt like tacit agreement, neither of them ever spoke about family, about mothers or fathers or brothers or sisters.

By the end of dinner, Jo's eyelids were falling, and even though she insisted on helping Graham clean up the table, when he gave her a brand-new edition of Encyclopedia of Flowers, she was thrilled to sink back into the couch to devour the pictures and flower descriptions, and dream of the garden store she would open one day. Finally, her exhaustion got the better of her.

Love was unmasked on Graham's face as he looked at Jo, fast asleep on the couch, her legs tucked up under her small, curvy body, her beautiful face resting on her hands. And when the baby started crying, he immediately went to the fridge to pull out a bottle of breast milk and got water heating on the stove for it before heading back into the nursery for the little girl he was absolutely crazy about.

Making shushing sounds against the baby's soft skin and stroking the cap of hair that so beautifully matched her mother's, he brought her into the kitchen just as the bottle was warm enough.

As the little girl greedily drank her fill, she stared up at him with big blue eyes. He told Leah what he was so afraid to tell her mother.

"I love you." The baby's little hand lifted to wrap around one of his fingers and he cuddled her closer, whispering, "I will never let anyone hurt you. Ever."

When the baby had finished eating, he rocked her gently in his arms, the lullaby he softly sang quickly soothing her back to sleep.

Jo had woken as Graham brought her daughter back into the living room, but it had been so nice, just for once, to stay in that quiet and serene half sleep while he fed Leah. She'd been watching the two of them from under her lashes, and even though she knew how much he loved her little girl, hearing the sweet words of love fall from his lips, and then the lullaby, was a shock.

Even more so was the shock of just how badly she wanted to hear those three words for herself.

In her secret heart of hearts she knew she'd been falling for him for much longer than she hated to admit. But tonight, as she watched him give his heart to the one person who meant absolutely everything to her, she not only fell the rest of the way in love... she realized she'd never had a chance of keeping her heart safe from him.

For the first time, instead of trying yet again to hide from her feelings, she decided it was long past time to act on them. Graham had helped her in a dozen special ways with both her pregnancy and the baby. Now she would do whatever she could to help him.

She had enough scars of her own to recognize how deep his own ran. Not only had she never been able to forget his expression when he'd spoken of his sister that one time, but when she'd searched his name on the internet, she'd learned of his painful loss.

Two years ago his sister had died. The stories she'd read on the internet had called it an accidental death. But there was more than lingering grief in Graham's eyes.

Jo sat up and, slowly but surely, moved closer to him. He made a move to hand her the sleeping baby, but she shook her head and stilled him with a hand over his.

His eyes darkened as she moved closer, then closer

*still, until her mouth was barely a breath from his.
The silent night wrapped around them, protecting
three souls, as her lips finally touched his in a soft
and sweet kiss that was just as much a declaration
of love as any words could have been.*

Twenty

It always took Valentina a few minutes to come back to the real world after a scene ended. The powerful emotion Smith and Tatiana brought to their work made resurfacing more and more difficult. Especially now that she'd sent her screenplay off to George and hadn't yet started on something new as an outlet for her emotions. Over the past few days she hadn't been able to get the forbidden-love story set on Alcatraz she and Smith had brainstormed out of her head. She knew she'd be putting words to paper soon.

Thankfully, she wasn't the only one who needed to take a deep breath and shake off the fictional world, because Smith's chatty sister seemed just as dazed as everyone else by what she'd seen play out on the set in front of them.

"Oh, my God," Lori exclaimed, "I think my heart just broke into a million pieces and then glued itself back together all at the same time."

"It's been like this since the first day of filming," Valentina told her.

Lori turned to her. "Is Tatiana ready to become a massive star? Because she will be after this comes out."

"I hope so. All I want is for her to be happy."

Lori nodded. "I feel the same way about Smith. So many of the things ordinary men take for granted, like picking up a cup of coffee or going out on a first date, are so hard for Smith to do without people freaking out when they realize it's him. But I've never heard him complain about it, even though it's got to totally suck sometimes. Everyone thinks being a star is so glamorous, but that's just a small part of it. Sometimes when I look at Smith's life it all just seems like long hours, superhard work and a horrible loss of privacy."

Valentina couldn't agree more. Some actors were in it for the fame. Others continued giving their best in spite of it. Smith was definitely in the latter camp, as she'd never seen him do one single thing to try to make sure his name appeared in the press. And from the past weeks she'd spent with him, she knew his sister was right—he was doing an amazing job of dealing with an often impossible situation.

Guilt churned inside her at the way she'd made being normal even harder for him. He'd wanted to take her on a date; she'd immediately said no without giving him a chance. He'd wanted her to spend more than just the one night with him after Alcatraz; she'd been too afraid that her sister, and then everyone else on set, would find out. He'd tried to show her a dozen different ways that he cared; she'd tried to pretend a dozen different times that she didn't, when the truth was, she cared more and more with every passing second. Yes, she had her reasons, even knew he understood them to some degree, but it still didn't make the situation any fairer for either of them.

Lori held Valentina's gaze, her expression uncharacteristically serious. "Smith has been the best big brother in the world, and has loved me and my siblings and my mother with everything he has." Her eyes softened. "He doesn't know how to love any other way. None of us Sullivans do."

Lori wasn't accusing her of anything, but Valentina suddenly wanted to beg for forgiveness, wanted to tell Smith's sister that she didn't mean to toy with Smith's heart, that she'd done everything she could to keep him as a friend, despite the attraction—and desperate need—that raged between them like a wildfire.

But before she could blurt out any of that, Lori's arms came around her in a warm hug. "I'm so glad I got to see you again today, Val." She grinned, the mischievous spark back in her pretty eyes as she said, "Now it's time for me to go harass my big brother."

Valentina met Smith's gaze over Lori's retreating back and the flash of heat—and emotion—that ran through her told her no amount of burying herself in work for the rest of the evening could possibly help her forget what had happened in his office that morning.

Or just how much she wished she could give him

everything he so rightfully deserved. But that would mean changing who they both were…and she already knew that neither of them would want to do that to each other.

Lori and Smith were heading over to his office when she grabbed his arm, grinned widely and said, "You're Valentina's mystery guy that she can't shake, aren't you?"

Knowing Lori was clearly beside herself with glee at realizing he was Valentina's un-boyfriend, Smith muttered, "This is making your day, isn't it, Naughty?"

"Are you kidding? This has just made my year!" she teased before adding, "Valentina's beautiful, but not at all your usual type."

Lori was right. He usually went for women who looked more like Valentina's younger sister. Small and soft, not tall and lithe.

"There's nothing typecast about Valentina," he told Lori, both drawn and frustrated by that fact. "I've never met anyone like her before."

As they walked into his office, Lori immediately took in the mess on his desk and the floor where the papers and stapler had fallen that morning, along with the fact that the desk was now sitting at a strange angle in the room. It couldn't have been more clear what he and Valentina had been up to.

"First woman you've ever really cared about, and the best you can do is drag her in here to have a quickie on your desk?" Lori shook her head in disgust. "No wonder she's still way up on the fence about you."

Damn it, he hated that he had to agree with his sister's annoying analysis of the situation.

Winning Valentina over was proving to be really, really difficult. Outside of the bedroom, anyway. It was far more tempting to keep her naked and panting with him until he could get her to finally agree that they were having more than just a film-fling.

But since sex wasn't the problem, clearly *more* sex wasn't going to fix it.

He knew Valentina trusted him with her sister... but still, the bigger questions remained; not only how to get her to trust him with her own heart, but also how to make her believe that between the two of them they could figure out a way around the spotlight.

"I like Val," Lori said. "A lot. So much, in fact, that I wouldn't mind hanging with her at family functions for the next forty or fifty years." His sister pinned him with a razor-sharp look. "Which is why I seriously hope you have a better plan than just more of that." She gestured to his desk again with another disappointed shake of her head.

He pulled off the tie his character Graham always wore and scowled at himself in the mirror. He hated that there was so much wisdom in what Lori was saying, in forcing himself to keep his hands off Valentina until he convinced her to actually date him with everything out in the open, rather than the two of them skulking around the set in a clandestine affair.

But as he threw his character's suit jacket over his

office chair, he absolutely refused to give up those precious moments when Valentina let down her walls and let herself be open and connected to him. Just as he'd told her that afternoon, he wasn't giving up on finding that still-hidden pathway to her heart.

Lori moved behind him and wrapped her arms around his waist. "Trust me," she said with a commiserating sigh, "if anyone knows how you're feeling, I do. Love sucks, doesn't it?"

"No," he told the little sister for whom he wanted nothing but the best, "love's the good part."

Somehow he'd figure out a way to deal with the rest of it.

It was dark and stormy in the city by the time Smith left his final meeting of the day. The battery on his phone had died a couple of hours ago and although he figured there had to be a couple dozen messages and emails waiting for him, he headed neither for his office, nor his house, to recharge it.

Instead, he drove the dozen blocks to the rental home Tatiana and Valentina were sharing.

All afternoon, his talk with Lori had grated on him. She was right about him playing things wrong with Valentina. Increasingly, as the days turned into weeks, he'd grown more and more frustrated.

Idiot.

That's what he was for not knowing she would be stronger than any of his attempts to woo her. After all, her strength was one of the things he'd fallen for, right from that day when she'd all but skewered him with the message that he'd better treat Tatiana right, or else.

Each sexual encounter he and Valentina had was hugely physically satisfying, but they weren't getting him much closer to stripping away her other layers. Not when what he wanted for both of them ran so much deeper than just desire.

Sure, any number of women would have fallen at his feet. But he wanted *her*.

And she was worth however hard he had to work to get her.

As he rang her doorbell, the hard rain splattered his clothes and shoes. He couldn't fight the rush of disappointment when Tatiana opened the door instead of her older sister.

"Great, you got my message," Tatiana said with a wide grin as she stepped aside to let him in. "I'm pretty sure Valentina's about to roll up the script and start hitting me over the head with it."

Looking past Tatiana, he caught the quick flash of pleasure—and desire—in Valentina's eyes at seeing him in her house before she quickly masked it with a polite hello.

"Can I get you anything to drink?" Valentina asked him.

"Sure, water's good."

When she moved past him into the kitchen, it took every ounce of control he had not to pull her against him and breathe her in. She smelled exactly the way she had when he'd taken her on his desk, like lavender shampoo and sex and her own intoxicating scent that had always driven him crazy. He hadn't come here for a friendly drink with two coworkers or to make more progress on the movie with her sister, but Valentina quickly cut off any advance he might have made.

"Thanks for coming to work with Tatiana tonight. I know how much she appreciates it. Especially," she said in a low voice that only he could hear, "when you're filming such a difficult scene tomorrow."

Damn it, he couldn't believe he'd forgotten what was coming tomorrow. The sex scene between Graham and Jo. More than ever, he needed to stay tonight and make sure Valentina understood that he and Tatiana were just going to be actors tomorrow when they had their hands and mouths on each other in front of the cameras.

"Valentina—"

Cutting him off, she shoved a bottle of water from the fridge at him and said, "I'm going to turn in early."

But before she could walk away from him yet one more time, he blocked her sister's view with his body and took Valentina's free hand in his. She sucked in her surprised gasp just before it left her lips, her eyes wide and full of the passion she never managed to conceal when she looked up at him.

He stroked his thumb along the inside of her wrist and felt her breath go in a soft *whoosh*. "Actually," he said loud enough for Tatiana to hear, too, "with Nicola and Marcus crashing at my house tonight instead of heading back to Napa in the storm, would either of you have a problem with me staying here tonight so I can let the two lovebirds have some privacy?"

The flash of fire in Valentina's eyes at how easily he'd trapped her had him grinning, even as Tatiana said, "You're always welcome here, isn't he, Val?"

Her "Of course" came from between gritted teeth at the same time as she yanked her hand from his.

"Sweet dreams, Valentina."

Valentina was almost surly enough to lock her bedroom door. But she refused to give Smith the satisfaction of hearing her make a lame attempt to keep him out of her bed. How sad would it be if she needed a padlock to keep her legs shut around him?

If he dared come to her tonight, he'd find that she was strong enough to turn him away, to tell him that it simply wasn't appropriate for the two of them to continue their secret tryst while her sister was only across the hall.

She decided to fight the chill of the rain pouring down outside by running a bath. Oh, yes, she would very much enjoy the fact that Smith would have to listen to the water running and know she was naked and wet—with only her rubber ducky for company—while he sweated out the final mechanics of tomorrow's scene with her sister.

Her gut clenched tight as she thought about what tomorrow would bring. Not just more of the gentle kisses Jo and Graham's scene had ended on today, not just the adoring looks they'd had to give each other while in character during the photo shoot earlier in the week, but—

No.

She shouldn't get all twisted up about it. She'd known all along this day would come where Smith and Tatiana would film a very intimate and sexy love scene, and that was one of the reasons why she'd been so careful not to let Smith get too close…so that what happened during filming wouldn't end up destroying her.

Valentina put her fingertips into the water to test the temperature, sucking in a breath when she realized she'd made it too hot. She ran the cold tap for a few seconds, but when she tested the water again it was too cold.

She muttered a curse, the one harsh word echoing in the tiled room, as she pulled the plug to let some water out so that she could try to get it right one more time. But as she watched the water swirl and drain out of the tub, she suddenly saw herself in the water, pulled deeper, faster, down down down by the inescapable force of gravity.

It didn't matter how hard she'd tried to fight her attraction to Smith, or how far away from the edge of the cliff she'd stood…she'd never succeeded at doing anything but falling straight into his wide-open arms.

What, she suddenly found herself wondering, *if she didn't fight it?*

What if she let falling in love with him be as natural as gravity?

And what if she let Smith love her the way she'd always secretly dreamed of being loved? Was there a chance that they could work through all of the potential problems and issues that came from his career and her fear of being caught out by flashbulbs and cameras?

Kneeling by the side of the tub with the questions going around and around inside her head, she stared blindly at the water. Only when the last drops going down the drain made a loud sucking sound did it jolt her into standing up to finish getting ready for bed.

As she slid naked between her sheets, with the comforting sound of Smith and Tatiana talking out in the living room lulling her toward an exhausted sleep, she dreamed, not of broken hearts and raw disappointments...but of strong, warm arms that held her close until the storm outside stopped raging.

After Smith said good-night to Tatiana, the seconds that he waited to hear her bedroom door close felt more like hours. Finally, he headed across the hallway to Valentina, silently opening, then closing her door.

In the dark he could see, just barely, Valentina's curled-up form under the covers. His heart skipped a beat as he watched her sleep. She was so beautiful, so peaceful, as she breathed deeply and evenly. Her long hair was spread over the pillow and there was a small smile on her face, one that had him hoping she'd been dreaming of him.

He slid in behind her, her sweet scent utterly intoxicating. He didn't want to wake her when he knew how badly both of them needed the rest, but he had to hold her.

"You came."

Valentina's voice was sleepy, and so damned seductive it sent every last cell in his body that wasn't already on fire up in flames.

Thanking God she wasn't angry with him for sneaking uninvited into her bed, he couldn't stop himself from slowly, softly, running one hand down her sleek curves. He wanted her, desperately, but just this chance to lie in bed with her was so precious that he would happily forgo making love if it meant getting to hold her.

Smith had always thought he had women under control, that they were a need he could turn on or off at will, that no woman could ever cause him pain.

Valentina had proved him wrong. So damned wrong.

It was how he knew for sure that he was in love with her. And love, as he'd seen first with his parents, and then with his siblings and their significant others, was worth the need, the hurt—worth absolutely everything.

He pressed a kiss to her shoulder, then to the sensitive skin at the curve of her neck. She shivered against him, then turned to put her arms around him so that her breasts were pressed against his chest and her legs were sliding against his. She whispered his name, but he knew she was more asleep than awake.

"Shh," he murmured against her lips before he pressed a soft kiss against them and felt her drop back into sleep just that quickly. "I've got you."

Forever, if she'd have him.

Twenty-One

The storm had washed away in the middle of the night, leaving behind brilliant blue skies and crisp, clean San Francisco air as Valentina headed into her office on the set. She pulled her laptop out of her bag and put it down on her desk, her skin still tingling from Smith's slow, sweet lovemaking that morning.

He hadn't woken her when he'd come to her bed in the dark, just wrapped her up in his strong arms and held her. She couldn't ever remember sleeping so deeply or so well. Nor could she remember ever waking up so needy, so hungry, so ready to be touched, kissed, stroked, *loved* by a man.

Their first night together—and all the quickies that had come after—had been about temptation, about discovery and inescapable pleasure. But this morning, their need for each other had been a demand that neither of them could, or would, deny.

Even now as she thought back to it, their early-morning lovemaking seemed more like a dream than flesh-and-blood reality. Perfectly silent, barely moving, they'd come together so naturally, so perfectly. Smith's body fit against hers as if he'd been made for her, and she'd been made for him.

She pressed her hand to the hollow of her throat where he'd left one kiss after another as she'd arched into him, and felt her heart beating the same rhythm it had beat beneath his lips. Not fast, but with a languid heat that rose more with every slow slide of his body into hers. She couldn't remember what any other morning had been like without him there, could barely imagine a time when Smith hadn't been hers.

The first rays of the sun had broken through the darkness as she'd given herself to him. His mouth had covered her sounds of pleasure, his tongue against hers driving her even higher still, before he'd given himself up to her, too.

All she'd wanted was to stay like that with him forever, to forget the rest of the world existed outside of their own private paradise.

But she couldn't forget that he had an early call. Knew, too, that she'd need to be on set soon to support Tatiana on what was sure to be a difficult day. Quite possibly the most difficult day of the entire shoot.

Plus, if Tatiana had seen Smith coming out of her bedroom, the jig would officially be up...and Valentina would have some pretty big explaining to do to the one person from whom she'd vowed never to keep secrets.

She'd thought for sure when Smith had shown up at their house last night that he'd been looking for a showdown, but in the morning he hadn't made her explain any of her swirling, conflicted thoughts. Instead, he'd said, "Today, when Tatiana and I are filming—"

She'd pressed her mouth to his to stop him from saying anything more. Filming sex scenes was part of his job. And since she hadn't managed to keep her walls up around him these past weeks, then she was just going to have to find a way to deal with it, wasn't she?

When she'd finally drawn back from his sinfully delicious mouth, he'd simply smiled his breath-stealing smile down at her, and said, "You make me very, very happy, Valentina." He'd kissed her once more and then was gone a moment later, back to the guest room for a quick shower, and then out the front door a short while after that.

Valentina finally realized she'd been daydreaming with her computer still in her hands for God knew how long, and gave herself a firm mental shove before briskly walking across the parking lot to her sister's trailer. Pausing outside, she took a steadying breath and worked on her smile before knocking.

Her sister opened the door wearing a blue silk robe. Valentina's breath caught in her throat. Tatiana had never looked lovelier, or more fresh and innocent. At the same time, her sensuality had been played up with professional makeup and clothes and hair.

"You look beautiful, T."

Her sister bit her lip. "Filming today is going to go okay, isn't it?"

Oh, God, what could she do but put her arm around Tatiana, smile as if it were no big deal and say, "Of course it will. You're two professionals doing your job. You know everyone always says that filming a love scene is not that different from filming a fight scene. One arm here. One leg there."

"You'll be there the whole time, right?"

The set was the very last place in the world Valentina wanted to be today. Just the thought of Smith's mouth, his hands, on her sister had her stomach on the verge of emptying out. It was a closed set, and only the most essential members of the cast and crew would be there.

"Of course I will," she promised. "And I won't move an inch until you're done." But when she could see that her sister still wasn't totally at ease, she said, "I'm sure it will be just like Smith said—you'll probably feel like all you're doing is playing Twister together." Valentina made herself joke, "Little does he know how cutthroat us Landons are about our Twister games."

When Tatiana laughed and grabbed her script to sit down with it for a few more minutes, Valentina breathed a silent sigh of relief.

Now all she needed to do was figure out a way to believe her Twister comment was true, as well. Valentina had been trying to pretend this day wouldn't come. But ignoring it hadn't made it go away.

When Tatiana had first wanted to be an actress, Valentina had made her sister agree to one hard and fast rule: no matter how big the incentive from a studio or producer, she would never film any sex scenes as a minor. If she couldn't legally drink, she wouldn't take her clothes off in front of a set full of strangers and roll around naked on a huge screen for millions of viewers to salivate over.

Valentina didn't expect—or even want—her sister to be a little girl forever. On the contrary, she celebrated what an incredibly lovely young woman she had become, despite the pressures from Hollywood to turn her into a carbon copy of every other actress out there.

The only problem with the fact that Tatiana could now order a glass of wine at a restaurant was the fact that sex scenes were no longer off the list.

Valentina also recognized that no one would ever call the sex scene in Smith's movie gratuitous. Rather, it was a crucial part of the plot and character development for Jo and Graham as they moved from friends to lovers.

Still, she had no idea how she was going to deal with watching him make love to her sister. And worse still, considering it had to be one of the most terrifying moments of her sister's career so far, how could Valentina ever forgive herself for caring more about her own feelings than Tatiana's?

Thankfully, when the production assistant came to get Tatiana, her sister looked as relaxed as if she was about to film a toothpaste commercial.

Whereas Valentina knew she herself must look as if she was heading in for a root canal…without anesthesia.

* * *

Smith still remembered the first sex scene he'd ever shot. He'd been cast as a bitter son who seduced his father's new wife for revenge. The actress had been ten years older than he and he'd been nervous, yet desperate not to show it. Fortunately, his costar had been as kind as she was beautiful. Not to mention happily married.

She'd made the experience so easy for him that he'd gone out of his way to make it easy on the costars he'd had over the years. Not all of them had wanted to keep things strictly professional, and he hadn't exactly complained during the projects where going from his costar's screen bed into her real one had been the natural progression of things.

But Tatiana was different. For all of the intense on-screen attraction that they were both manufacturing for their roles, in real life he couldn't imagine actually making love to her. There was less than no chance that anything they portrayed today for the cameras would ever actually happen. It was all fantasy. Nothing more than make-believe.

From a screenwriting and directing standpoint, the sex scene was simply part of the story being told. Still, he understood how difficult it was for actors of both sexes to open themselves up in such a physically intimate way in front of a dozen crew members and cameras that picked up even the slightest movements.

Over the past few weeks, he'd made sure to take the scene apart and look at it from every angle. He'd created a shot list that was by far the most technical of any so far. He knew exactly how the scene would play out so that the core sensual connection wasn't only coming to its ultimate conclusion between Jo and Graham, but was in fact a new beginning for both of the characters as they realized just how much they needed each other to fully come back to life.

And yet, the truth was that he hadn't been turning the scene into a technical exercise just for Tatiana's benefit.

He'd done it for himself, too.

Sex scenes had never been an issue for him before. Until now...when he'd finally learned the true power of lovemaking in real life.

Because when he touched Valentina, when he kissed the bare skin at the curve of her shoulder, when he slid into her and felt her gasp of pleasure all the way down deep in his soul, sex became something so much bigger, so much more important than just pleasure and orgasms.

He looked up from the notes he'd made in the margins of his script just as Tatiana walked onto the set, with Valentina flanking her from behind. It was difficult to keep his focus on his costar when his every sense came alive around the woman who had started to mean so much to him, but if there was ever a time he needed to stay completely in tune with the younger Landon sister, it was now.

"Ready for our game of Twister?"

He was glad when she grinned at him. "You bet. Let's do this thing."

When Tatiana went to take her place on set, Smith felt Valentina touch his arm.

"I know you can't go easy on her today," she said, "and that you need to film the scene exactly as you wrote it, but—"

"I'm going to make this as painless as possible," he vowed in a soft voice. "For all of us."

But Valentina wasn't looking at him. Instead, she was staring at her sister's back with such a bleak look in her eyes that he wanted desperately to reach for her, to pull her into his arms and swear to her that nothing that was going to happen on set today had a damn thing to do with what the two of them were building together.

Smith was a heartbeat from doing it, her protests and rules about keeping their affair secret be damned, when her eyes finally met his.

"I trust you with her." She nodded as if trying to convince herself that what she was saying was true. "I really do."

Considering her sister meant everything to her, her trust that he wouldn't hurt Tatiana today meant a great deal to him.

But not nearly as much as it would have meant to know for sure that Valentina trusted him not to hurt *her*.

Valentina's hands were clenched so tightly that the skin on her palms was shredded by her nails within minutes of Smith and Tatiana taking their marks. But she didn't feel the physical pain, not when she could barely breathe past the tightness in her chest.

Smith said something that had her sister laughing and then, the next thing she knew, the cameras were running and Tatiana was in his arms, his mouth coming down over hers. In the moment that their mouths touched in passion for the first time, bile rose up so high and fast in Valentína's throat that she had to cover her mouth with both hands and swallow hard to keep from actually being sick in front of everyone.

Again and again, the kiss was captured from different angles, but it never got easier for her to watch, never hurt any less to see her sister act as if she was melting into Valentina's real-life lover's arms. It didn't matter how many times Valentina reminded herself that it wasn't real, that they were just acting, that their paychecks necessitated the kiss that never seemed to end.

But that endless kiss was better, so much better, than when the scene moved forward…and clothes started coming off as Smith and Tatiana moved together toward the bed in character.

Were it not for the promise she'd made her sister not to move an inch, Valentina would have run as far and as fast as she could. But she couldn't. She had to stay right where she was, with a front-row seat to an on-screen seduction that was more than believable.

She all but forgot how to breathe as she watched Smith-as-Graham gently lower Tatiana-as-Jo onto the bed. His large hands stripped her out of her robe and he reverently stared down at her as though he was seeing beauty for the very first time.

Feeling as though a thousand knives had been thrust into every inch of her skin, Valentina couldn't believe she wasn't bleeding out all over the set. On and on the scene seemed to go, as her sister arched into his touch, as his mouth roamed over her skin and his hands followed everywhere he kissed.

Black spots were starting to dance in front of Valentina's eyes when Smith abruptly lifted his head from her sister's stomach and said, "Cut." It was exactly the splash of cold water she needed, just enough of a break to keep her from sliding off the chair and onto the ground.

A moment later, both actors were off the bed and watching playback a few feet away from where Valentina was sitting.

Even without editing or effects, it was one of the most beautifully filmed love scenes she'd ever seen. Her heart was almost broken in two by the realization that Smith was just as good in bed with her sister as he was with her—when she finally tuned in to the discussion the two most important people in her life were having.

"I need to remember to keep my eyes open in that part, don't I?" Tatiana said. "Otherwise, it looks like I'm grimacing rather than having a good time."

Smith nodded. "Our hands are also off here. How about we try this instead?" He moved her hands to his shoulders, then slid his arms around her waist.

Valentina's breath was just catching again when

her sister said, "What about my legs? I feel like they're just flopping around down there."

The director of photography piped in with his suggestion about the best angle for shooting their lower extremities, and Valentina had a moment of clarity. She was watching the choreography of two bodies on film being done in real time. She'd seen it a hundred times over the years, knew that even in nonsex scenes there was important blocking, but she'd never thought anything of it. Because it hadn't felt personal back then.

And she hadn't wanted to keep one of the actors all to herself.

Twenty-Two

Unfortunately, it turned out that a handful of moments of clear thinking didn't go that far in a too-long day of watching Smith and Tatiana roll around on a bed with each other.

Hour after hour, Valentina tried to fight back the insidious thoughts, each one of them more and more convincing as they whispered that everything Smith had felt for her when she was lying beneath him, he now would start feeling for her sister, too.

And how could she possibly discount the fact that he was an actor? One of the best she'd ever seen. Smith could convince any woman on earth that he had feelings for her. He wouldn't even have to try to have half the population falling at his feet and begging him not to leave them as they pathetically declared how much they loved him.

Even when he swore that he wasn't acting with her, that he never had…well, how could she possibly trust that?

Only a fool would trust a world-class actor.

A fool who was that desperate to be wanted. To be desired. But most of all, to be loved.

When, at long last, filming ended for the day, every muscle in Valentina's body hurt. She couldn't have faked a smile, couldn't have gotten up from her seat without toppling over, not when her limbs felt numb, lifeless.

As numb and lifeless as her heart.

From what seemed like a long distance, through a lens darkened on the edges with jealousy and self-disgust, she watched Smith make her sister laugh and the two of them hug each other before shrugging on their clothes. And as she watched them tease each other, it struck her just how perfect they were together, the ultimate beautiful couple, two actors who complemented each other both on-screen and off.

Smith hadn't looked her way one single time during filming and she'd been glad. If he'd tried to connect with her while seducing her sister in front of her, it would have been the final straw.

It had been easier, better, to simply be forgotten.

At least, that's what she'd told herself over and over again as the pain from each kiss, each caress, dug another knife in so deep that she wasn't even capable of bleeding anymore.

Finally, Smith turned and, when he looked at her, his frown came swift and deep. All she could do was stare as he came toward her, purpose in every step.

She had no idea what she'd say to him, not when

every instinct screamed at her to hurt him the way he'd repeatedly hurt her today. Worse still, she wasn't strong enough to keep it inside out of fear of being heard by the crew. If he tried to speak to her here, if he tried to touch her, she'd explode.

Even knowing the additional pain it would bring in the future, the way people would talk about how she'd been foolish enough to believe Smith Sullivan could have wanted more from her than just a couple of rolls in the hay, she couldn't possibly have kept her emotions from bubbling up and over.

All this time she'd thought that if she kept him from getting too close, she'd be protected from the inevitable pain of losing him later. Only, every second that she watched him act the sex scene out with her sister made it more and more clear that not only had she not protected herself from *anything* at all... but also that she had no idea how to let him go.

Because he'd already gotten past every single one of the barriers she'd tried to erect.

The closer he got, the louder the blood rushed in her ears. This was it, the end to a beginning that should never have happened. And, really, it was for the best, wasn't it? Not only was he so far out of her league it wasn't even funny, but how could she possibly withstand a lifetime of scenes like this, where he was kissing and touching beautiful women on other sets?

Ice settled in over the flames that had been burning her up from the inside out as she prepared herself to cut every single emotional tie to the only man who had ever found his way past the walls around her heart.

"Uncle Smith!" Summer, his eight-year-old niece-to-be, barreled into his midsection. "I wanted to come on set earlier, but they said I couldn't because you were filming inappropriate stuff. No one will tell me what it was you were doing. But you will, right?"

The air she hadn't realized she'd been holding in burst from Valentina's lungs, leaving her feeling so dizzy she had to put both hands on the arms of her chair.

"Val?" Her sister was suddenly there in front of her with a cup of cold water. "You don't look good."

Valentina drank from the plastic cup as if she'd spent a week in the desert.

"You look like you need to lie down." With a strong arm around her waist, Tatiana had her up off the chair and heading toward her own trailer.

As Tatiana got her settled on the leather couch with a blanket tucked over her, it was the first time Valentina could remember her sister taking care of her, rather than the other way around. Sure, she'd had the flu or a cold a couple of times over the years, but even then she'd made sure not to be a burden when her sister had to hold focus on whatever job she was working on.

Tatiana sat next to her, her beautiful blue eyes full

of concern. "You haven't been sleeping well, have you?"

Oh, God, how could she admit that she'd finally had a good night's sleep, but only because Smith was there with her?

But she was already lying to her sister by her omissions, so rather than add to those lies, she simply shook her head. "Last night was good, but the past few weeks, no, I haven't."

How badly had she wanted to stay in his arms this morning? More than she'd ever wanted anything before.

Knowing she was blowing it on a day when she should have been there a hundred and ten percent for her sister, she somehow focused enough on Tatiana's well-being to ask, "How are you feeling? I know today was hard on you."

"I feel fine," her sister said in a soft voice, one with a note of something that had Valentina's senses coming back to life from where they had been beaten into submission by pure, unfettered jealousy. "You're the one I'm worried about, Val."

Valentina tried to smile, tried to raise a hand to brush off her sister's concerns. But her lips wouldn't curve in the right direction. And when she lifted her hand, she saw dozens of little crescent-moon cuts from holding her hands so tightly fisted all day long.

Tatiana took her hand and gasped. "Oh, Val, I was so wrapped up in myself today that it never even occurred to me to think about what watching the scene would do to you." Her sister lifted deeply concerned eyes to hers as she curled her hands around Valentina's. "Smith is great, but he's like a brother to me. Everything you saw between us today was acting and nothing more than that, I swear."

Valentina felt her mouth opening, then closing on words she didn't know how to say. All she could do was shake her head and try to deny the emotions that had grown deeper with every passing second she spent with Smith.

"I can't—" She tried again. "He shouldn't—"

But when Tatiana squeezed her hands and smiled so gently at her, she knew there was no point in even trying. Less so when her sister softly said, "I know how you feel about him." When Valentina's eyes widened in surprise, Tatiana said, "You haven't told me, but I'm your sister and I know you better than anyone else. You've never looked at a man the way you look at him."

Even knowing how useless the knee-jerk reaction was, weeks of telling herself lies had Valentina saying, "Everyone looks at him like that."

"No. They all look at him with stars in their eyes. They all want him for the fantasy, for the star, for everything but the man he really is. You've never seen anything but the man, Val."

Oh, God, it was true. And even worse than having to face it was the fact that she hadn't managed to hide even the smallest of her feelings from her sister.

Who else had seen it? More to the point, who could possibly have missed it?

Suddenly, all of her excuses were gone. All she had left was a single admission. "I tried not to. I'm still trying."

"But, Val," her sister said in an urgent voice, "can't you see that he looks at you the same way? Half the time when we're supposed to be working on figuring out a scene, if you're in the room he's busy mooning over you."

"Don't be crazy. This movie means everything to him."

"It means a great deal to him," her sister agreed, "but not even close to everything."

One of the tears Valentina had been working so hard to hold back all day finally slid down her cheek and as she wiped it away, she said, "All these years I've warned you against falling for one of your costars and here I'm the one who did it. I'm sorry for completely falling apart like this."

Tatiana made a sound that was part frustration, part resolve. "I'm not ten years old anymore. You have always been there for me, but don't you see—I want to be there for you, too."

For the second time in one day, Valentina was struck by their role reversal. All these years she'd spent taking care of her sister, had she ever let Tatiana take care of her? She could suddenly see herself in Smith's trailer that first day on set. *Your sister is lucky to have you to protect her... But who's protecting you?*

She'd told herself she'd accepted the fact that her sister had grown up, that she was old enough to drink, that she could film a sex scene. And yet, had she really wanted to treat Tatiana like an adult? Had she ever thought she could burden her sister with her own fears, her own pain?

And if not, why had she been so afraid to let Tatiana be one half of their support team?

Knowing she had so much ground to make up, Valentina struggled to admit, "I don't know what I'm doing. I should stay away from him, but I can't."

Tatiana's frown deepened. "Why do you need to stay away from him?"

It was so painfully obvious to Valentina, she couldn't believe she had to actually say the words aloud. "He's one of the biggest movie stars in the world. I'm me. A relationship with him could never go anywhere."

"Are you kidding? You two are beautiful together."

Panic knocked through her. "You've seen us?"

"No one else has," her sister quickly assured her, "but I've spent more time with the two of you than everyone else. He's always touching you when he thinks I'm not looking." Tatiana's eyes lit up with mischief. "And then there was that time I walked in on you guys kissing."

Heat flamed on Valentina's cheeks. "When?"

Tatiana grinned. "That night you were in the screening room, I realized I'd left my marked-up script. The door was open so I walked in without

knocking." She fanned herself. "All I can say is, wow.
I was seriously impressed. With both of you." Tatiana
leaned in closer and lowered her voice as she grinned.
"On the chair, huh?"

Frantically working to stuff away the huge wave
of embarrassment rolling over her at the thought of
her baby sister witnessing her completely losing control in Smith's arms, Valentina asked, "Why didn't
you say anything?"

Hurt briefly flashed in Tatiana's eyes. "I could tell
you were feeling a little weird about it, so I was waiting for you to tell me."

"I'm sorry I didn't confide in you," Valentina said,
and she truly was.

Why hadn't she talked to her sister? Especially
since she'd been so tormented by emotions and feelings she didn't understand. She'd tried to tell herself
that it was because she didn't want to accidentally
derail the success of the movie by putting her sister
in the middle of what was going on with her and Tatiana's powerful costar..But while there was certainly
truth to that concern, the bigger truth was that she
hadn't wanted to accept that her sister was all grown
up…so she'd treated her like a child instead of the
incredible woman she was.

Trying to explain, Valentina said, "I swear I didn't
think there was going to be anything to tell, that once
he got past the challenge, he'd lose interest." She was
still waiting for that, and was more than a little confused about why it hadn't happened yet.

"He obviously hasn't lost interest, Val. He won't. How could he?" Tatiana looked at Valentina with all of the love the sisters had for each other. "You're amazing. Beautiful. Smart. Funny. And the best sister in the world. I know he sees all of that. And all of you."

She couldn't make up for the weeks of hiding her feelings from her sister, but she could change things by sharing them now. She took a deep—and shaky—breath and tried to put in words the emotions that had been knocking around inside her for the past few weeks.

"The thing is, sometimes I don't feel like myself around him." It was already a night of admissions, so she added one more. "And that scares me. Badly." Especially when she lost control, the way she had again and again from nothing more than a look, the brush of his fingertips over her skin, his mouth claiming hers.

"I don't understand," Tatiana said, and Valentina wasn't surprised to hear it. Her younger sister had very rarely been afraid. And if she had, she hadn't let fear get in her way. "Who do you think you are?"

Valentina opened her mouth to answer, starting with "I'm—" but nothing came out after that.

She was happy with her career, would likely have gone to business school regardless of whether she managed her sister's business affairs or not, and had really enjoyed working on her screenplay these past couple of years.

But *Who do you think you are?* was less about what

she wanted to do for her job…and more about what kind of life she wanted to have as a woman.

For so many years she'd denied the emotional woman inside of herself, along with the sensual one. Sure, she'd had some fairly good sex with some perfectly nice men, and she hadn't completely tamped down on her emotions by any means, but at the same time, she'd kept everything in reserve just in case her sister needed her for any reason. Valentina's entire being had been wrapped up in Tatiana for so long, and she'd been so convinced she needed to avoid the pain her mother went through with all of her boyfriends, that somewhere along the way she'd lost sight of who *she* was.

And yet, despite all the things she'd held back for too long, her sister was perceptive enough not to miss a beat of her thoughts.

"I love you too much, Val, not to want the fairy tale to come true for you." Tatiana smiled, her beautiful smile that had lit up screens all over the world. "What if you gave Smith a chance to love you the way you deserve to be loved? Don't you think there's a chance that he could be up to the challenge? And don't you think you could be up to whatever challenges come, too?"

Love?

Oh.

Oh, my.

Even as Valentina had accepted the pulsing, unavoidable attraction between her and Smith, she'd been careful not to let herself dream of anything more than pleasure. No matter how sweet, how heartfelt, how gentle or loving, he was every time he kissed her.

The whispered words, "But what if he isn't? And what if I'm not?" came out of her before she could pull them back.

She could feel Tatiana's blue eyes on her, still concerned and so full of love, as she said, "You know Jayden?"

Valentina tried not to show how surprised she was by the abrupt conversation shift. "Sure. He's really nice."

A flush appeared on her sister's cheeks. "I think so, too. In fact, I've kind of been waiting for him to ask me out for a couple of weeks."

The first thing that hit Valentina was how perfect Jayden was for her sister. He was quiet and focused, cute and young and sweet. He wasn't about the limelight, but because he worked on film sets, he'd have some idea of how to deal with Tatiana's life because he worked with stars all the time.

How had she missed the budding romance between her sister and the on-set techie? Here she'd claimed she would do anything to be a good sister, and yet she was even blowing that.

"The thing is," Tatiana told her, "I don't think he's ever going to ask me out."

Now it was Valentina's turn to say, "Why not?"

Her sister's gaze was so direct Valentina had to sit back deeper into the couch cushions. "Because he

thinks I'm a big movie star and he's *just him*." She
used her fingers to put quote marks around the words.

Looking at the situation from her sister's view-
point, Valentina could see how frustrating it must be
to be put on a pedestal. And yet, wasn't that exactly
what she'd done with Smith, despite how many times
he'd proved to her that he was just as human as the
rest of them? But she'd been so busy trying to protect
herself from a future she couldn't define or clearly
see that she'd used his fame as the perfect excuse to
keep her distance.

Clearly, her suck-a-tology was at an all-time high.

Especially since flashes of her sister in Smith's
arms kept coming at her and nailing her flat, despite
everything that they'd just said to each other.

This time she was the one squeezing her sister's
hands and saying, "Where are you going to go with
Jayden when he says yes?"

"I'm going to take him to a restaurant with a romantic table for two." Her sister licked her lips. "And
then I'm going to seduce him."

If Valentina had been trying to convince herself
that Tatiana was still just a girl, she knew now that it
was time to give up. Her sister was a woman, with a
woman's needs. And a woman's heart, one that longed
for love, yet was smart enough to know how to reach
out and grab it when it was within reach.

Valentina put her arms around her. "I love you, T."

"I love you, too," Tatiana said, and when a knock
sounded on the door a second later, she added,

"Enough to tell you I think you should give Smith a chance. A real one, this time, so that he can show you exactly what he's made of. And so you can show him what you're made of, too."

Tatiana didn't wait for Valentina to respond before hopping off the couch and opening the trailer door for Smith. "She's inside," Tatiana said, and then in a lower voice that Valentina couldn't hear she told him, "If you hurt her, I'll hurt you," before leaving the two of them alone.

Twenty-Three

Valentina was standing in the middle of the trailer when Smith stepped inside. God, even looking at her now away from the lights and cameras and the crew, he couldn't get her expression when they'd finished filming out of his head.

Knowing how thin his thread was where Valentina was concerned, as soon as they'd started shooting the sex scene, Smith had steeled himself not to look at her, and to keep his full focus on Tatiana. But it had been impossible to block Valentina out. For the first time in his acting career he felt completely ripped in two.

All it would have taken was one look into her devastated eyes and he would have made the split-second decision not only to cut the scene that needed so badly to be in his movie, but also to call a halt to the day's filming altogether. Were it not for the cast and crew and studios and investors that were counting on him to get it right, he would have walked off the set, taken

Valentina's hand and disappeared with her to a place where Hollywood and make-believe didn't exist.

And yet, after he and Tatiana finally finished filming what had been the most difficult scene of his career, and he'd let himself turn to Valentina again, Smith hadn't been close to being prepared to see how pale her skin had become, how horrified her eyes had been…or how the mask of betrayal and sadness enveloped her face.

Had he made the wrong choice? And had he just lost the only thing that truly mattered?

Unexpectedly, Summer and his brother Gabe had come to see him on set, and even though he loved the kid to pieces, every second away from Valentina had been excruciating. He'd needed to go to her, to try to make things right. Thankfully, his brother had been able to tell something was wrong. On a promise to bring Summer back to the set soon, Gabe had distracted her with a visit to the craft services table full of treats for the crew.

After they left, Smith had all but sprinted off the set to get to Valentina. No one dared to get in his way, and if they had, he would have mowed them down. Now that he was finally with her, he couldn't think, could barely string two thoughts together when she was near. He just pulled her into his arms…and prayed she wouldn't pull away.

"I'm sorry. I didn't mean for today to hurt you. I don't want to hurt you. I won't ever hurt you again, I promise." With every sentence, he stroked one hand down her back, her hands trapped against his chest.

She had to feel just how hard, how fast, his heart was beating.

"It did hurt," she said softly into his neck, and the one short sentence felt as if it had reached in and ripped his heart out. "But—" the breath she took shook her chest "—it wasn't you who hurt me. I did it to myself."

He drew back so that he could look into her eyes. He didn't completely understand what she'd just said and he needed to. "I screwed this up so bad, I can't believe it. I prepared Tatiana for today, but I—" Damn it, he should have tried harder to talk with Valentina about today before it happened, but he'd been afraid. Afraid that even talking about it would make her run. "My entire career, I never had a problem with filming sex scenes. But it killed me today. Please, tell me it isn't too late to tell you how much it kills me to touch anyone but you."

"It's part of your job, Smith, one I don't want to steal piece by piece from you because you're worried about what I might think or feel about you playing a certain role."

But didn't she see? He'd been so worried about the importance of investors and the studio and his reputation that he hadn't realized what was truly important until it was nearly too late.

Her.

"I didn't think today would be so hard. Not after all the times I've had to pretend to make love with married actresses, with women I don't like, with complete strangers, even with friends." He dropped his hands from her shoulders and moved away in self-disgust, his hands going to his hair, pulling the dark strands up straight. "Being with your sister on-screen today was the hardest thing I've ever done."

He could see in Valentina's eyes the same bleakness that he felt down deep in his soul. He hadn't cheated on her, but nothing felt right anymore. A simple, pure love story without strife or complication was what he'd wanted so badly to give her. But he'd given her just the opposite today.

And still, even though it wasn't fair to ask her for anything else, he wanted so much from her.

So much *more* than he'd ever wanted from any other woman.

"I'm not going to lie to you," she said softly, "today was bad. Really, really bad."

When he winced at the terrible part he'd played in causing her so much pain, she reached for him. He looked down at her elegant fingers on the muscles of his forearm, then found himself holding his breath as she slowly slid them down to his hand.

Her fingers entwined with his and he lifted her hand to his mouth to press a kiss to it.

"I didn't know I was capable of that much jealousy," she admitted with a rueful twist of her lips into something that no one would ever call a smile. "I know there is nothing between you two. I even know that there never could be, that you're like brother and sister, but..." She took a shaky breath that was like a punch to his chest. "But it was so hard to remember any of that when you were—" She shook her head. "No. I don't want to relive it anymore, not with the crazy soundtrack from today still playing in my head." She moved closer, close enough now that he could feel the heat of her body all along his. "Help me make a new one, Smith."

All he wanted was to kiss her, to love her, but not just for those reasons.

"I've never wanted a woman more than I want you, but I want our lovemaking to be more than just a way for you to forget what happened today. I need us to be more than that, Valentina."

He saw the effect of his words laid bare on her face. He wasn't going to hold back anymore. He couldn't. Not when he'd come so close to losing her today.

"What—"

When she paused, Smith found it so damned difficult to let one of the most extraordinary women he'd ever met stumble on her question, but as much as he wanted to steamroll her into loving him the way he knew he loved her, he forced himself to wait.

Finally, she asked, "What do you want? What do you need?"

"You."

It was as simple as that. He suspected it always would be. From that first moment he'd met her, he'd been drawn to her. Making love with her had taken that sudden spark and magnified it until he'd become utterly consumed with her. Not just her body, not just her unbridled passion, but everything she was, inside and out.

"I want you, too."

Her words came so softly that he'd barely have been able to hear them if he hadn't been praying for them with every fiber of his soul.

For all the suffering that today's filming had caused, maybe it was exactly the turning point they both needed.

He slid the pad of his thumb across her full lower lip and she shuddered at his touch, the strong woman who always trembled so beautifully in his arms. "You already have me, Valentina. You know that. So tell me—" he paused to draw on his self-control so that he didn't give in to the almost overpowering urge to take before she had a chance to give "—what else do you want?"

"I want—"

She paused again, but this time when she looked into his eyes, he could see her strength, clear and present on her beautiful face. And the determination that was so much a part of her.

"I want to try. I haven't given you—*us*—a chance. I mean, I know I've taken a chance on sleeping with you," she said with a heated flush that had him wanting to pull her down to the floor to take her right then and there, "but I haven't let myself think that anything more could be possible." She looked incredibly contrite as she said, "I've been unfair to you. And I think," she said slowly, "to myself, too."

She was still holding his gaze straight on, and hot damn if that didn't do it for him just as much as her momentary lapse into softness did. Oh, yes, all the contours and shapes, the sharp edges and rounded curves, the fire and the ice...every last cell that made up Valentina Landon did it for him.

"Would you like to go out on a date with me?"

Joy at her question came so sharp and sweet he could all but taste it as he grinned at her. "There's nothing I'd like more."

But instead of grinning back, she said, "Nothing?" in a seductive voice that sent every last pint of blood rushing south.

"Well, now that you mention it," he said as she closed the final distance between them and pressed herself against him, "there might be one or two things."

Her mouth lifted up to his, and even as he tried to let her lead their sensual dance, he was lost to his need for her. There was no one but Valentina as whatever remnants from more than twenty years of women were completely erased from his consciousness as her tongue slid out over his lower lip to mimic the way he'd been touching her just minutes before. He sucked her tongue inside so that it tangled with his as her hands tugged at his shirt.

Buttons flew as she yanked the fabric open and shoved the cotton off his shoulders and onto the floor. Smith loved that no one who had met Valentina, not even her close friends, would recognize her right now. So much passion drove her that it floored him every single time they were intimate with each other.

And all of that passion was *his*.

"It should have been me today." She followed her words by pressing a kiss to the hollow just beneath his

Adam's apple. "I love my sister so much and what you two were doing wasn't even real and I still wanted to shove her off the bed and take her place beneath you."

Every spot her sister's mouth had been during filming, Valentina now covered with her lips, running kisses over his shoulders, and then his collarbones. She made hungry little sounds as she reclaimed him for herself and each one reverberated through him, from chest to groin.

Lord, if he was going to stay upright, he needed something to hold on to. Thank God her hips were right there, surprising him yet again with how full and round they were beneath his palms.

Valentina was a continual surprise—and pleasure— to him, from her passion and her unexpected softness, to her incredible intelligence and her boundless well of love for her sister. Life with her would never be boring. She would never tell him what he wanted to hear, would never spend a second massaging his ego because he was a wealthy superstar. It made him uncomfortable the way so many people kowtowed to him, but Valentina never had, and never would.

And she would please him every single second, whether she was stealing puzzle pieces from him…or stealing his heart every time he looked at her, kissed her, touched her, loved her.

The next thing he knew, she was pushing him down onto the couch. Satisfaction lit her eyes as she stared down at him. He was sprawled on the leather cushions, bare from the waist up, legs open from where she'd pushed him so that his throbbing desire for her was clearly evident in the wardrobe suit pants that he still wore.

One second she was moving away to lock the trailer door, the next she was pulling out the band that held her sleek ponytail in place as she came back toward him. Her black fitted jacket came off next, followed shortly by a silk camisole. The sight of her breasts rising up from sheer lace had his vision dimming enough that by the time it cleared again, she was standing in front of him in lingerie and heels.

A raw curse left his lips at the most beautiful sight he'd ever had the pleasure of witnessing.

Her mouth curved up at his crude language. "How'd you know that was exactly what I was hoping you'd say when you saw me wearing another one of your gifts?"

"You're the gift," he told her, meaning it so deeply he could hardly get the words out.

She seemed to wobble on her heels for a moment at the emotion in his voice. But then she was coming toward him and, as if in slow motion, she dropped to her knees between his legs. She didn't reach for his belt buckle, but simply pressed her mouth to his in a soft kiss that stole his breath, even as the sheer knowledge of what was coming had him almost losing it.

Sweet Lord, he was never going to survive this. They'd have to find someone to take over for him on the movie because he was going to die of pleasure tonight.

And he wouldn't have it any other way.

"I know there will be other actresses that you'll

have to kiss," she said when she took her mouth from his and pressed her palms flat over his pecs, "but the only woman I ever want you to think of is me." Her nails lightly scored his chest, down over his abs, which rippled beneath her touch as she marked him as hers.

"You *are* the only woman I'm thinking about," he swore.

From the first moment he'd touched her, she'd been all he wanted, all he desired, his only obsession. He couldn't deny the truth, didn't see the point in wasting any energy when there were so many better places to put it.

Not when winning Valentina's heart was the only thing that mattered anymore.

Instead of giving any indication that she'd heard him, she lowered her head and licked his chest. The tips of her soft hair flickered over his skin, teasing him just as unbearably as her tongue and teeth did to his sensitive skin. He couldn't hold back a groan of pleasure that mingled closely with frustration.

He was bigger, stronger. He could have her flat on her back and be inside of her in seconds. It would be so good, better than good. But he'd hurt her so badly today that for her to reclaim her power, she'd need to run their lovemaking from start to finish. And, damn it, since he couldn't give her the gift of not filming the sex scene, he'd at least make sure she had this. Still, he couldn't keep his hands from tangling in her silky hair as she roamed his skin with her lips and tongue and teeth.

Did she have any idea how sexy she was kneeling between his legs in the bra and thong and heels, as sensual in their private darkness as she was conservative in front of everyone else in daylight? Finally, she lifted her head from his stomach and licked her lips.

"That's much better," she murmured, more to herself than to him as she deftly unlaced his shoes and slid them off, along with his socks. He would have smiled at the sweetness of her comment if she hadn't reached for his belt buckle just then.

He sucked in a breath as her fingertips teased over his stomach while she smoothly slid the leather buckle open. It didn't seem to matter how many times they had each other, every time was a new beginning, a voyage of discovery that blew his mind apart all over again.

She held his gaze as she slowly pulled down his zipper. He was pretty sure he'd forgotten to breathe as he stared back into her beautiful hazel eyes, more green than brown, a color he knew he would always associate with passion. And then, she was tugging at his trousers and he was instinctively lifting his hips so that she could get them off. His boxers came off with them until he was sitting in front of her, naked and as hard as he'd ever been in his life.

Deep pleasure lit Valentina's eyes, her mouth a sensual curve as she watched his hard flesh bob and pulse in a silent plea for attention.

"Mine," she said in a soft voice, close enough to him that he could feel the warm rush of air over his skin as she spoke.

Another low groan sounded from his chest as she licked her lips again, and then—*oh, hell*—she was bending over and her tongue was on him, slicking a devastating path over his hard shaft. His fingers tangled tighter in her hair as he unconsciously pulled her down to take him deeper.

He thought he heard the sweet sound of her laughter, but then she was opening up and taking him inside and he was lost to everything but the heated pleasure she was giving him.

"Valentina."

Her name was a prayer. A plea. A benediction.

And a vow that he would give her just as much pleasure as she was so unselfishly giving him. Soon.

If he were a better man, a stronger one, he would have stopped her to make sure she was satisfied more than once before he even thought about himself. But the way Valentina so openly tasted him, the fact that she wasn't holding anything back from him as she hummed her pleasure at his loss of control, stripped him bare.

He'd had to be in control his whole life. For his family, for his mother, for his siblings, on movie sets and with the press. But with her he could let go of all of it.

And just *be*.

On a roar of pleasure that reverberated throughout the trailer, he gave himself entirely up to Valentina's mouth, her hands, the greedy little sounds she made as she used her hands and mouth to take him to the edge and then all the way over it.

When she sat back on her heels, licking her lips like a contented cat, Smith couldn't manage to do anything but stare down at her. Her hair was knotted from his hands, her lipstick was long gone, her skin was slightly damp, her cheeks flushed.

The words *I love you* were on the tip of his tongue, but even as far gone as he was after what she'd just done to him, he knew better than to tell her now. When he finally told her how he felt, he would make damn sure she didn't try to write his feelings off as driven by the heat they generated between the sheets.

Or on the couch, for that matter.

But even though he couldn't tell her tonight, he could show her. He knew she was afraid to hear the words he wanted to say, but he would make her listen in other ways, using his mouth, his hands, his body.

The same way she'd just made him listen with hers.

Twenty-Four

Valentina had never done anything so crazy, so wild…or so wonderful in her entire life.

She could still feel the rush of exhilaration in her veins from the way Smith had lost control beneath her hands and mouth. It had been perfect. And so sweet.

Shockingly so.

"Your turn now." Smith punctuated his words by wrapping his large hands around her waist and pulling her onto the couch. Before she knew what was happening, he'd reversed their positions and he was the one kneeling between her legs.

Feeling suddenly vulnerable, she knew she should make a joke or say something sexy. Instead, all that would come out was, "But I just had my turn."

His eyes, already so dark, went even closer to black as he put his hands on either side of her face and kissed her. His tongue slipped and slid against hers in a shockingly sensual rhythm, so much like what they'd just been doing when she'd been the one on her knees.

"In that case," he said in a low voice that reverberated up, then back down her spine, "it's *my* turn now, isn't it?"

All she could do was swallow. And maybe nod just a little bit so that he'd know what a good idea she thought it was.

Only, he didn't do anything more than stare at her, his dark gaze roving hungrily, possessively, over every inch of her skin exposed in the naughty lingerie he'd bought for her.

He was so tall that even on his knees, when he straightened, she had to look up at him. Even after his climax his erection had barely abated and now, as she used her legs to pull him so close that the sheer silk of her bra was brushing against his bare chest, his erection pressed against her, right where she was so desperate for more of him.

"Smith, I can't wait. Not tonight. I want you. I need you. *Now.*"

Yet again, she openly admitted just how much she wanted him.

Needed him.

His dark eyes flashed with pleasure and so much heat she lost her breath just as his mouth crashed into hers. And then his hands were cupping her hips and he was moving them so that she was lying beneath him on the couch, still in her thong and bra and heels.

As his mouth found her neck and she arched into the bite of his teeth on the sensitive skin just beneath her ear; as his fingers slid silk away; as he found protection, then moved inside of her in one hard thrust so that her gasp of pleasure joined his desperate groan; as her nails dug into his shoulders and her ankles crossed tightly across the small of his back while she urged him for even more—Valentina realized the foundation for her fears was disintegrating.

Because when they were loving each other like this, with no boundaries and even less control, he wasn't a movie star anymore, wasn't any part of the famous Smith Sullivan that millions of women fantasized about.

He was simply a man whom she couldn't stop falling for, deeper and deeper with every laugh, every hug, every kiss. And every one of the dark, heated looks he gave her, every stroke of his hand across her skin, was full of something she'd been afraid to let herself acknowledge.

"Valentina."

She opened her eyes to find Smith staring down at her, his beautiful face awash with pleasure and need and something she'd been trying so hard to pretend wasn't there.

Love.

And it was with the word resonating in her head and Smith's hands slipping through to hold hers on either side of her head that the first tremors of release tore through her.

"You're mine," he said. And she was.

Entirely his.

For as long as he wanted her, she would be his, because he had come to mean more—so much more—to her than she had ever thought he would.

And then there were no more thoughts, no more fears, no more words. Just the potent and oh-so-sweet pleasure of Smith holding her so tight, and thrusting so deep, that when her climax came with enough force to take her completely under, she let herself go, finally trusting Smith with not only her body...but, for the very first time, with a piece of her heart, too.

A half hour later, when their clothes were back on and their stomachs rumbling, Smith looked at her with clear disbelief in his eyes.

"*This* is where you're taking me for our first real date?"

Kids rushed in and out of the dingy building followed by parents who were too harried to notice the star in their midst.

Valentina flushed. "Tatiana and I sort of have this thing about miniature golf. It started when we were kids and we never stopped. Plus, no one ever seems to care who she is when we're here, so I thought—"

She never got a chance to finish her awkward explanation, because Smith's grin was a mile wide. "You thought exactly right."

And then he was pulling her inside with at least as much excitement as the eight-year-olds who were hopped up on Slushies and Sno-Cones. Her stomach growled at the smell of hot dogs and French fries and she'd been beyond pleased when Smith ordered the fast-food meal-deal for both of them. Junk food was just what the doctor ordered after the long day they'd both had.

The kid working the register was doing okay until it finally hit him who was standing in front of him. "Oh, man, you're Smith Sullivan."

"Nice to meet you, Mark," Smith said, making it a point to look at the kid's name tag on his bright blue shirt.

"My friends are going to freak out when they hear you're here! The best movie we saw last year was *Forces of Destruction.*"

Mark was reaching for his phone when Smith said, "Can I ask you for a special favor?"

The kid nodded. "Sure. Anything, dude."

Smith lowered his voice and acted as if she couldn't hear him say, "I'm on a pretty important first date and I'm really afraid of blowing it with her. I was hoping to keep things low-key tonight so I could make a good impression."

The kid's eyes were huge as he finally registered Valentina standing next to Smith at the counter. After a few seconds of studying her as if she was a bug under a microscope, he leaned toward Smith and said in a stage whisper, "Dude, she's hot."

In the same voice, Smith said, "I know. Seriously hot." Buddies now, he said, "So are we cool?"

"Sure," the boy said. "No problem."

"Thanks. And if you want to come by the set sometime, why don't you give me your number and I'll call you to set it up."

"Seriously?" The kid scrawled his number on a napkin, then said, "I'll make sure no one bothers you tonight."

After Smith grabbed their food and they sat down, despite how hungry Valentina was, she knew she wouldn't be able to eat a thing. Not yet.

"There's not one single thing you could do to blow our first date."

Smith didn't reach for his food, either. "You sure about that?"

The look in his eyes suddenly reminded her of the way he'd gazed at her when they'd been making love—as though he couldn't imagine living without her.

Maybe before tonight she would have lied to him, would have told him that she was fine. But after what they'd shared with each other, after how close she felt to him, she had to tell him the truth.

"No, I'm not completely sure, but—" she paused and stared into his eyes "—I want to be. So, so badly."

She knew it wasn't what he wanted, that it wasn't nearly enough. It wasn't enough for her, either. But he simply picked up the mustard and ketchup and made two straight yellow and red lines along either side of her hot dog. It was just the way she liked it and he must have been paying attention when, on rare occasions, she indulged in a hot dog from the craft services table.

As she took it from him, she had to wonder how he could possibly have had a chance to notice the way she liked her hot dogs? But then, was that really such a stretch from his noticing her at all in the first place?

Smith grabbed one of her fries and popped it into his mouth. "So, what are the stakes for this little game?"

She raised an eyebrow. "You want to turn a friendly game of miniature golf into a bet?"

"I'm a guy. It's what we do," he said, his dark eyes sizzling with wicked intent.

She rolled her eyes. "At least you recognize how ridiculous you are, acting so competitive about a fun game."

"Do you really mean to tell me you and Tatiana aren't the least bit competitive with each other? Or that you haven't tried to rig the windmill hole to close at least once before her ball could get in?"

She laughed at his far-too-insightful question. "Well, maybe there was that one time she 'accidentally' slipped on a ball in front of my shot that was sure to be a winning hole in one."

He shook his head. "Little sisters are a pain in the butt, aren't they? But then again, I'm sure you got her back for that, didn't you?"

She gave him her most innocent look, before saying, "Who knew putting Vaseline on a golf ball would make it nearly impossible to hit straight?"

"Now that I know how much the win means to you," he said through his laughter, "I may have to do a full body search for any hidden jars of Vaseline before we start playing."

Valentina was struck yet again that it didn't matter where they were—on the set, in a conference room, in his living room doing a puzzle or sitting in the middle of a golf 'n' games arcade that hadn't been updated, or cleaned, since the early seventies—she wanted him.

And she liked him very, very much.

"If I win," he said in a low voice that sent shivers running over her already too-sensitive skin, "you have to hold my hand for the rest of the night."

Tatiana's advice from earlier that day came fast and furious at Valentina: *What if you gave Smith a chance to love you the way you deserve to be loved? Don't you think there's a chance that he could be up to the challenge? And don't you think you could be up to whatever challenges come, too?*

So even though Valentina's hand was starting to shake on her lap beneath the sticky Formica tabletop, she made herself raise it. With her heart hammering so hard she wouldn't have been surprised to see it actually pop through her ribs and skin, she reached across the table for his hand.

Valentina thought she heard Smith's breath catch as she slowly slid her palm against his, before interlacing their fingers.

The heat of his touch immediately melted the ice that was trying to close her heart back in.

"You don't need to win a bet to have that."

After their game of miniature golf had ended in a perfect tie, they decided to head home. Valentina and Smith walked into her rental house hand in hand and found Tatiana lying on the couch reading a book.

She smiled at them over the top of her paperback. "Are Marcus and Nicola spending the night at your house again, Smith?"

He grinned back at her. "Nope."

Valentina had never had a man stay over before.

She'd told herself it was because she hadn't wanted to make her sister feel uncomfortable. But the truth was, she'd never wanted to give away enough of herself to a man in exchange for the intimacy of waking up together.

Now, for the first time, she wanted to give that to Smith.

"You don't mind if my boyfriend stays over, do you, T.?"

At the word *boyfriend,* Tatiana grinned widely and said, "Nope, I'll just make sure I've got my earplugs handy."

Smiling at her sister's sassy response, Valentina was plugging her phone into its charger when she realized she had a message waiting from George, one that must have been there all afternoon. Even though she wanted nothing more than to get into bed with Smith, she couldn't ignore a decade of work ethic that had her dialing her voice mail and listening to what he had to say.

When she put down the phone, her hands were shaking. She looked at the two people who meant the most to her, and was glad they were both there to hear her news.

"George says there's a bidding war going on for my screenplay." She wondered how her voice could sound so calm, when her insides were doing cartwheels. "A big one. And he said he thinks I'm going to be really happy with the studio that's in the clear lead."

"Oh, my God!" Tatiana jumped up off the couch and hugged her.

Smith put his hand on her chin and pulled her face up to his so that he could say, "Congratulations, Valentina," before kissing her, before grinning even wider and teasing, "If only I'd had a chance to see your screenplay…"

She laughed as she danced around the room with her sister, pulling him in so they were a wiggling, happy threesome. "I promise you'll be the first person to see the next one."

Tatiana found a bottle of champagne, and after they'd all toasted and finished a glass, it was the nicest, most natural thing in the world to brush her teeth with Smith standing by her side at the sink, to strip the clothes from each other, then slip between the sheets together.

Valentina had no doubt her sister would need the earplugs on other nights, but for tonight, Smith simply wrapped his arms around her and held her tight.

And she held him right back.

Twenty-Five

By the time Smith and Valentina made it into the kitchen for breakfast the next morning, Tatiana was already up and drinking a cup of coffee, a half-eaten bowl of oatmeal on the table in front of her. She smiled at them both when Smith said, "Good morning," but when Valentina reached into the cupboard to grab two mugs, Tatiana mouthed to him, *We need to talk.*

"Hey, Val," she said, "remember the earrings I loaned you last week? The ones with the rubies in them? I've looked everywhere and can't find them. Would you mind checking to see if they're in your bedroom?"

As soon as Valentina left the kitchen, Tatiana reached under the table and plopped a printout from the internet into Smith's hand. "Look at this."

The page showed one of the "romantic" staged pictures of him and Tatiana that had been shot the week before to promote the movie while they were in character as Graham and Jo…and then another, slightly fuzzy picture of Smith and Valentina holding hands last night at the arcade. The headline between the photos shouted: Smith Sullivan Introduces Gorgeous Costar to Pleasure While Having Secret Affair with Older Sister! Details About Movie Star's Torrid Love Triangle Inside.

The paper crumpled in Smith's hands as Tatiana said, "I don't want Val to see this. She'll freak out." Both of them knew what a major understatement that was. "But if it's already in this online magazine, that means every major entertainment show and blog is bound to pick up the story by this afternoon. I just don't know how we can keep her from seeing it."

Twenty-four hours, thought Smith. Had that really been too much to ask?

Yes, since last night, it felt as if they'd come a long way from the point at which he and Tatiana had finished filming the sex scene. But was it far enough for Valentina to trust that they could get past this kind of crap, especially with the echo of her saying, *I can't imagine anything worse than being in the spotlight,* ringing in his ears?

Or would this headline, along with a picture of the two of them from the very first time they'd held hands in public, only confirm every single one of her fears about how hard her life would be with him?

"I know how much Val cares about you," Tatiana said as she put her hand on his arm in what he knew was supposed to be a reassuring manner. "I mean, she hates stuff like this, but you guys are so great together."

Valentina was coming back into the kitchen with the earrings in her hand, saying, "Sorry, I thought I gave them back to y—" when she looked between the two of them and frowned. "What's wrong?"

There was no point in pretending it hadn't happened, or trying to hold off the truth any longer. Smith held out the paper to her. "This."

He slid his hand into Valentina's as she read the article, all the way through the part about how "confidential sources" said not only couldn't he keep his hands off Tatiana, but he was also having double the fun with the older sister who managed the business side of her career.

Tatiana's voice shook as she said, "I know we can't control this kind of stuff, but it's not fair if it hurts you, Val, not when you haven't signed up for this life like we have."

Fair. Smith knew there wasn't much that was fair about Hollywood, or the world that revolved around it.

"But," Tatiana added, "once everyone realizes the two of you are actually together and that Smith and I are just working on this movie, I'm sure this will all blow over and everything will be okay."

Maybe Tatiana was right about that, Smith thought, but even if she was, it meant the spotlight would turn entirely on Valentina.

Valentina hadn't yet said a word, and that was what worried him most of all. Because if this had just been a picture of him and Tatiana, he knew she wouldn't have been thrilled about the false story, and she would have been trying to comfort her sister the way she normally did.

Smith had spent so long trying to convince himself that he had control over this crazy circus life, that even as he could feel it all crumbling down around him, he told Valentina, "We make up stories to tell to the world in movies and TV shows and plays and books. These people are doing the same thing."

The big difference, of course, was that the characters in his movies were pretend, whereas the photographers and blogs were playing with real lives. His life and Tatiana's had been fair game for a while now.

Now, Valentina's was, too. Because of him.

He'd known that once she'd agreed to be with him, at some point the press would want to know more about her. But he hadn't thought it would come this soon.

Or be anywhere near this ugly.

Finally, Valentina spoke, her voice hoarse with the barely restrained fury that was choking them all. "I knew it would be hard. I knew this would happen, even though it all seemed like everything was starting to go so well, and things were so easy and perfect this morning with the three of us having breakfast together. I knew better, knew I didn't want—"

She stopped abruptly in the middle of her sentence and both he and Tatiana held their breath as she put down the paper. When Valentina finally looked up at him, Smith was struck by the way the beautiful green and brown of her eyes were in sharp relief to her starkly pale face.

And then, she reached for him, her hands even colder than they'd been that night when they'd boarded his yacht to head to Alcatraz. His heart stopped beating in his chest as he waited for her to tell him she was done. That she couldn't do this. That it was over.

She took a deep breath. And then another. Finally, she said, "I meant it when I said I'd try. I'm not looking forward to more of this, but it's one thing to say I want to try. It's another to know that I can keep trying when everything's not perfect and sunshine and rainbows."

Relief swamped him as he immediately dragged her into his arms and held her so tightly that only later would he realize he could have bruised her ribs. Her words meant even more with Tatiana there to witness them. Because, finally, she wasn't trying to hide them anymore.

Was it possible, Smith wondered, that the fake story might end up being a blessing, rather than a curse?

Smith soon found out that he'd never been so wrong about anything in his life. The paparazzi lying in wait for the three of them on the sidewalk outside Valentina and Tatiana's house were anything but a blessing.

Already late heading to set, having ignored the last five texts that had come in from his assistant director,

Smith led them out the front door of the house. The flashes from cameras went off in their faces while the paparazzi got big money shots of the three of them. While it was happening, a half dozen images flashed in Smith's mind.

Valentina with fire in her eyes as she faced him down in a way few other people ever had when she warned him to stay away from her sister.

The sweet joy—and longing—on her face when she'd congratulated Marcus and Nicola on their engagement.

Holding her in his arms in front of the fire while they talked about their families, and the pain of losing a parent.

The shocking heat of their first kiss in his office, and then again at Alcatraz, out on the rocks beneath a full moon.

Her tears falling as they filmed another emotional scene from his movie.

And then, the way she'd bravely faced him and told him she wanted to try, that she was willing to see if they could make things work despite his career and her aversion to ever having to be in the spotlight with him.

Smith had fifteen years of experience at dealing calmly with this kind of situation. A week before, he might have bragged that he could have taught a class on it to new actors. Hell, just minutes ago he'd been telling Valentina that they should just look at it as being similar to the kind of make-believe they created with their movies and stories.

But as he tried to shield Valentina from the paparazzi, as he told them again and again to stop and they didn't, and as he heard one of the photographers tell another, "Talk about living the dream by banging two hot sisters," all he could think was, *She's going to leave me now. She's going to leave me now. She's going to leave me now,* until the words blurred together inside his head into something that resembled the hard shape of a fist.

Smith's fist crashed hard into one of the cameras first, before crashing even harder into the jaw of the man holding the camera.

Twenty-Six

Oh, God, Valentina thought as she sat in the passenger seat of Smith's car with Tatiana in the backseat, *I don't want this life. I've never wanted this life.*

Smith gunned the engine and flew down the street, away from the paparazzi who were still taking pictures. Valentina's mind felt at once totally full, yet completely empty. She didn't know what to think, didn't know how to deal with the strange sense of satisfaction over watching him defend her and her sister that was combined with her fear that he'd get hurt in the scuffle. Not to mention the fallout that was sure to come from his complete loss of control.

In the backseat, Tatiana had immediately called the film's head publicist so that they could get started on damage control. But Valentina couldn't even begin to concentrate on what her sister was saying.

She couldn't look away from Smith, from the way his knuckles were bruised and bloody where he'd come in contact with the edge of a camera…

and then the bones of another man's jaw. His own jaw was clenched tight, and she could feel the fury, the frustration, pouring off him.

"Are you okay?"

Her voice sounded strange to her own ears— strange enough that when Smith didn't answer, she thought maybe she hadn't actually said the words aloud.

She tried again. "Your hand. It's bleeding. Are you okay?" But this time, even though she was sure she'd said it out loud, he still didn't answer. "Smith?"

He hit the brakes hard at a red light, and when he turned to her, what she saw in his eyes had her breath catching in her throat.

"You're right," he said, his voice even deeper than usual. And raw. So raw.

Whatever it was she was right about, she didn't want him to say it. She just wanted everything to—

"I'm no good for you. My life is no good for you."

Oh, God. She'd already thought things were bad, but this—*this*—was a thousand times worse.

Smith had been sure from the start. Sure that he wanted her. Sure that she wanted him. And he'd been unfailingly sure that they could figure out how to make things work when all signs pointed in the opposite direction.

She was so stunned and so deeply wounded by his declaration that she felt frozen in stone, only her sister's hand on her shoulder thawing a tiny part of her.

How badly she wished she could tell him he was wrong, and that she could handle this life. But how could she when she'd been caught in what felt like an impossible web? One made out of her beliefs that she was not, in fact, capable of dealing with the spotlight—along with intertwining threads of a ravenously hungry media and paparazzi who would always be intent on shining that light over whomever Smith chose to be with.

And if she couldn't say it, if she couldn't get out the words to make everything better, what then?

Did it mean they were over?

Just the thought of it had her stomach twisting, her chest clenching, her breath faltering. What she'd felt after seeing the horrible story about the three of them, or even when the paparazzi had been taking pictures of her, was nothing compared to actually losing Smith.

Smith pulled into the cast and crew parking lot and Tatiana squeezed her shoulder once, then said, "I'll let everyone know you're both coming soon," before getting out of the car.

Valentina looked at Smith's hand again, saw the dried blood on it and wished she knew what to say. What to do. She always had before, had been so sure about what to go for, what to avoid. Until now. Until Smith had come into her life and everything she'd believed, everything she'd been so damn sure about, had twisted and turned and flipped around until the only thing she knew anymore was how much she wanted him, how much she enjoyed being with him, how much she *needed* him.

But even though she had no idea what to say or do

or feel anymore, she knew one thing: they couldn't leave the car like this. Couldn't go about their day on set with, *You're right, I'm no good for you,* ringing in both their ears on repeat.

But just as she was about to finally reply, she saw the flashes coming from the sidewalk just beyond the set. Of course the paparazzi had come. She'd just been too shell-shocked by everything that had already happened this morning to think ahead.

Smith saw them at the same moment and reached for the door handle to get out of the car and away from the cameras when Valentina put her hand on his arm.

"Smith."

Her voice caught on his name, turning one syllable to two.

When he turned back to face her, his expression as bleak as she knew hers had to be, she had to say something. Anything. If only so he'd know that she wasn't ready to give up yet, and that she still wanted to see if they could find a way to make their happily-ever-after work out.

She opened her mouth to try to find the words, but fear had them clogging in her throat.

The faint hope that had flared in his eyes for a brief moment burned out.

Finally, he was the one who spoke. "We need to get away from the cameras."

Knowing he was right, she went with him in silence from the car to the set, which had been beefed up with extra security. Anything she could have said to him was swallowed up by the concern of the cast and crew who had become like family to them both. No one made a big deal out of Smith and Valentina being together, only about the indignity of the paparazzi cramming its way into their private business.

Business that, due to the extreme expense of shooting a movie on location, had to go forward as usual.

For the next six horribly tense hours, everyone did their damnedest to do their job, and do it well. And when Valentina watched the married camera operator and lighting designer give each other a quick kiss between takes, her chest clenched tight at their easy affection.

What would it have been like to be able to kiss Smith without worrying about what people would say?

But as the cameras started rolling again, Valentina knew that hadn't really been the problem. After all, she'd never cared what anyone thought about her.

She'd been a coward about trusting their relationship to keep moving forward, especially past filming when they both moved on to other projects. She'd tried to back up that cowardice by telling herself that things with Smith had come from so far out of the blue and had moved too fast that she hadn't come into this project looking for a man that she would fall in l—

"Cut!"

When Valentina looked at Smith in surprise, and realized he was holding his phone to his ear, she froze again, thinking it must have to do with the fallout from this morning. But that wouldn't explain the quick flash of joy that moved across his face. And then she saw the name on his lips—*Sophie*—and she knew.

His sister was having her twins.

She was already up out of her seat as he headed toward her. "I know I'm not family," she said, "but—"

"Come be happy with me, Valentina."

God, yes, please. She wanted so badly to share in his joy. He called out for everyone to take the rest of the day off, and then they were racing each other to his car. The cameras started flashing again as soon as the two of them came into view, but even though Valentina's gut twisted again, and she could see a muscle in Smith's jaw jumping, she did her best to ignore the paparazzi.

She loved babies. The way they smelled. Their innocence. Their soft skin. Even the way they scrunched up their little faces when they were furious at the world for keeping them hungry or wet or sleepy.

She still remembered the day Tatiana was born, the immediate love she'd felt for her baby sister. Her mother had let her hold the newborn within minutes of the birth, and when her sister had looked up at her with her big blue eyes, Valentina had tumbled heartfirst into a love so strong it had shaped her entire life.

"My mother said she's been having contractions for most of the morning and that they're close enough now for all of us to come."

God, she thought as despair rolled through her, she loved the sound of his voice. It was going to be so hard not to hear it every day…especially the way he whispered her name in her ear with such passion as he came into her.

Still, she needed to try to keep it together right now. At least until Sophie had her babies.

"Did Mary say how Sophie was doing?" Valentina couldn't help but worry that the sweetest, softest Sullivan was dealing with something more difficult than she could bear. Especially when she knew that Smith and Sophie shared a special closeness. "Is she in a lot of pain?"

"Sophie is far tougher than she looks," he told her, but Valentina could see how worried he was for his younger sister. "For all her big talk, Lori's the pussycat. Sophie can hold her own."

She could hear the tension in his voice, tension that was only partially due to his concerns over how Sophie was doing.

They'd been so close that morning…and now?

Valentina took a breath that shook through her, hard enough that Smith turned his intense gaze to her for a moment. It hurt too bad to think about what had happened to them between last night and this afternoon.

Somehow she managed to think clearly enough to ask him, "Tell me about Sophie and her husband. How did they meet?"

Smith paused for a long moment before answering. "Jake is a family friend. As far back as I can remember, he was always in the house. Sophie fell in love with him when she was just a little girl."

When he said the word *love,* for a moment, Valentina felt as if she was going to shatter.

Especially when he said, "They were so different, Valentina. Too different, it seemed," and his smile fell away. "She's a librarian. He owns pubs. She's quiet, calm. He's loud, came from a rough background, is covered in tattoos."

Valentina's throat was so tight she could hardly get words out. "But they made it work."

Smith pulled into the hospital parking lot and turned his dark gaze to her. "He loves her just as much as she loves him. So, yeah, they make it work."

Stepping into the waiting room was like walking into a Sullivan family party. All of Smith's brothers and his sister were there, ready and excited to meet two new additions, hopefully tonight.

The only thing that could possibly dim their happiness was the concern he could see etched on all their faces. Everyone was worried about him. Because he'd never even come close to punching out a photographer before.

Marcus and Nicola greeted them first with hugs. Smith hadn't been too sure about them as a couple the first time he saw them together. In fact, he'd warned his brother away from getting too close to a pop star because he hadn't thought her lifestyle would suit the most low-key and serious of all his brothers. But he'd been wrong. They were perfect together. Just like Sophie and Jake were, despite his reservations when he'd heard that Jake had gotten Sophie pregnant after a one-night stand.

Smith knew he and Valentina had been perfect together, too. Until his glittering world had come crashing down onto them and blown their new, too-fragile connection to pieces.

When Nicola moved to hug Valentina, Marcus shot Smith a look that was easy to read.

What the hell is happening to you?

Smith shook his head. He didn't want to talk about it now, didn't want to let all the crap that came with his fame overshadow one of the biggest, most important moments for their family. He knew his brothers would have happily hunted down the paparazzi and kicked their asses to protect him, that they hated not being able to defend one of their own. But he also knew they would continue to respect his wishes that they not engage, or get themselves into trouble on his behalf. He was the one who had chosen this career, not them.

Damn it, it was just the reason why he needed to let Valentina go. He was trying so hard to do what was right for her…even as he knew that nothing had ever felt so wrong.

Ryan's fiancée, Vicki, and his sister Lori greeted Valentina as if she was an old friend. Smith was grateful to them all so much for making her laugh, especially after the way her voice had broken in the car that morning when she'd said his name.

But then, another woman in labor was pushed past them in a wheelchair, moaning in pain as she gripped her stomach, and suddenly all Smith could think of was Sophie.

He tried to be an honest man, with others and himself, but until this moment he hadn't really wanted to think too hard about the reality—and the risks—of Sophie giving birth to twins. And even though she'd insisted to him a hundred times that she was the healthiest pregnant woman on the planet, he found himself spinning off into worries he could no longer control.

Damn it, why hadn't he seen Jake making his move on his sister? Maybe then he could have stopped all of this from happening and she wouldn't now be in the hospital where anything could go—

"Smith."

He hadn't seen Valentina move in front of him and was surprised to hear her say, "I think this is the perfect time to use your infamous movie-star charm to convince a nurse to let you check on Sophie so that you can see for yourself that everything is going to be fine."

Her calm broke through the fog clogging his brain like the beam from a lighthouse. It was another reason why they were a perfect match: if he ever started to go off the rails—which was pretty damn easy to do in his line of work—he could count on Valentina to lovingly, but firmly, bring him back to center. He'd seen her do the very same thing at least a dozen times with her sister during filming, so in tune with Tatiana that she always honed in on just when her sister needed her most.

How could he let her go? Even if it was the right thing to do for her? Even if she'd have a better life without him?

The flash of a camera came through the waiting room's glass door. A split second later, Valentina was saying, in a voice laced with fury, "You all need to stay here for Sophie. I'll handle this."

"This isn't okay."

Valentina walked right up to the men and women holding the cameras. They had obviously been tipped off as to where she and Smith were going when they left the set. Or maybe, she thought, they'd gotten here first and had been lying in wait for the perfect chance to take pictures of the whole family when they finally emerged into the more public area of the hospital. The hows didn't really matter, though, not when the only thing that mattered was that they leave.

"I know he's a star, that his picture sells papers and advertisements, but can't you at least give him this? Just a few hours to be alone with his family?"

The cameras kept clicking as she spoke and she knew she was feeling just what Smith had that morning on her doorstep. That she'd do anything she had to if only she could get them to leave.

"Please." She hadn't had the words earlier when Smith had needed them from her, wasn't sure she had it in her to sacrifice her privacy, or to sign up for the circus that would always be his life. Now, even though it was too little, too late, nothing could stop her from saying, "Tell me what you want so that you'll leave the Sullivan family alone today. Tell me and I'll do whatever I can to make sure you have it."

She didn't even have time to take her next breath before the first question came. "Is it true that Smith has been dating both you and your sister secretly?"

"No."

"Then who is he really with?"

"Me. Just me."

"How long have you been with Smith?"

"Four weeks."

"Were you dating in secret?"

"Yes."

"Did your sister know?"

"No."

"Does he love you?"

She shook her head, knowing tears were going to start falling soon. "I don't know."

"Are you in love with him?"

Tears began to fall down her cheeks, one after the other. "Yes, I love him."

And with that, she knew she'd given them exactly what they wanted. A clear shot of the endless depth of her love for Smith…and the fear and uncertainty that came right alongside it.

"Now, please," she asked them, "go."

Amazingly, they did, but she still stood right where she was to make sure they didn't change their minds at the last second. When she finally turned around, she walked right into a hard chest.

"Smith?"

"I don't deserve you."

He cupped her face in his hands and looked down at her, his eyes blazing with dark, intense heat, and she realized he must have seen and heard everything.

"I know you deserve more than this," he told her. "You deserve better than to be thrust into my crazy life, but I'm too much of a selfish son of a bitch to let you go."

His mouth came down on hers, crushing her lips in a kiss that held nothing back. And just like every one of their kisses that had come before, she couldn't hold anything back from him, either.

"I love you, Valentina. I love that you're here with my family. And someday I can't wait to remind you how stunned you looked that day I told you I loved you while we were standing in a hospital waiting room, surrounded by bright fluorescent lights and cheap blue plastic chairs."

"Smith Sullivan?" a middle-aged nurse called. "I'm ready to take you back to see your sister now."

He gave her one more breath-stealing kiss and then he was heading into the maternity ward to make sure his sister was okay.

The swinging doors had barely closed behind Smith and the maternity nurse when Lori moved to Valentina's side.

"I knew it."

Valentina still felt so stunned, so overwhelmed, by what Smith had told her not just once but three times in a row, and by what she'd told the photographers—*Yes, I love him*—that she couldn't have made her lips form a response to his sister for the life of her. Smith's brothers and their significant others weren't nearly as overt, but she could tell they were all paying rapt attention to the way things would play out from here.

But for all of Lori's energy and enthusiasm, she clearly wasn't without empathy, because she linked her arm through Valentina's and said, "Anywhere I find myself waiting for something important, I check to see if there's a coffee machine, and if there is I make sure to buy a cup. Kind of a little superstition, I guess. Want one?"

A minute later, Valentina was holding a cup of truly disgusting-looking coffee. Looking down at the watery sludge, then back at Lori, she said, "Thank you."

Smith's sister smiled at her. As beautiful as Smith was, each member of his family reflected a different aspect of that beauty. Lori's beauty, however, was so stunning that Valentina had to wonder if she'd ever had a difficult time moving past her looks the way Valentina's sister and mother had.

Suddenly noticing how tired Lori looked and that she was wearing tights, a sparkly skirt and ballroom dance shoes, Valentina asked, "Would you mind if we sat down for a few minutes?"

As Lori gratefully sank onto one of the chairs, Valentina thought she saw more than tiredness on her pretty face. There was sadness there, too, all but rippling outward to Valentina as Lori momentarily dropped her perky cover. For all that she was reeling from Smith's declaration a few minutes ago, Valentina found herself wanting to reach out to Lori.

"Is everything okay?"

Lori's eyes widened with surprise and for a moment it looked as if her face might crumple. But then she was shaking her head and saying, "I'm just thinking about Sophie. You know, the whole twin connection and her pain is my pain, and all that."

Valentina didn't doubt that Lori was, in fact, very concerned about Sophie's well-being...but she also didn't fully believe what Smith's sister had just said.

Only, before she could let Lori know that she was happy to listen anywhere, anytime, if she had something she wanted to talk about, Lori sipped at her coffee and made a face.

"My God, I think this just might be the worst machine-dispensed coffee I've ever had." A beat later, she was turning her attention back to Valentina.

"Smith is the most driven of all of us," Lori told her, and Valentina knew how extraordinary a statement that was, considering how successful each and every one of the Sullivans was. "I used to think that he was waiting to hit a certain stage of his career before he gave his personal life the same priority. But now I know that wasn't it."

Lori smiled at her with such open affection that Valentina felt the tightness in her chest start to fade.

"He was simply waiting for the right woman." She squeezed Valentina's hand. "I'm so glad he's found you."

* * *

Smith found Sophie and Jake bracing for a contraction when he walked into their room wearing the scrubs the nurse had given him. His heart stopped for a moment as he saw his elegant and soft-spoken sister gritting her teeth and groaning low and long as the pain hit her. Her husband had one hand in hers, the other brushing back the damp hair from her forehead as he whispered encouraging words into her ear.

His mother put her arm around him and said in a low voice, "The anesthesiologist has just been in. Her pain should be lessening soon."

Smith could barely swallow past the lump in his throat. He couldn't stand to see his baby sister in pain, even if giving birth was supposed to be the most natural thing in the world. Yes, he and Tatiana had played this out on-screen, but pretending to be in labor was very, very different from actually going through it.

Finally, when the contraction finished having its way with her, Sophie looked up through eyes blurred with pain and gave him a weak smile.

"Smith. You're here."

He quickly moved to the open seat at her other side. "Of course I am, sweetheart." He pressed a kiss to her cheek, and took her hand in his.

Seven months ago, the four of them—Sophie, Jake, his mother and Smith—had been in another hospital room together. He'd flown in from Australia not just to make sure his sister had come through her emergency surgery in one piece, but also to give a piece of his mind to the man he'd called a friend. The man Smith believed had betrayed them all by seducing his sister.

It hadn't taken him long, fortunately, to accept the love between Sophie and Jake, and to understand just how long in coming it had been. His mother, it turned out, had always seen it, but then again, when had she ever missed one single thing about any of them? And, of course, Mary Sullivan was the first one Smith had confessed his own feelings to. Because he'd known she'd understand and support him, no matter whom he loved, or how difficult it would be to convince that one precious woman to love him back.

Yes, I love him, Valentina had said. And there had never been sweeter words spoken, or ones that touched his heart so deeply. And even if the first time he heard her say those words had been to a bunch of paparazzi, instead of directly to him, he wouldn't ever want her to take them back.

"How is Valentina?" Sophie asked him as if she could read his mind. She grinned before he could reply and said, "You knew Lori would tell me about the two of you."

"Amazing," he told his sister as he thought of the way Valentina had faced the paparazzi and sacrificed herself to their spotlight—for him and for his family—without fear, without hesitation. "She's absolutely amazing."

"Oh, Smith, I'm so h—"

Her words were cut off by another contraction. Her hand clamped down on his so hard he heard his joints crack at the force of her small, strong fingers wrapped around his much bigger fingers.

Every last ounce of Jake's concentration was on his wife, and soothing her pain, even though it was clear to Smith that he was barely holding on to his own control. If Smith had any final reservations about his friend's love for his sister, they were all dispelled as he witnessed Jake's utter devotion to Sophie.

When the contraction finally passed, and her grip had loosened the slightest bit, she gave them both a watery smile. "I think that one was a little better."

"You're doing so great, sweetheart," Smith told her, his voice thick with emotion. "I'm so proud of you."

She smiled at him, such a pure sweet smile full of love, and in that moment she was again the quiet little girl he'd always taken special care of, making sure that his louder brothers and sister didn't run roughshod over her.

But, just as he'd said to Valentina, Sophie was a heck of a lot tougher than people gave her credit for. Tough enough to withstand the pain of yet another contraction as it hit her like a Mack truck.

Smith turned to meet his mother's eyes, and even though he knew she didn't like seeing her daughter in pain any more than the rest of them, it was clear where Sophie had gotten her strength from. Mary Sullivan looked delicate, and was just as beautiful now as she'd been in her modeling days...but they'd all learned their strength from her.

Looking back at his sister, Smith saw that Sophie's

head was buried in the crook of Jake's shoulder as she worked to get her breath back between contractions. Smith would always be there for her, but now he finally realized she didn't need him to protect her from the world anymore.

She had Jake. And Smith knew with utter certainty that her husband would never let any of them down. Especially not the woman who meant absolutely everything to him.

With another kiss to her cheek, Smith said, "I love you, Soph. And I can't wait to meet your babies." He silently passed on his trust, and faith, to Jake, who accepted it with a nod.

Smith slipped his fingers from hers and left his sister with the two people he trusted most with her. Sophie had found the forever love that she'd been looking for.

And so had he.

Twenty-Seven

Valentina was sitting with Lori in the waiting room when Smith emerged from Sophie's room. Both of them immediately jumped up as Lori asked, "How is she?"

Smith smiled. "She's great. Better than great. The contractions are pretty rough," he said as he flexed his hand to try to get the bones back in the right position, "but I don't think it will be long now."

Chase's wife, Chloe, was holding on to her baby daughter in the waiting room, clearly close enough to her own birth experience to sympathize. "God, I swear I can feel her pain even from here."

Baby Emma chose that moment to reach out and grab Heather's ponytail with a happy giggle. Everyone laughed along with the baby, who looked around at her big family with glee.

Zach's fiancée took the baby when Emma reached out for her and together Heather and Zach pressed kisses to each of her soft cheeks so that she giggled even louder as she really got a good hold on Heather's ponytail.

But even though Smith absolutely adored his little niece, he couldn't take his eyes off Valentina. Every moment he'd been with Sophie and Jake, he'd been thinking of her. Now, even with his entire family surrounding them, it was as if they were the only two people in the room.

For the first time in his entire life, he was so overcome with love he simply couldn't get any other part of his body to work, save his heart, which beat only for her.

"Do you feel better now?"

"Yes," he said, both for the knowledge that Sophie was in good hands...and for the very, very sweet knowledge that Valentina loved him.

Conversation flowed around them, but Smith was happy just holding Valentina in his arms. She was quiet and warm against him. A short while later, his mother burst out of the double doors with the biggest smile he'd ever seen on her face.

"She did it!" Her eyes overflowed with happy tears. "Oh, they're so beautiful. Sophie and Jake can't wait for all of you to meet their little girl and boy."

Mary Sullivan was one of the most even-keeled women on the planet. She'd had to be to deal with eight rambunctious children, but for the first time ever she almost seemed unable to pull herself back together.

Marcus and Lori were standing close to their mom

and they flanked her on either side as she said, "They named their daughter Jackie, after Jack."

Smith felt his own eyes go damp at the tribute to his father, and was glad when Valentina moved even closer to him. This moment wouldn't be nearly as good—or anywhere as complete—without her there to share it with him.

"And they named their son..." Mary looked at Smith and smiled through her happy tears. "They named him after you, Smith."

Jesus. He'd never thought how much something like that would mean to him, but now he knew.

It meant the world.

"Oh, Smith," Valentina said as she looked up at him with eyes that were so soft and warm they took his breath away just as much as hearing his sister had named her son for him. "That's so sweet."

Their mother wasn't the only one sniffling now and when Marnie, the obstetrician who had also delivered Chase and Chloe's daughter earlier in the year, came out, she graciously accepted their thanks for another delivery gone well.

"Sophie and Jake were the ones doing all the work, but I'd be lying if I said a bottle of bubbly would be refused," she said with a wink in Marcus's direction. As everyone laughed, she said, "They're all cleaned up and ready to meet their aunts and uncles now, although two or three at a time should be more than enough chaos for our nursing staff back here."

Marcus, the oldest Sullivan, took a silent vote from his siblings before turning to Smith and saying, "Go meet Smith, Jr., and Jackie. But remember, the rest of us are waiting."

Smith pulled Valentina through the double doors before she could protest. Of course, he'd also been banking on the fact that she clearly had a thing for babies.

There were scrubs and hand sanitizer waiting for them both outside Sophie's room and he had to press a kiss to the back of Valentina's neck when she automatically turned to have him tie the cotton strings together in the back. He loved the little shivers that moved through her as she leaned back into his arms for a moment.

But neither of them could wait another second to meet the two new additions to the family, so they quickly broke apart and stepped into Sophie and Jake's room.

A soft sound of wonder fell from Valentina's lips as she got her first look at the newborns. It shouldn't have been easy to tell the little baby girl from the boy, but there was something undoubtedly male about Smith and sweetly female about Jackie.

Smith's hands were already outstretched by the time he made it across the room to his sister's side. She didn't hesitate to place her son into his hands.

"He's perfect, Sophie."

Valentina was still standing by the doorway when Jake said, "Would you like to hold Jackie, Valentina?"

She was clearly overwhelmed by the offer. "I would love to," she said softly, before finally saying,

"Congratulations, they're absolutely beautiful. I'm so happy for both of you."

Smith could barely take his eyes off his little nephew, but when Jake handed Jackie to Valentina, he was beyond glad he didn't miss the moment when she smiled down at the baby. Valentina looked as open, as joyous, as she did whenever she was in his arms.

A moment later, she looked up and her gaze connected with his. This time Smith was the one with tremors moving through him.

Some people would say that as a movie star he'd already had everything. But he hadn't. Not until Valentina. And now, he wanted it all. Not just Valentina's love, not just a promise of forever in his arms and with her by his side, but family and babies and laughter and tears. He wanted to share every precious moment with her, every single one that really mattered.

Neither of them noticed the look Sophie and Jake gave each other, or the pleasure on Sophie's face at the realization that she was getting to witness her beloved big brother finally giving his heart completely away.

Valentina quickly turned her attention back to the soft little package in her arms and Smith did the same, both of them murmuring how pretty and handsome and strong the babies were.

The obstetrician knocked on the door, and poked her head in with a grin. "Just want to let you know, your other brothers and sister are about to mutiny out there if they don't get some face time with the little ones soon."

Smith very reluctantly relinquished the baby boy

to his sister. "You're amazing, Soph. Anything you need—" he looked at Jake, too "—I want you both to call me. Day or night."

Valentina clearly was having just as hard a time letting go of the sweet little bundle in her arms. "Bye-bye, pretty girl." She gave the baby back to her father and hugged both Jake and Sophie.

Her eyes still held all of that softness as he put his arm around her and they headed out of the room to let his siblings know Sophie, Jake, Smith and Jackie were ready for more visitors. Lori went next, along with Marcus and Nicola, and even though Smith loved spending time with his family, he also knew there were other things he needed more right now.

He pulled Valentina toward the exit.

Fifteen minutes later, Smith helped Valentina out of his car and his mouth was on hers less than a heart-beat later. Then she was in his arms and he was kicking the car door shut and carrying her into his house, just as he had their first night together after Alcatraz.

His kiss was full of passion, but also something so soft and sweet that she melted in his arms as she wound her arms around his neck and kissed him back just as passionately. Every time she'd been with Smith, she'd wanted him, but never more than in this moment.

Want. Need. Desire.

None of those words, none of those emotions, were big enough to hold everything she felt for Smith.

For his family.

For the way they'd included her in one of their most special moments.

And, most of all, for the chance to hold a miracle in her arms.

Smith laid her down on the bed, never breaking their kiss, not even for a second, as his hands found the zipper on her skirt and pulled both the metal teeth and then the fabric from her hips. With only her panties and the thigh-high stockings he'd bought for her covering her lower body, she wrapped her legs around his waist and pulled him in tighter. Moments later, Smith slipped open the buttons on her blouse and pushed the silky fabric open. The front clasp on her bra was next and then her sensitive flesh was in his hands and she was arching into the warm scratch of his palms and fingertips on a gasp of pleasure.

Moment by moment, her skin grew more heated, her bones seeming to liquefy with every kiss, with every caress, with every thrust of his clothed hips into hers. And yet, instead of their kiss growing more out of control, Smith's mouth gentled on hers.

Amazingly, the whisper of his lips over hers only intensified her emotions, her needs, her passions, so that by the time he finally lifted his head to gaze down at her, she didn't have a prayer of holding back anything from him, even if she'd wanted to.

"The babies, Smith." Her mouth felt swollen and hot from his kisses and she sighed at the extreme pleasure of it. "Weren't they just the most beautiful thing you've ever seen?"

"They were beautiful," he agreed in a low voice

that rumbled over her skin and brought up thrill bumps over every inch of her. He lifted a hand to her cheek and brushed it over her full lower lip, which trembled at his touch. "And so are you."

Holding the babies in her arms had completely erased their horrible morning with photographers and fights from which she'd been so sure she and Smith could never recover.

But, amazingly, they had.

Later, they would figure everything else out. Now, they would celebrate new life…and their love for each other.

This time she was the one pressing her mouth to his skin, first to the short, dark stubble that covered the lower half of his jaw, then to the strong, steady beat of his heart at the side of his neck. She'd never let herself be sure of a man before, and Smith had been the last man on earth she had been looking for.

But how could she even think of looking anywhere else when he was all she could see?

She was so happy for him that it could have been her own sister giving birth instead of Sophie, whom she'd only met a couple of times. Now, even with her nearly naked body wrapped around him, heated and ready for anything he wanted, he didn't make a move to take off his clothes. He simply continued to stare down at her.

All she could hear was the sound of her heart— and his—beating in time with each other.

And all she knew was that she was deeply, truly, madly in love with him.

Not because he was the most physically beautiful man she'd ever known. Not because he was famous or rich. Not even because of the way she felt when he was kissing her, touching her, making her cry out his name in pleasure.

But because of the way he loved his family, his mother, his sister—and now, the babies—with every last piece of his heart.

Heat and wild desire had always pulled them together, even when she'd tried so desperately to stay away. Now, there was so much she wanted to tell him, and yet all that she could manage was to whisper his name.

"Smith."

"I love you, too," he replied.

They shared a kiss full of joy and passion, happiness and desire—everything she'd always wished for, but had never truly believed she would ever have. Dreams, reality, passion, affection, all melded into a perfect sensual combination as she began to strip him of his shirt and then his pants and boxers. They made short work of the rest of their clothes until they were naked and reaching for each other the second Smith put on protection.

Together, they tumbled into each other, strong and soft, wild and steady, as he moved into her in one beautiful thrust. She urged him deeper as she arched into him, her head falling back against the pillows while he ran his hands down her back to cup her hips and pull her tighter against him. Everything she gave he took, everything she craved he offered, as finally, neither of them held anything back.

In the exact moment that Valentina began to crest the wave, Smith took her mouth in a kiss so soft, so sweet, so full of love, that the tears she never let herself shed began to slide down her cheeks one after the other, faster still as the tremors of release racked them both. The tears were still falling as Smith began to press soft kisses over her closed eyelids, her cheeks, her chin, everywhere that was streaked with wetness.

And when the waves of pleasure finally settled down, Valentina knew that she had never been so sated, so well loved, in all her life...or so shocked by what had happened to herself while in Smith's arms.

A part of her felt born again, as if she'd been baptized by her own tears. But those same tears had been her last defense against the pain she'd refused to acknowledge. Even her own sister had never really seen her cry.

Only Smith.

Finally, when he'd kissed away every last hint of her tears, he lifted his head to look down at her. He didn't say anything, but he didn't need to when she could read everything in his eyes: the love, along with the lingering desire fueled anew by the soft kisses he'd never stopped giving her.

"I love you," she said simply. It was the first time she'd ever said the words directly to him.

As joy suffused every inch of Smith's face and as she said it again and again between his kisses, Valentina realized that as amazing as it had felt to hear

Smith say, "I love you," it was not only a million times better to say it to him…it was also easy. Sweet.

And oh so perfect.

With her lips on his she whispered the three little words she'd been so afraid to even feel. He whispered the words back to her before he curled her into his arms, her head on his chest, her legs still entwined with his.

All she wanted to do was close her eyes and rest for a short while, knowing Smith was there with her to hold her all through the night. She didn't know how many hours it had been since they'd abruptly left the set, and for as long as it had taken Sophie to have her babies, Valentina hadn't cared about the responsibilities she was ignoring. But now that it was just her own pleasure on the line, didn't she have to drag herself back into the real world? No matter that it was the very last thing she wanted, that all that seemed to matter anymore was Smith and the joy she'd felt every single moment she'd ever spent with him.

As if he could read her mind, Smith pulled her closer and said, "The world will keep spinning without us for a little while."

The last thing Valentina felt was the press of his mouth against her forehead as she finally let herself lean all the way into him…and dropped every last defense around her heart as he whispered, "I love you so much," one more time before sleep claimed her.

Twenty-Eight

With her stomach grumbling, Valentina woke to the fantastic smell of pepperoni pizza. As she pushed her hair back from her face and sat up against the pillows, she noted the sky outside the windows was black.

The lights were on in the room, but dim enough that she had to carefully scan the large bedroom for Smith. His eyes were on her from where he stood in the sitting area, obviously having just laid out food for both of them on the coffee table.

She'd worked with him for long enough now to recognize when he was in director mode, almost as if he was framing the scene with her on the bed with the intention of pulling out a camera to shoot it. She began to move off the sheets to go to him, but her name on his lips held her captive where she was. A flush of heat spread slowly, and then faster, across her skin as he drank her in from across the room, until she was the one saying his name in a voice made slightly hoarse both by sleep and by the way she'd been calling out his name earlier.

"I love seeing you in my bed."

"I love being in it."

Moments later, he was standing in front of her and pulling her up to her knees, the covers completely sliding away from her naked body as she wound her arms around his neck to press her mouth against his with a passion that never seemed to abate, but only grew hotter, bigger, deeper, with every kiss.

In the back of her mind, she noted how easy it was—and how easy it had always been—to allow herself to be innately sensual with Smith. For so long she'd worked to suppress that side of herself, to make sure no man ever "took advantage" of her need to be touched, kissed, held. But she'd always felt safe with Smith, despite the dangerous hunger that was so often in his eyes when he looked at her. Was it because she felt the hunger, too, that the danger seemed not only okay…but was, in fact, a shockingly lovely bonus?

He brought over the shirt he'd been wearing the night before. She slipped her arms through the long sleeves, but she didn't button it, simply rolled up the sleeves and wrapped the fabric around herself as they went to sit on the couch together.

He didn't reach for the food and neither did she. Instead, he took her hands in his just as she was reaching for him.

"Hungry?" he asked her, his deep voice at once soothing and arousing.

She nodded in answer, but knew she wouldn't be able to eat a thing until they talked. Even the biggest stars in the world needed food and sleep just like anyone else. But when it came to the ones those stars loved, and to the potential damage fame could do to their relationships, "normal" came to a crashing halt.

And yet, Smith made her want to believe. Not just in love—she already knew that was real, knew that what she felt for him couldn't possibly be merely the result of close proximity and great sex—but that their love could withstand not only the pressures of life, but of his fame, too.

For so long, she'd thought being strong meant not letting herself be vulnerable. But all this time had she had it backward? Instead of being a weakness, wasn't risking everything to love actually the strongest, bravest thing she'd ever do?

She looked down at their hands entwined together, and knew he already held so much more of her than she thought she'd ever be able to give him.

Now—finally—she wanted to give him even more.

She looked up into his dark eyes, so beautiful, and so full of love. *For her.* "I don't want to be a mystery anymore. Not with you."

His hands didn't tighten on hers. Instead, his thumbs stroked over her palms, sending both warmth and shivers through her at the same time.

"I'm here, Valentina. Now and always." He continued to stroke over her skin, slowly, surely, steadily. "All you have to do is let me in."

He made it sound so simple.

And then, suddenly, she realized it was.

"My mother was different when my father was alive." As she began to speak, he pulled her closer, so that her legs came over his and she could feel his heart beating from where he was holding her hands against his chest. "She was always beautiful, but she was warm, too. It wasn't until my father died that I realized just how much of that warmth had come through him." She made herself keep thinking back to those first months after her father had died. "And after he was gone, it was like she crumbled away, one layer at a time, until she was gone, too."

"You lost them both."

Smith's gentle words surprised her, then a moment later, resonated, even as she said, "She was still there, just—" She took a shaky breath. "The first actor she dated was barely a few years older than me. That was weird enough, but then one time when she was taking a long time getting ready, he—"

She stopped and shuddered as Smith scowled.

"What did he do? Who is he?"

She shook her head. "Nothing. He was all talk, innuendo. But I think if I had been willing…" Disgust came at her now just as hard and fast as it had those times her mother's too-young actor boyfriends had come on to her.

"Did you tell your mother what he said? What he tried to take from you?"

"No," she said softly, "I couldn't figure out how or what I would have said. And I didn't want her to feel bad, not when she was just doing her best to deal with her own grief. It was easier—" she paused for a moment, hating to have to use that word, but she wouldn't hide the truth from Smith anymore, not even for pride's sake "—*easier* just to pull back. And to focus on my worries about Tatiana, about all those strange men my mother was dating coming in and out of the house. My sister was so pretty even then, and so innocent, that it was a relief to leave school and the dorms to move back in with them and take over managing her business affairs so that I could get her to all of her auditions and jobs." She reassured Smith, "No one ever tried anything with Tatiana. Honestly, the only reason I think they ever came on to me was because I was their age."

"You know that's not the only reason, Valentina. You told me once that I could have any woman in the world." He stared into her eyes with such intensity that she couldn't possibly look away. "I want you."

Valentina couldn't have possibly held back the words, "I want you, too. I just wish—"

Again, she knew it would be easier not to say any of this to Smith, but painful experience with her mother had taught her that easier wasn't better. Trying to avoid or deny pain in the short run only made everything hurt worse later...and become very difficult to fix.

While memories of her mother flitted through her mind, Smith was right here, holding her hand, letting her spill it all out.

"I would never ask you to change what you do, or change who you are," she told him. "I love you too much to even think of stopping you from sharing your incredible gifts with the world. But I've been on plenty of sets over the past ten years. And I've seen what happens, how inevitable it all seems when men and women who've professed their love to other people end up falling for their costars, how marriages happen too fast and then end even quicker once they move on to other projects on other sides of the world."

"You're right, my work is important to me," he told her. "So are you. So important that I don't want to make big life and career decisions all alone anymore. From here on out, I want to make them with you."

Even as his words had warmth filling her from head to toe, she had to tell him, "But it scares me that we met on a film set. And that it all happened so fast. It's so hard to keep a normal relationship together. Apart from Paul Newman and Joanne Woodward, I don't know how many Hollywood relationships have ever really worked."

It wasn't that she didn't believe he could want her. She could no longer deny his desire for her, or hers for him. No, she was simply trying to make sure that both of them went into this relationship with their eyes wide open.

"The first couple of years after my breakout movie were difficult to adjust to," Smith told her. "Really difficult. I loved acting, and I knew if I was really good at it I'd become famous, but I had no idea what it would actually be like to lose my privacy. To have the press calling up my family and friends to ask them questions about me. I'm not going to lie to you and say that we won't have more hurdles, that there won't be a thousand other journalists and photographers trying to make a buck by sticking their noses into our relationship."

Determination and love were reflected on Smith's face as his voice remained as steady as hers had been shaky. "But I've waited my whole life for somebody like you, for a woman I wanted to be with forever, and I refuse to give you up. I was afraid you'd never come, that there'd never be a woman who didn't want me because of who I am, what I have, who I know. Until you."

He lifted her hands to his mouth and gently pressed his lips to each of them before saying, "Tell me what love means to you, Valentina."

She didn't have to think. *"You."*

His mouth found hers then, at once gentle and firm, sweet and passionate. If anyone had asked her before she met Smith if those contrasts could possibly coexist, she would have known the answer. She had been utterly certain that if she finally let herself love it would make sense—she would be in control of her heart, from the first beat to the last.

But every moment they'd been together, Smith confounded her expectations…and exceeded what she'd believed to be the limits of her heart.

"I know we can love each other enough to make our relationship matter more than anything else ever has," Smith said. "Yes, Hollywood is crazy, but even though I just broke rule number one today by bashing in a photographer's face," he said with a slightly rueful half grin, "I'm convinced we can transcend the pitfalls from here on out."

He got down on his knees before her. "I want you by my side not only for red-carpet events, but for the nights when we're both exhausted from a long day on set, too tired to do anything but hold hands and fall asleep. I want to kiss the sugar off your lips while you're eating sweets for breakfast. And I want you there to drag into the shower with me to make up for not having the energy to make love to you the night before."

Nothing Smith had said was flashy. There were no big diamonds blinding her, no expensive promises or glittering, sweeping vistas before them. He wasn't like any other man she'd ever met, and he'd definitely broken the movie-star mold by being beautiful not only on the outside, but on the inside, too. He would never hurt her or her family, just as he would never hurt his own family.

Weeks ago she'd asked him why love couldn't just be as pure as two people who simply realized that they would always be happier together rather than apart because they made each other's lives complete in a way no one else could.

Now she knew it could be.

Finally finding her voice, Valentina put her hands on either side of his face and told him, "You can have it, Smith. All of it. And I want you there, too, to grill Tatiana's new boyfriend with me. I want to share the paper with you on a Sunday morning. I want to sit with you under a blanket on the couch in front of a fire and work on puzzles of every dog and cat in the family."

And as he picked her up and carried her over to the bed, food still forgotten, they fulfilled their most important hunger of all.

Hunger for love.

Twenty-Nine

Three weeks later

Valentina stepped out of her office on the *Gravity* set for the last time and took a few moments to take a final look at the place that had ended up feeling more like a home than a temporary film set. Tomorrow morning all of the lights, temporary walls and furniture would be emptied out, leaving the space bare for its next occupant.

Everything would change again for the cast and crew who had worked on the film. Some, like Smith, would be moving on to postproduction work. Others would take a much-needed vacation. Most of the actors would go back to Hollywood to audition for their next role, or to take their place on the next set. Tatiana had just committed to star in a major historical piece set in Boston…but for the very first time in a decade, Valentina wouldn't be going with her.

It made her chest hurt thinking about not seeing

her sister every single day, even though she knew it was the right thing for both of them.

She needed to let her sister have her wings. And, Valentina thought as she caught sight of Smith walking toward her smiling that devastatingly sexy smile she could never get enough of, she finally admitted to herself that she needed to give herself room to let *her* wings unfurl all the way, too.

Only, she hadn't expected to see her mother beaming at her a moment later from Smith's side. She was also surprised to see her mother's boyfriend, David, with them. He was several weeks past her mother's usual sell-by date for actor boyfriends.

"Oh, honey, wasn't it so sweet of Smith to invite us to the final day of filming?"

It was. So sweet that Valentina immediately felt ashamed for not thinking of it herself. Smith slid his fingers through hers and pulled her against him to give her a kiss, one that lingered far longer than Valentina's previous rules of PDA dictated. But his kiss was completely irresistible all the same, even though anyone around them could snap a picture and send it off to a tabloid.

The strange truth was, however, that a part of her was glad that they'd been through the wringer with the paparazzi and the press when their relationship was brand-new. Even though it hadn't been fun to watch the tabloids run pictures of her and Smith, or see the way they'd tried—and failed—to make Smith look like a bad guy, she'd survived it. And knowing that she could survive it again made her bound and determined not to worry about whether one of their kisses ended up in the press.

She knew her skin was flushed, not from embarrassment but pleasure, when he finally pulled his mouth from hers.

"Can I get either of you anything?"

He had asked both her and her mother the question, but she knew from the way he squeezed her hand that he was making sure she was okay being left alone with her mother. When they told him they were fine, he lifted her hand to his mouth for one more kiss before steering David away with him.

Valentina and her mother watched the two men go, until they turned a corner and were out of sight.

"My friends can't stop talking about how one of my daughters caught a movie star," Ava Landon said on a happy little sigh. "I still can't believe you're dating Smith Sullivan."

Normally, Valentina would have tried not to feel hurt by her mother's disbelief. She would have told herself that it was better to just let the comment roll off. But she knew why Smith had asked her mother to come to the set today. It wasn't just so that Ava could cheer Tatiana on the last day of filming, but because family meant the world to him.

And he loved her so much he wanted her family to be whole again.

"Why?" Valentina's voice was quiet, but her question was still firm. And riddled with the hurt she could no longer hide. "Why can't you believe it?"

Her mother blinked up at her with the big blue eyes

that had captivated young actors throughout Hollywood for the past decade…and her husband for two decades before that.

"Not because you aren't beautiful, Val." Her mother put her hand on her arm. "Your looks have always been far more exotic than mine or your sister's. I'm not surprised he can't take his eyes off you. It's just that I know how much you disliked actors, probably because I've always dated them."

"You knew that?"

"You have a very expressive face, honey," her mother told her.

"I don't get it." If there was something to be said, it had to be said now. After all, once upon a time, she and her mother had been so close. Not just mother and daughter, but friends. "After Daddy died, why—" She pushed aside the image of her father to get through her question. "Why have you always dated actors?"

"I could never replace your father, and I never even wanted to try." Her mother's voice was full of the same sadness Valentina herself felt whenever she talked about him. "Early on I realized the nice thing about dating an actor is that even if they don't really think I'm young and beautiful and desirable, they know how to fake it. Well enough that I can believe them for a while."

This time Valentina was the one reaching for her mother. "You don't need anyone to pretend that you're beautiful, Mom. You *are*."

Her mother's eyes glimmered with tears. "I know

I haven't told you often enough, but I'm so proud of you, honey."

Valentina knew it would be easiest just to take her mother's compliment at face value, and to smooth over years of hurt. But Smith had taught her just how easy love could be once you had it. She'd also learned just how much hard work had to go into getting it.

Smith hadn't given up on her. He hadn't underestimated her strength, her convictions…or the love she had to give. Maybe, Valentina found herself thinking, it was time for her to stop giving up on her mother. Which meant no more dancing around each other, no more talking without saying anything.

"We used to be so close. Before Daddy died." She'd started her relationship with Smith with a "Why?" when she'd needed to understand his reasons for pursuing her. Now she would try to restart her relationship with her mother with that one little word. After all those years, Valentina couldn't stand not knowing anymore.

"Why did you leave us, too?" She felt a tear slide down her cheek and wiped at it with the back of her hand. "We needed you." Another tear fell, too fast for her to catch before it plopped onto the cement. "*I* needed you."

Her mother's slim arms were surprisingly strong as they abruptly reached around her. "Oh, honey, I'm sorry."

But instead of falling apart, for once her mother was the strong one, another role reversal Valentina hadn't seen coming.

"You and your sister were always so close. I loved that you were so tight as a unit, loved knowing that you would always be there to look after her, if anything ever happened to me and your father. And then, when he died so unexpectedly—" Ava Landon shook her head. "Honestly, I don't remember much about those early months. But when I finally came back to the world, the two of you were closer than ever. Just like you are now. So close that it sometimes seemed like you didn't need me at all. That you only needed each other." Her mother wiped away her own tears now. "Will you forgive me?"

Valentina had never thought about how the bond with her sister might have affected her mother. "Of course I do." She was the one hugging her mother this time, the familiar scent of her perfume, and her softness, as comforting to her now as they had been when she was a little girl.

They had a lot to catch up on, far more than they could possibly cover in the next five minutes before filming started for the day. But she did have one more question before they headed over to the set.

"Are things serious with you and David?"

Her mother answered her question with one of her own. "Would it be okay with you if they were? I know how much your father meant to you, how much he still does."

Valentina instinctively put her hand over her heart. She paused to think, and to feel, before she said, "It would."

Smiling, their arms still around each other, they

walked across the lot and onto the set. And when Smith looked up at her, she could see not only the love for her in his eyes, but also his joy at the obvious emotional breakthrough she and her mother had made.

And then the lights were dimming. Smith and Tatiana were taking their places on set on the bed beside each other as the cameras started to roll. Valentina's mother squeezed Valentina's hand and she pressed an impromptu kiss to her soft cheek before turning her attention to the scene just starting to play out before them.

Jo and Graham had made love many, many times over the past few weeks. And they had both fallen helplessly in love with each other from that first clash on the street all the way through shared nights caring for her baby.

But despite both of those facts, Jo knew they hadn't truly shared love with each other.

From the first moment she'd collided with him, Graham had been full of purpose, determination, intensity. And still, after they'd made love that first time, and after she'd watched him give his love to her daughter without any barriers or borders, she'd believed that no one could sustain himself on endless intensity without eventually running out of steam. When she watched him sleep, instead of the lines in his beautiful face softening, they still held the heartbreaking edge to them that tore her apart a little more every day.

When, she wondered as she reached to stroke back

a lock of hair that had fallen across his forehead, would he ever let go of the demons that drove him?

He murmured her name and pulled her into him, her back to his front. She loved the feel of his strong arms around her, loved lying together with him like this when they were both barely awake.

Safe. He had said he would always keep her and her daughter safe.

Which was why, at long last, in those fragile minutes between night and day, believing in him as she'd never let herself believe anyone else, she began to speak.

"I never knew my father. Just the men who came in and out of my mother's life."

She could tell by the way his muscles tightened slightly against hers that he had just come fully awake. Maybe she should have been frightened. Maybe this was the one risk she shouldn't take—to trust him with a story that only she knew, that could die with her and her alone.

But somewhere along the way, she'd realized she could live with taking that risk. But she couldn't live without love.

"Some were nice. Some were scary. Some wanted things from me that I didn't want to give." His hand tightened over her chest and she tried to calm him by saying, "I was small. And fast. And I knew how to stay hidden when I had to. I also knew I needed to get out before I was ever found."

Her name was on his lips. She knew it would be so

easy to turn into him, to let him kiss away her ugly memories. And she would. But not yet.

Not until she'd bared herself to him. Fully. Completely.

And not until she'd risked everything for him so that he could do the same for her.

"His name was Bryan. I thought I'd seen it all, thought I was so smart when it came to picking a boyfriend, a man to finally give my virginity to. He had a good job working with computers. He wasn't creepy or scary. He was nice. He didn't treat me like I was stupid, or worthless because of where I came from." She sighed, remembering how naive she'd been. "I didn't get pregnant on purpose. I don't know what happened. Maybe the condom broke. But when I went to tell him, I knew I couldn't do it. Not because I didn't want to trap him into having to stay with me." She swallowed hard. "I didn't tell him because I couldn't trap myself."

She didn't realize she was crying until she tasted the tears on her cheek, nor did she realize Graham had turned her in his arms so that he could kiss them away, one by one.

"There had to be more. I knew there was more."

The sunlight had come up just enough to bathe the room in a soft glow. When she lifted her eyes to his, he would see everything she felt for him. And she wanted him to.

"I love you. And I'm not saying that to trap you into staying with me for any longer than you want to."

Now, he was the one brushing the hair back from her forehead as he said, "Marry me."

She sucked in a shaky breath, knowing the only reason she could keep the slightest bit steady was because he was holding her. There was nothing she wanted more in the world than to belong to this man.

Nothing, except for him to trust her with his pain, so that she could help him the way he'd helped her a thousand times over.

"Yes," had to come first, because she couldn't bear to keep him guessing if she wanted to share his forever. There was nothing she wanted more.

The kiss they shared after she accepted his proposal was sweet, and could so easily have turned into something even sweeter. But she hadn't been afraid to come to San Francisco with five hundred dollars in her pocket and a baby growing inside of her...and she wouldn't be afraid now.

"I don't want your money."

"I know." And he did, knew that he could lose every last one of his billion dollars and she would remain at his side without so much as blinking an eye.

"I don't even want you to be less domineering or bossy," she said with a little smile that had his mouth curving up in a smile as he stared down at her. "All I've ever wanted is a family."

"I want to be Leah's father. Legally."

She reached up and touched his face, the sunlight starting to stream over them now like a spotlight, knowing he'd understood her perfectly, but had deliberately tried to deflect her request.

"We're both yours. Always. I want you to be my husband and Leah's father." He was closing the distance to kiss her again when she said, *"But we also want a grandmother. A grandfather. We want uncles. And aunts."*

He stilled above her, his eyes shuttering, but she was young and strong.

And not the least bit afraid of a fight with the powerful man leveraged above her.

"It was my job to protect my sister." Each word of the emotional confession she hoped he'd finally feel safe making with her was raw. And filled with unbearable pain. *"Leanora was the baby of the family. She used to tell me I was her hero, and I believed she was right, that I was invincible, that there was nothing that could touch me. Or her."* He was looking right at Jo but she knew it wasn't her he was seeing. *"I was busy screwing some woman whose name I couldn't even remember when the call came in. I didn't get it until the next morning, didn't know that they'd found her with some punk, both of them overdosed. His heart was still beating. But hers—"*

This time she was the one wiping away his tears, putting her arms around him, soothing him with words that meant nothing, and everything, all at once.

She was surprised when his hand moved to her stomach. *"She was pregnant. I was the only one in my family that she'd told. I told her I thought it was a good idea that they weren't going to get married. I told her I would take care of her. I read every book on pregnancy, on being a single parent. I promised her I'd be there for her when she told the rest of our family. I thought she knew we loved her, and that she didn't need to keep her pregnancy a secret. I thought I was still her hero, the one she could depend on for anything."*

This time, when his eyes met Jo's he saw the woman he loved and he would continue to love her with everything he had, with every last piece of his heart.

"She never told me about the drugs. And I never guessed. Because I didn't want to guess, I didn't want to see it. But I should have seen it."

Jo wasn't going to pretend she didn't know the story—at least up until the part where it turned out his sister had been pregnant—or that she hadn't read about it on the internet once she'd realized who he was.

But all this time she'd thought it was grief that had hardened him. Finally, she realized it wasn't just grief that tore him apart every hour of every day.

It was blame. For himself.

"It wasn't your fault."

His head was on her chest and she was holding him just as steadily as he'd held her moments before.

"I should have been there for her. I should have protected her."

"No," she argued. "You should have loved her. And you did." She rocked him as she rocked her baby girl so much of every day and night, the baby that he'd asked her to name after the sister he'd loved so much. "You did."

Thirty

In near-perfect silence, the entire crew watched as the final scene was filmed—where Graham introduced Jo to the family he'd walked away from two years earlier. Everyone on the cast and crew had to reach for tissues, especially when the prim and proper matriarch of Graham's family had taken Leah onto her lap, kissed the child's soft hair, then softly said to Jo, *"Thank you for bringing my family back together, and for becoming a part of it."*

Hours later in her rental house, it was only the fear of ruining her perfectly applied mascara that kept Valentina from blubbering like a fool over the movie's end. Thankfully, she hadn't had to say her goodbyes to the friends she'd made on the set this afternoon. The wrap party tonight would give them all time to hug and laugh and reminisce and drink just a little too much together.

Over the past weeks, Valentina had begun to adjust to the spotlight, little by little. She was used to holding Smith's hand in public, she'd absolutely loved spending Thanksgiving at his mother's house with Tatiana and the rest of his family, and she'd even accepted that stories and pictures of the two of them snapped by strangers in San Francisco would often end up on blogs and in newspapers.

But tonight was different.

The Maverick Group, a multinational corporation made up of a group of powerful billionaires who had a golden touch when it came to business, was the main investor in Smith's film. They were throwing the wrap party for *Gravity* tonight.

Most women, she knew, would be thrilled to put on a stunning couture dress made by one of the top designers in the world and slip their feet into heels that cost more than the average month's rent in most places around the country. Valentina had never been like other women, though. Even as a girl, she'd been just a little more serious, far more likely to get excited over a book than a pop star.

Fortunately, Tatiana knew her inside and out. Her sister had gone out of her way for the past two hours to make it seem as though they were simply having a fun makeover day together. Instead of going to a fancy salon for a blowout, manicure and makeup, Tatiana had suggested they make each other up instead.

Of course, her sister didn't need Valentina's help. Tatiana was such a pro after all she'd learned over the past few years that if she ever decided to give up acting, she'd have no problem launching her own hair, nails and makeup line.

Now, Valentina tried not to see the panic in her own eyes as she looked in the mirror. Tatiana had a blow dryer in one hand, the other smoothing Valentina's hair.

"There," her sister said as she finally turned off the dryer. "Perfect." She didn't give Valentina too much time to study herself before pulling her out of her seat and handing her the shockingly gorgeous dress.

"Time for the finishing touch." Tatiana smiled as she looked down at the dress Valentina hadn't yet taken from her. "Smith has some seriously great taste. I can't wait to see it on you."

The large dress box had been yet another gift waiting on her desk this week. She loved that he hadn't stopped surprising her, and she knew he never would.

Her sister was right about his taste. The soft yellow fabric was elegant while somehow hugging all of her curves at the same time, and the bodice glittered just enough to make the dress something special. In fact, it would have been the perfect dress if not for the long slit up the side of the leg.

She took a deep, steadying breath as her sister all but shoved the dress into her hand. Telling herself to stop being such a baby, Valentina quickly slipped off Smith's button-front shirt that she'd been wearing while Tatiana did her hair and makeup, and stepped into the dress, putting her arms through the spaghetti straps. After Tatiana zipped her up, Valentina slipped her feet into the stunning heels.

She closed her eyes for a moment before turning to face her sister.

Tatiana's eyes were wide. "Val." Her pretty mouth curved into a huge smile. "You look *amazing!*" She grabbed her hand and took her over to the full-length mirror. "Look!"

Valentina stared in the mirror with surprise. She'd expected to see a stranger. But even though she'd never been done up like this before, the woman looking back at her was the same one she saw every morning and evening in the bathroom mirror when she brushed her teeth with Smith standing right there beside her.

Granted, her hair had never looked quite so glossy or well styled, and her eyes had never seemed so smoky and mysterious, nor her mouth quite so plump and red.

A knock came at the door, followed by Smith's deep voice asking if he could come in. Tatiana called out for him to enter, which was good because Valentina's throat had gone completely dry.

She stood perfectly still as he walked in.

"Valentina."

Tatiana slipped out unnoticed as Smith stood where he was in the middle of the room and stared at Valentina. "My God, you're beautiful. I'm never going to get used to it, am I?"

Despite her own worries about how the evening was going to go, she couldn't doubt for even one second that he meant what he said. Even the best actor in the world couldn't have seemed that genuine if he hadn't really believed every word.

"Thank you." She tried to smile, but her lips had a hard time moving up at the corners.

This wasn't her first Hollywood party by any means. She'd been to dozens with her sister over the years. The difference was that she'd always been in the background, just one of the support staff for her sparkling, beautiful sister. No one had ever noticed her. She'd been as invisible as the ice sculptures melting in the middle of the vegan buffet.

Tonight she wouldn't be invisible. And not just because of the dress, the shoes, the hair and makeup.

She'd be with Smith. On his arm. As much a target for dissection as the actors and actresses who had willingly signed up for a career in the spotlight. Yes, they'd already been in plenty of tabloids, blogs and magazines, but this event was on a whole different level.

Before she'd met him, she'd been utterly certain that this kind of life was crazy, and that any woman who walked willingly into a relationship with a man like him was a fool. Now, Valentina was one hundred percent certain that he was worth being crazy and foolish for—worth even the terror that rode her.

And still, her heart raced and her palms dampened just thinking about all those...

She was stunned out of her frantic thoughts by the sound of the door being locked by Smith. By the time she got her brain functioning at least halfway as fast as it should, he was moving toward her and taking her hands in his. He lifted them to his gorgeous mouth, pressed a kiss to each of her fingertips, then gently turned her to face the wall while lifting her hands up to put her palms flat against the cool painted plaster.

She stood there, turning her face from the wall to look at him over her shoulder. "Smith, what are you—"

Her question slid away on a gasp as he easily found the long opening along the right side of her dress that ran from ankle to midthigh. It was the one part of the dress that had given her pause, more than a hint of sexy on an otherwise perfectly elegant dress. She loved how sexy she felt any time he kissed her, touched her, whispered how good she felt in his arms, relished how natural it was for her to let go whenever they were making love. But it was one thing to let her inner sensual self out in the privacy of his bedroom; it was another entirely to let the rest of the world see it.

But now, as his warm fingers ran a devastating path up her sensitive skin, she gave silent thanks for the cut of the dress. He didn't rush as he lightly caressed the skin on her upper thigh, first on the outside and then in toward her inner thigh.

From the first touch of his lips on her fingertips, her arousal had spiked. And as his hand slid over the thin lace of her thong and he cupped the sensitive flesh between her legs, she couldn't think, or worry, or even remember how those thoughts got there in the first place. All she could do was arch her hips into his in a silent plea for more.

Her name was a heated whisper against her neck as

he answered her plea by slipping his fingers under the edge of silk and into her. His tongue traced the curve of her neck as she rocked into him, the delicious— and oh so unexpected—pressure quickly sending her straight into a heady climax.

Still braced against the wall with her hands, her neck arched back into his mouth as a brilliantly colored fireworks display shot off inside of her.

"Beautiful." Smith's teeth found the lobe of one ear as she came apart with him pressed tightly against her back, his hand moving in a perfect rhythm between her thighs as he kept her release going on and on. "So damn beautiful."

By the time she remembered to breathe again, it came out in hard, fast pants. Everything inside her was spinning, twisting, buzzing.

His large hands were gentle on her bare shoulders as he turned her to face him. She licked the spot on her lower lip that she'd bitten into when he'd sent her reeling and his eyes were hungry as he gazed down at her mouth.

"You were worrying," he said in answer to the question she hadn't been able to ask. He lifted his hand to brush the pad of his thumb across her lower lip. "I've decided that any time I see you overthinking things, or if you start panicking over the Hollywood circus, that's what I'm going to do." His gaze darkened even further with sensual intent. "I won't care where we are, or what we're supposed to be doing. You come first, Valentina. Always."

She believed him, knew he never said anything

he didn't mean. But she also knew that it was going to be a long time before she could figure out how to keep from freaking out about being in the Hollywood spotlight alongside him. If ever.

Only, instead of the usual panic that accompanied that thought, a shudder of sweet anticipation came at Smith's incredibly sexy promise about how he would help her cope with the pressure.

But it wasn't until he pressed a soft kiss to her mouth and began to step away from her that she realized the only thing he'd been concerned with was helping her, not taking his own pleasure, too.

Thank God her brain had started functioning well enough by then for her to take his hands in hers and ask, "What if I'm still worrying?" When renewed concern moved across his beautiful face, she quickly put his hands on her hips and brought her mouth a breath away from his to whisper, "What else will you do to make me stop?"

She felt his answering grin right before he said, "This," and took her mouth in a possessive kiss.

He deftly slid down the zipper along the back of her dress and helped her step out of it, before carefully laying it across the back of a soft chair in her bedroom. He stood holding the yellow silk in his hands, his gaze filled with awe as he took in her naked body, now clad in only a silk thong, thigh-high, lace-edged stockings and heels.

And then he was threading his hands into her hair and lowering his mouth to devour hers in a deeply passionate kiss. He rained kisses over her face, down her neck, her shoulders, before finally laving the peak of one breast with his tongue, and then the other.

She loved the rough scratch of his jacket against her bare breasts as she pulled him down over her, using her calves to pull him even closer as he slid her panties off. And this time she was the one kissing him with the passion he revealed within her more and more every time they made love. If they had more than a few stolen minutes, they might have kissed for hours, until both of them were utterly, completely desperate for more.

Very reluctantly, Smith pulled his mouth from hers and his hands from her skin to undo his tie and the buttons on his dress shirt. Valentina knew better than to help him—she needed him so badly that she was in danger of ripping the shirt off him—and curled her hands into fists on the soft bedcover to keep from ruining his dress clothes. Fortunately, he was able to undress quickly enough that it felt as if he'd barely stepped away from between her thighs to kick off his pants when he was right back with her, a condom already rolled down his thick, hard length.

A heartbeat later his hands were once again threading into her once perfectly done hair, his mouth was kissing off her expertly done makeup and he was sliding into her on a pleasured groan. Her skin was slick against his as they moved together, Smith going deeper even as Valentina opened herself all the way up to him.

As he rocked into her again and again, and her pleasure grew higher, sharper, she forgot all about

Hollywood, about billionaires and cameramen and gossip rags.

She felt as though her entire body was tightening down around him when he lifted his head from her mouth and looked into her eyes.

"I love you."

The simple vow was all it ever took to send Valentina hurtling over the edge, and Smith was right there with her, not only to catch her as she fell…but also to show her just how incredibly good it was to leap, knowing his strong, warm arms would be around her every single second.

Minutes later, as they both worked to catch their breath, and Valentina stroked Smith's slightly damp hair from where he'd laid his head across her breasts, she felt wonderfully drained of nerves.

He pressed a quick kiss to her lips before pulling her up off the bed, stripping off her stockings and heels, dragging her into the bathroom for the world's quickest shower. He held her hair up out of the way of the spray as she soaped both of them up, his body responding again as if he hadn't just finished taking her.

But even though she could see that he would have also been happy to do just that, she turned off the water and reached for the towels, handing him one before taking another for herself.

Smith had never used his fame as an excuse to hide, and she wouldn't make him hide for her.

"Come on, slowpoke," she teased as she purposely dropped the towel to the tiled floor and left the bathroom to put her dress back on. "Race you to the limo."

She'd almost reached her dress when his strong arms came around her.

"I love you."

His breath whispered against her neck as he once again said the three words that never ceased to fill her with awe. Not because she hadn't believed it was possible for a movie star to love her, but because she hadn't thought it was possible for love to find her at all.

She turned in his arms, the press of their nakedness forgotten as she put her hands on either side of his face. "I love you, too."

A few minutes later, he'd zipped her back into her dress and she'd straightened the bow tie on his tux. Her hair was a lost cause and she'd had to settle for a quick lash of mascara and a swipe of lipstick, but when she and Smith finally went down to meet her sister, who had been patiently waiting for them in the living room, Tatiana's eyes widened as she looked at the two of them.

"You looked amazing before, Val, but now you're simply perfect." Tatiana grinned at Smith, one good friend to another after their long weeks of working together. "Nice work, Mr. Sullivan."

He grinned back as the three of them headed to the limo outside. Valentina slid in between the two movie stars who meant everything to her and, instead of being terrified by the night they were about to have, Valentina felt happy.

Content.

And utterly, completely loved.

Thirty-One

New Year's Eve
Gabe and Megan's wedding

Snow was falling outside the floor-to-ceiling windows of the large wood-framed building. The pine trees outside were covered in soft, cold flakes, while the forest floor was blanketed in thick white fluff, turning all of Lake Tahoe into a winter wonderland.

Gabe Sullivan and Megan Harris had fallen in love in Lake Tahoe last winter, with some help from Megan's daughter, Summer, who had a brilliant knack for matchmaking. Today, the warmth of love surrounded Gabe, Megan and Summer as two hundred family members and friends gathered to celebrate their wedding.

Smith held Valentina's hand tightly as he watched another one of his brothers say "I do" to the love of his life. As Gabe slipped the ring onto Megan's finger, Summer standing close to both of them with an enormous smile on her face, Smith played with the white-gold band on Valentina's left hand.

His Christmas gift to her this year had been the easiest one in the world to pick out. Still, his heart had beat like mad as she'd opened the succession of boxes each one smaller and smaller until, finally, all that remained was one small velvet box.

She'd stared at it for a long moment, so long that his heartbeat had reversed from racing too fast to barely beating. He'd known how much he was asking from her, that being his wife would never be easy, simply because what he did for a living meant the world thought he was theirs.

"I'm yours," he'd told her in a voice made raw with emotion. "Be mine, Valentina."

And then, she'd smiled at him and the joy and love on her beautiful face had told him everything he needed to know, even before she said, "I've always been yours."

He'd made love to her beneath the twinkling lights of their Christmas tree and they'd been lying naked in each other's arms when she'd put her gift for him on his stomach. Feeling like a kid again, he shook the package, and her laughter at his antics wrapped around him like a blanket. Finally, he'd ripped open the wrapping paper and saw that she'd given him a photo album from the *Gravity* set. Inside were dozens of pictures in black and white, and color, too, of Smith and the cast and crew he'd just spent the best seven weeks of his life with. Laughing, working, eating, goofing around—everything was there. Including one final picture that he'd cherish forever.

Valentina had her arms around his neck, and his were around her waist. The two of them weren't kissing, or even smiling. They were simply holding each other. There was no caption for this picture, but it didn't need one. Not when anyone could see how close the man and woman in the picture were…so close that nothing could ever break them apart.

Carefully setting the album aside, he'd lifted her back on top of him, and loved her again.

They'd joined the rest of his siblings at their mother's house later that day to open presents, and the margaritas had been flowing again as this time their engagement was the one being celebrated. Christmas with his family had always been special and full of love. With Valentina at his side, love ran deeper than he'd ever known it could.

Now, on New Year's Eve in Lake Tahoe, everyone stood to applaud the bride and groom as they first shared a kiss with each other, and then with Summer, one smooch to each of the little girl's cheeks, followed by one from her for each of them. Summer jumped up into Gabe's arms and he held tight to her as the three of them began to walk back down the aisle hand in hand.

Valentina's eyes were soft and dreamy with love as she looked up into Smith's, her curves warm and sensual as he held her in his arms. "What a beautiful wedding."

She was holding her free hand over her heart, and he covered it with his as he leaned down to press a kiss to her lips.

They'd already discussed the fact that their wedding would be small and private, but after seeing her reaction to his brother's, he had to ask, "Do you want a wedding like this one? We can make it work, Valentina, if it's what you want." It wouldn't be easy to pull off a large wedding given his level of celebrity, but he would move mountains for Valentina.

She smiled up at him. "All I want is you."

If they'd been anywhere else, Smith might have forced himself to hold tight to his control. But these were his friends. Family. And he didn't need to hold back in front of them.

Not when they knew that Valentina held not only his heart, but his soul.

Her mouth against his was as warm and soft as her eyes had been and, silently, he made every one of the vows to her that Gabe had just made to Megan…all the while knowing that Valentina was making them right back to him.

"I love you."

They whispered the words aloud to each other and Smith knew it didn't matter if they had a large wedding, or if it was just the two of them in front of a priest. Every time they laughed together, every time they kissed, every moment they spent with each other's families, they became more and more entwined in each other's hearts.

Hand in hand they walked out into the large reception room. The children, including Summer, had begged their parents to let them go play out in the snow before it was time for lunch to be served, and the sound of hooting and hollering warmed the already cozy space.

Smith had introduced Valentina to his cousins Rafe, Adam and Dylan, who had all flown in from Seattle earlier that day. Their sister, Mia, was flirting with one of the guys from Gabe's firehouse. Unfortunately, the oldest Seattle Sullivan, Ian, had his flight in from England canceled and wouldn't be arriving until later that night.

Smith whisked a tray of champagne from a pretty young server who blushed profusely at his thank-you, then passed glasses around for a toast to the bride and groom.

"To love," Smith said, grinning at the way his single cousins could barely refrain from rolling their eyes.

"And to what looks to be one heck of a snowball fight outside," Rafe added.

Smith wasn't at all surprised to see Summer kicking serious butt against some of the older boys. After all, he'd spent a couple of hours the previous afternoon teaching her everything he knew about snowball warfare.

Valentina squeezed his hand as she pulled his gaze over to the dance floor. "Look at how sweet that is."

Chase and Chloe's daughter, Emma, had crawled onto the empty dance floor and a boy who looked to have just learned how to walk had toddled up to pat her hair. The two babies plopped down in front of each other and began to have a wordless conversation of *goo*'s and *ga*'s that had everyone smiling.

Until the boy suddenly reached out a chubby little hand and gave Emma a shove.

The baby girl's eyes went wide for a moment before she toppled slowly over onto her back. She was kicking up her heels in a wail just as Chase scooped her up into his arms.

"Poor thing," Valentina murmured. "And she was having so much fun flirting, too. Now whenever she sees him, she's going to be worried that he'll do it again."

"What about you?" he asked softly. "Are you feeling worried about anything?"

He could feel Valentina's pulse quicken against the pad of his thumb where he was stroking her sensitive skin. She bit her lip, and he watched her channel her inner actress as she said, "A little."

"Excuse us, guys."

His cousins gave him a look that said they knew exactly what he was about to do with his beautiful fiancée, and he knew they were more than a little jealous, too. A couple of them had brought dates, but he could tell that the women weren't anything special to them.

Love made all the difference...and meant so much more than money or success or fame ever had. But he wasn't going to waste his breath explaining that to his cousins. Not when it would be so much more fun to let them suffer through figuring it out for themselves.

Fortunately, after all the clandestine sex he and Valentina had had on set, he had the knack of scoping out the perfect spots for their trysts. Not to mention the fact that he knew just how much she secretly loved that tiny threat of discovery, of having to be extra quiet so no one heard them, and especially of knowing what they'd just been doing while everyone else had simply been going about their day.

Of course, he would never let anyone find them, would never let another man or woman ever set eyes on Valentina's naked body, but that didn't mean he didn't get off on fulfilling her secret fantasies.

They'd gone to several industry events together during the past month and, with every one, Valentina's nerves came with less force. Even though Smith liked to think that her increasing confidence mostly had to do with his brilliant distraction technique of making sweet love to her right before they got dressed—and often after, as well—he knew the truth came from her inner strength, and her willingness to do whatever she needed to do to make their relationship work.

The laundry room smelled of fabric softener and was still warm from the dryers that had been recently running. The door had a secure lock, and the room was far enough away from the festivities that Valentina's sounds of pleasure would be for his ears only.

They came together in each other's arms, clothes stripping off, hands and mouths wandering wherever bare flesh was revealed, and as Smith's passion for Valentina took him a thousand miles away from movie-star perfect, or from any semblance of control, he knew she was right there with him.

And she always would be.

Epilogue

Lori Sullivan watched the dance floor fill up with her brothers and cousins. Even Sophie and Jake were dancing together with their tiny little twins wrapped in pink and blue blankets snuggled between them. Lori had been so busy lately that she didn't get to see any of her family enough. She knew she, of all people, should be out there on the dance floor with them.

But, for the first time in her life, she didn't feel like dancing.

She wasn't at all surprised when her mother moved beside her a moment later and slid a hand around her waist so that they were watching the action on the dance floor together. Mary Sullivan had a sixth sense about when her children were happy…and when they were hurting.

Their mother's unconditional love—knowing that Mary was there for her children, and only them—had been something Lori could always count on. Still, as she turned to take in her mother's stunning profile, one that had sold many, many magazine covers before she retired from modeling, Lori was caught by the sense that things were changing.

Not only because each and every one of her siblings had found love, but also because even her mother suddenly looked different. Almost glowing.

Could there be a man in her mother's life?

Lori shook off the silly question. Of course there wasn't. There never had been, not one in all the years since her father had passed away. If Lori hadn't been feeling so off-kilter, she would never have had such a crazy thought.

Just then, Smith and Valentina emerged from a back door Lori hadn't noticed before, both of them flushed and laughing, their hands linked together as Smith pulled her in for a lingering kiss.

"Aren't they beautiful together?"

Her mother gave a happy little sigh. "Oh, yes. So very beautiful."

Everyone was thrilled with the news that not only were Smith and Valentina engaged, but they would also be working together to produce a film in San Francisco next year based on an Alcatraz love story.

"Not in the mood to dance yet?" her mother asked softly.

"No, not yet." Her mother could probably see the dark smudges under her eyes even though she'd worked to conceal them with makeup.

"When you were a little girl," Mary said as she rubbed small, soothing circles on Lori's back, "you used to talk all the time. So much so that other mothers would shoot me sympathetic looks whenever we were out." Mary smiled and leaned in closer, close enough that their foreheads touched for a moment. "But I loved it, loved that you wanted to share everything with me."

Lori could feel the tears coming, knew she could tell her mother anything—anything at all—and Mary wouldn't judge her.

But she couldn't. Not yet. Not if there was still a chance that—

"I love you, Mom."

"I love you, too, honey."

The next thing Lori knew, her hands were full of a soft, sweet baby. She looked down into little Jackie's face, then up into her twin sister's eyes.

"They wanted their favorite aunt to come dance with them," Sophie said, as if her infants could say or even think something like that at this stage in their development. But she knew her sister loved her too much to let her stay on the sidelines.

As Lori and her mother were drawn onto the dance floor, each of them holding a baby in their arms, they moved to the music of the wedding band. Her brothers each danced over to tickle a little foot or grasp a small hand, and amid all the laughter Lori let herself pretend that everything was going to work out in her love life, too.

* * * * *

From *New York Times* bestselling author

SUSAN MALLERY

**comes a poignant new story in her
Blackberry Island series, about love, family and
finding the courage to reach for your dreams.**

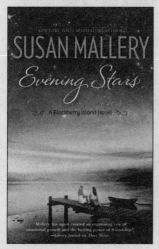

Small-town nurse Nina Wentworth
is more "Mom" than her own
mother ever was. She sacrificed
medical school—and her first love—
so her sister could break free.
Which is why she isn't exactly
thrilled to see Averil back on
Blackberry Island, especially
when Nina's life has suddenly
become…complicated.

Nina unexpectedly finds herself
juggling two amazing men, but as
fun as all this romance is, she has real
life to deal with. Averil doesn't seem
to want the great guy she's married
to; their mom is living life just as
recklessly as she always has; and
Nina's starting to realize that the control she once had is slipping out
of her fingers. Her hopes of getting off the island seem to be stretching
further away…until her mother makes a discovery that could change
everything forever.

Available now, wherever books are sold!

Be sure to connect with us at:

Harlequin.com/Newsletters

Facebook.com/HarlequinBooks

Twitter.com/HarlequinBooks

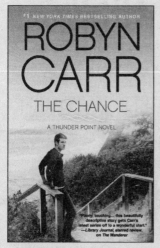

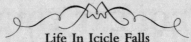
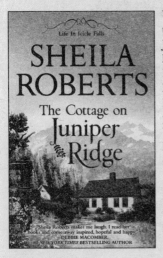

REQUEST YOUR FREE BOOKS!

2 FREE NOVELS
FROM THE ROMANCE COLLECTION
PLUS 2 FREE GIFTS!

YES! Please send me 2 FREE novels from the Romance Collection and my 2 FREE gifts (gifts are worth about $10). After receiving them, if I don't wish to receive any more books, I can return the shipping statement marked "cancel." If I don't cancel, I will receive 4 brand-new novels every month and be billed just $6.24 per book in the U.S. or $6.74 per book in Canada. That's a savings of at least 22% off the cover price. It's quite a bargain! Shipping and handling is just 50¢ per book in the U.S. and 75¢ per book in Canada.* I understand that accepting the 2 free books and gifts places me under no obligation to buy anything. I can always return a shipment and cancel at any time. Even if I never buy another book, the two free books and gifts are mine to keep forever.

194/394 MDN F4XY

Name _____
(PLEASE PRINT)

Address _____ Apt. # _____

City _____ State/Prov. _____ Zip/Postal Code _____

Signature (if under 18, a parent or guardian must sign) _____

Mail to the Harlequin® Reader Service:
IN U.S.A.: P.O. Box 1867, Buffalo, NY 14240-1867
IN CANADA: P.O. Box 609, Fort Erie, Ontario L2A 5X3

Want to try two free books from another line?
Call 1-800-873-8635 or visit www.ReaderService.com.

* Terms and prices subject to change without notice. Prices do not include applicable taxes. Sales tax applicable in N.Y. Canadian residents will be charged applicable taxes. Offer not valid in Quebec. This offer is limited to one order per household. Not valid for current subscribers to the Romance Collection or the Romance/Suspense Collection. All orders subject to credit approval. Credit or debit balances in a customer's account(s) may be offset by any other outstanding balance owed by or to the customer. Please allow 4 to 6 weeks for delivery. Offer available while quantities last.

Your Privacy—The Harlequin® Reader Service is committed to protecting your privacy. Our Privacy Policy is available online at www.ReaderService.com or upon request from the Harlequin Reader Service.

We make a portion of our mailing list available to reputable third parties that offer products we believe may interest you. If you prefer that we not exchange your name with third parties, or if you wish to clarify or modify your communication preferences, please visit us at www.ReaderService.com/consumerchoice or write to us at Harlequin Reader Service Preference Service, P.O. Box 9062, Buffalo, NY 14269. Include your complete name and address.

ROM13R

BELLA ANDRE

31600	LET ME BE THE ONE	___ $7.99 U.S.	___ $8.99 CAN.
31560	IF YOU WERE MINE	___ $7.99 U.S.	___ $8.99 CAN.
31559	I ONLY HAVE EYES FOR YOU	___ $7.99 U.S.	___ $8.99 CAN.
31558	CAN'T HELP FALLING IN LOVE	___ $7.99 U.S.	___ $8.99 CAN.
31557	FROM THIS MOMENT ON	___ $7.99 U.S.	___ $9.99 CAN.
31556	THE LOOK OF LOVE	___ $5.99 U.S.	___ $5.99 CAN.

(limited quantities available)

TOTAL AMOUNT	$ _____
POSTAGE & HANDLING	$ _____
($1.00 for 1 book, 50¢ for each additional)	
APPLICABLE TAXES*	$ _____
TOTAL PAYABLE	$ _____

(check or money order—please do not send cash)

To order, complete this form and send it, along with a check or money order for the total amount, payable to Harlequin MIRA, to: **In the U.S.:** 3010 Walden Avenue, P.O. Box 9077, Buffalo, NY 1426-9077; **In Canada:** P.O. Box 636, Fort Erie, Ontario, L2A 5X3.

Name: _____

Address: _____ City: _____

State/Prov.: _____ Zip/Postal Code: _____

Account Number (if applicable): _____

075 CSAS

*New York residents remit applicable sales taxes.
*Canadian residents remit applicable GST and provincial taxes.

HARLEQUIN® MIRA®
™ www.Harlequin.com

MBA0314BL